Praise for Ann Warner's *Dreams for Stones*

Indie Next Generation Book Award Finalist

"Dreams for Stones is wonderfully gripping... I could not stop reading it, and I held my breath right to the end."

~ *Joyfully Reviewed*

"Just remember to keep a box of tissues handy when starting this."

~ *Literary Nymphs Reviews*

Look for these titles by
Ann Warner

Now Available:

Persistence of Dreams

Dreams for Stones

Ann Warner

A Samhain Publishing, Ltd. publication.

Samhain Publishing, Ltd.
577 Mulberry Street, Suite 1520
Macon, GA 31201
www.samhainpublishing.com

Dreams for Stones
Copyright © 2008 by Ann Warner
Print ISBN: 978-1-59998-974-7
Digital ISBN: 1-59998-712-0

Editing by Jennifer Miller
Cover by Scott Carpenter

First Samhain Publishing, Ltd. electronic publication: December 2007
First Samhain Publishing, Ltd. print publication: October 2008

Dedication

To my husband who loves me for ordinary reasons in an extraordinary way.

And to my critique partners. Your thoughtful comments have helped make all my stories, including this one, so much better: Robin Borche, Jayne Close, Sharon Cullen, Roger Collins, Angelene J. Hall, Daphne Wedig-Griffis. Thank you! This book would not be the same without you.

And to Joe and Emma, muses and friends, who showed me how to face difficulties with grace.

Chapter One

Alan Francini smoothed a saddle pad onto Sonoro's back. The horse danced sideways before settling and nudging the man's shoulder, blowing softly. Alan stood for a moment, his forehead against the animal's neck, then reached for the saddle and, with one smooth motion, swung it into position. He tightened the cinch, mounted and, turning Sonoro toward the foothills, loosened the reins.

Their swift passage through the brisk air chilled Alan's face, pulling tears from his eyes. He ignored the wet on his cheeks, focusing instead on the dull staccato rhythm of hooves on frozen ground, the click of iron shoe against cold stone, and the huff of Sonoro's breathing visible in the icy air.

When they reached the alpine meadow with its tiny topaz lake, he left the stallion to graze and walked to the edge of the water. The day he and Meg discovered it, the lake had been blue and mirror still, reflecting mountains, trees and sky in all their perfection, like a second reality.

Now that day was the only memory he was able to look at directly, without flinching. The only day in all their days together that hadn't shifted and splintered into sharp-edged, constant pain.

A cloud slid across the sun and the lake darkened, its opaque surface shivering with each gust of wind. Early April. An uncertain time of year. As uncertain as the possibility of joy.

He picked up a stone, tossed it into the gray lake and stood waiting until the widening ripples from the splash touched the shore at his feet.

Then he remounted and rode back the way he had come.

Alan was halfway through chores Easter morning when his sister showed up. Elaine swung on the door of the stall he was cleaning, chewing a stem of alfalfa, looking more like a young girl than a woman of thirty-three.

He reached over and pulled the hay from her mouth. "Bad habit, Laine."

She wrinkled her nose and yanked a fresh stem free. "So how go the Denver State tenure wars?"

"Dossier's due next fall." He went back to forking used straw into the wheelbarrow.

"You have a take on how it'll go?"

"New department head might be the sticking point." At Hilary Hilstrom's first faculty meeting she'd laid out her "vision" to turn DSU into a fiction-writing mecca.

"So? Send her roses and a box of *very* expensive chocolates."

He took in a deep breath of air scented not with roses and chocolate but with hay and horse and turned to tell Elaine he couldn't think of a worse thing to do.

She grinned. "Gotcha. So why's she the sticking point?"

"She came to observe my class. Unannounced." He continued to work, his muscles loosening and warming, sweat dampening his shirt, as he recalled Hilstrom's visit. He'd done the math. The woman was at least fifty, but fighting it with short skirts and too much makeup.

The day she came to his class, she sat in the back of the room, a perfectly groomed, lavender-garbed apparition, while he struggled to get a reaction to a piece of experimental fiction out of students more likely to have lavender hair than lavender clothes. Eventually he succeeded, and caught up in the discussion, he forgot Hilstrom until the students filed out.

She had paused in the doorway, tapping her reading glasses against her teeth. "That was certainly an interesting approach, Alan." Her tone made it unclear whether she considered it a *good* interesting or a *bad* interesting.

Elaine wiggled her fingers at him. "About that visit?"

He didn't want to rehash it, bad enough to have lived through it once, but maybe he *could* come up with a story to amuse her. It would be nice to keep her hanging around for a while.

"We were reading *The Taming of the Shrew*. I invited her to read Katherine's part."

"Tell me you're joking."

"Trust me, Hilary Hilstrom is no joke." And wasn't that the truth. He kept his face turned away, as he continued to work.

"Did she do it?"

"She did."

"And?"

He leaned on the pitchfork and thought about where to take the story as the horses chomped steadily through their morning hay and oats.

And then he had it. "Hilstrom was so dramatic, the football player reading Petruccio forgot he was acting and kissed her." Alan smiled at the vision of Hilstrom, those damn glasses on her nose where they belonged for once, and a block-shaped lineman with no neck, leaning in, eyes closed, lips puckered.

"If that really happened, your goose is cooked."

"Yep. Unless he was a damn good kisser." He tossed the last of the used straw into the wheelbarrow. "She appeared bemused."

Elaine laughed. "By the muse or the guy?"

Alan shrugged, pleased with the success of his tale. As he passed her, Elaine turned and followed him.

"You made that up, right?"

He dumped the contents of the barrow, straightened and met her gaze with a solemn look. "Nope. Cooked goose. That's me. Easter dinner."

He saw she half-believed him, although as a clinical psychologist, she usually recognized bullfeathers immediately. But then it had been a very long time since he last joked with her.

Her grin fading, she stepped closer and touched his arm.

11

"Alan, there's something I need to tell you."

"Knew it was too good to be true you actually came to help me muck out," he said, hoping to lighten her up.

"We're making the announcement at dinner, but..." She bit her lip, her fingers worrying the fabric of his shirt. "I didn't want to spring it on you in front of everybody. But, well, we're going to have a baby."

He sucked in a quick breath and let it out slow, trying not to let the emotions set loose by her words take hold. "Hey, that's great news, Laine." He pulled her into his arms. "Bet Ted is thrilled, and the folks will be ecstatic."

"It's just. Times like this." Her voice caught, and she pressed her head against his shoulder. "Meg...she ought to be here. You know."

"Yeah." He spoke softly, because suddenly he found it impossible to get all the air he needed.

"Sometimes I can't stand it." The fierce words were interlaced with tears. "I miss her so much."

Yeah. He did, too. And always would.

Elaine scrubbed at her eyes. "Sorry. I didn't know I was going to do that." She stumbled out of his arms and went over to the nearest stall. The occupant stuck its head over the door, whickering a greeting, and Elaine stroked the shaggy neck, lifting and untangling the mane with her fingers.

The sun slanted across his sister's hair, burnishing the honey with gold, and for an instant it was as if Meg stood there, saying, "Alan, look at this. Her mane's all tangled and after I just combed it. Bet she got into those brambles going after berries again, the greedy gut."

The twist of pain was so powerful, he doubled over. When he straightened, he was relieved to find Elaine hadn't noticed.

He shook his head to clear it, then hooked a bale of fresh straw and hauled it over to the clean stall. When he looked up, he found Elaine watching him, a worried look on her face.

He spoke as gently as possible. "It's okay, Laine. I think your having a baby is wonderful."

He led Sonoro back into the clean stall and took his time unclipping the lead, stroking the soft muzzle, running his hands down each leg, picking up and checking each hoof. By the time he finished, Elaine had gone back to the house.

He breathed a sigh of relief, glad to be alone again in the quiet of the barn with creatures that couldn't speak.

Chapter Two

Kathy Jamison stood at the entrance to the botanical gardens, her gaze focused on the man walking toward her. She had the urge to pinch herself to make sure she wasn't dreaming. Instead, she rubbed her thumb against the diamond ring Greg had placed on her finger a month ago and knew she was most definitely awake. And reality was better than any dream.

Greg reached her and bent his head to kiss her before taking her hands in his and swinging her into an impromptu waltz, singing, "California Here I Come".

Kathy's smile slid away and her whole body stiffened with alarm. "California?"

"Yep. Can you believe it? The fellowship came through. San Francisco. Only the best toxicology residency in the country. My pick of positions when I finish."

Kathy stepped away, trying for perspective, dread replacing joy. "But-but, I thought... That is, we agreed. You'd apply for the residency here, and we wouldn't need to move."

People eddied around them as they faced each other in the center of the path.

"Well, yeah, but that was only if San Francisco didn't come through." Greg recaptured her hand. "You knew I went for the interview."

Because he didn't want to upset the head of Emergency Medicine at St. Joseph's who'd recommended him, but it wasn't supposed to mean anything. "You said you didn't have a chance."

"You know how it goes. Want something too much, it practically guarantees you won't get it."

Like her wanting to stay in Denver.

But if he wanted San Francisco, why hadn't he shared that with her? Instead he'd joked about what a disaster the trip had been, how he forgot to pack dress shoes and worried about it until an inept waiter made it a moot point by dumping coffee on him at breakfast.

They'd laughed about it, and somehow she'd failed to notice how much it mattered to him. But he had to know leaving Denver mattered to her.

He pulled on her hand. "Come on. We're blocking traffic."

She went along with him, her thoughts still churning, numb to the sight of daffodils and budding trees as he led the way to the Japanese garden where he'd asked her to marry him. When they reached the bench in the corner, he sat and pulled her down beside him wrapping his arm around her. She leaned away.

"What is it?" He cocked his head, giving her what she thought of as his doctor look. "You aren't coming down with something are you?"

"I may be." Her throat tightened, and her nose itched.

"A cold?"

She shook her head. "About San Francisco. Have you accepted?"

"Of course."

Of course? Could the man she loved be oblivious? "Don't you think we need to talk about it?"

"What's to talk about?" He looked puzzled.

That we agreed. We wouldn't leave Denver. "The University of Colorado, maybe. Did you hear from them yet?" It was a struggle but she'd managed to keep her tone calm.

"They called last week."

"And?"

He shrugged. "They offered me the spot."

For an instant his image wavered as if she were seeing it in a funhouse mirror. "You didn't tell me." *They offered you the spot. They offered you the spot!*

"I was waiting to see if San Francisco called. Look, Kit, if you wrote a novel, and you got an offer from Random House and another from Podunk Press, which would you choose?"

If she said anything more right now she'd likely regret it. Instead, she switched her focus to a middle-aged couple walking through the garden. The man leaned toward the woman and said something that made her laugh. Kathy watched the two until she thought she could speak without raising her voice. "The University of Colorado isn't exactly Podunk U."

"True, but San Francisco, Kit. It's the opportunity of a lifetime."

Did Greg's rich baritone carry a hint of irritation? But what right did he have to be irritated? Her life was the one being uprooted, and he needed to show some sensitivity to that fact.

"It's only two years, babe. No biggie. Besides, it's not like you've lived in Denver your whole life or anything."

He gave her his most ingratiating smile, and an overwhelming urge to shake him had her clutching her hands together.

"You'll love San Francisco."

Wrong. Denver was her home now. She'd chosen it, let herself get attached. Promised herself she wasn't moving again. And two years was more than nothing. It was as long as she'd lived any one place when she was growing up.

Moving. With a father in the Air Force, she knew all about it, and she'd had enough. Enough of leaving behind all that had become familiar and dear. Enough of starting over with new friends, new neighbors, new schools. New dentists, new doctors, new jobs. Enough of packing and unpacking. Enough wrong turns and ending up in wrong places.

Just enough.

She tried to speak, but her throat felt like it was full of sand. She swallowed. "So, tell me. Is this how you plan to handle decisions affecting the two of us once we're married?" Her voice began to spiral, like a car going out of control on an icy curve. "You decide, then you tell me what you've decided." She clamped her lips shut, moving her fingers in a silent count.

"Of course not. But it's my career so really that makes it

my decision."

"So. Does that mean since I'm the one who gets pregnant, it's my choice whether we have children?"

"That's ridiculous. Kids would affect both our lives."

"And your decision to go to San Francisco doesn't affect my life?"

Greg cleared his throat, lifted his eyes to hers and spoke with apparent sincerity. "I'm sorry. I shouldn't have accepted without discussing it with you."

Darn right, he shouldn't have. She took three more breaths, staring at him, willing him to look away. He didn't.

"I'm really, really sorry," he said.

He *did* look sincere. And regretful. She continued to glare at him.

Finally he lowered his gaze. "I didn't think. Being engaged— it's so new. I just didn't realize. I didn't mean to hurt you."

"I accept your apology." Her voice was stiff and jerky, but she made no effort to smooth it.

He reached for her hand, and she let him have it.

"You are so damn beautiful."

He almost got away with it—distracting her from her anger, not to mention from the fact they hadn't resolved anything.

"We still need to figure out what we're going to do," she said.

"I thought we had."

She tipped her chin to meet his eyes.

"We're going to San Francisco, and..." His voice drifted to a halt.

Her world sped up, then abruptly slowed. Images hurtling by too quickly for her to identify came into stark focus. Beyond the clear blue of his eyes and the gold of his hair. Beyond the breadth of his shoulders and the corded muscles of his arms, how well did she know this man? And was this what being married to him would be like? Sudden announcements—he'd bought a house, a car, changed jobs—without it ever occurring to him to consult her before he did it?

A fleck of lint clung to the side of his mouth. Her eyes

locked on that speck.

"What?" Greg swiped at his face, dislodging the lint.

Kathy blinked, noticing for the first time his hair was beginning to thin at the temples. A sudden image of Greg with thinning hair and an expanding paunch made her smile.

He grinned back. "Good. It's settled then."

She closed her eyes, shutting out the vivid blue of the sky and the fresh spring green, struggling to come to terms with the idea.

"You're scaring me, babe. Come on. It's not the end of the world, you know."

But it was the end of something.

"What can I do to make this easier for you?"

She wished she knew.

Later, she decided if this had happened to a friend—a fiancé announcing a major decision without any consideration for her friend's wants and needs—she'd have advised that friend to tell the fiancé, now downgraded to eye-of-newt, what he could do with his decision.

But look at her. Note how *she'd* handled her fiancé's announcement—made without any concern for her dreams and hopes—that they were moving to San Francisco.

Yeah, look at her.

She was packing, dammit.

And why was that, exactly?

Because she loved him, of course. It was their first...no not a fight. A difference of opinion. He hadn't stopped to think, but once he did, he'd apologized. Sincerely.

Sitting next to him, listening to his reasons, seeing how much he wanted to go to San Francisco, she'd been unable to deny him.

Compromise. Essential to any relationship. This time, his turn, next time, hers. Sacrificing for someone you loved was noble. And since that afternoon, they'd worked things out. Everything was fine again. Would be fine. The bright glow had dimmed only a little. After all, his dedication to his career was one of the reasons she loved him.

She'd dated enough to know a man who treated her with such care and thoughtfulness—well, most of the time—wasn't as rare as hens' teeth. But men like that sure weren't thick on the ground either.

With a sigh, she opened the bottom drawer of the dresser, lifted out a pile of sweaters, and plopped them willy-nilly into one of the cartons Greg had dropped off.

San Francisco. It was, as he'd pointed out, only two years. She could manage two years. Except...

She froze in the act of adding a pair of jeans to the sweaters and sat back on her heels. How could she have overlooked that one, casual line. "My pick of positions when I finish."

She'd been so focused on the main issue of the move, she'd let him slip right by her the hint that after his residency he might accept a position someplace he considered more prestigious than Denver.

But would he, really?

Before he announced his plan to go to San Francisco, she would have said no way.

And now? She narrowed her eyes, staring at the photo of Greg on the small table to her right.

Darn right he would.

So, was this how she planned to handle it? Pack and meekly tag along? As if everything she wanted, needed was unimportant when stacked up against Greg's "career".

Startled, she stared at the shreds of cardboard in her hands and realized she was halfway through tearing apart a box.

Listen to your heart, Kathleen. It's telling you what to do.

Well, this was certainly a fine time for her Emily tape to start.

Except, it was really. The exact right time.

Because whenever she was confused or worried, all she needed to do was tap into an Emily memory or dig out one of Emily's diaries, the way some people do the Bible. She'd pick up one of the small, leather books, open it at random and read. It always calmed her, and from that calm, her answer would come.

"Kathy dear, how is the packing coming?" Kathy's tiny landlady stood in the doorway, her halo of white hair backlit by light from the hall window.

Kathy shifted her gaze from Mrs. Costello to the shreds of cardboard. "Oh, just peachy."

"That's good to hear." Mrs. C raised her eyebrows a notch, eyeing the demolished box. "You know, dear, we're going to miss you something fierce when you leave."

"Oh, and I'm going to miss you, Mrs. C." Kathy scrambled to her feet to give her landlady, who smelled of warm bread and cinnamon, a hug. Mrs. C's foundation garment made her feel stiff, but Kathy recognized the returned affection in the pats the older woman gave her.

Mrs. C stepped back and used her apron to wipe moisture from her eyes. "What a couple of sillies we are." She patted Kathy's arm. "You go on with your packing, dear. You don't want to hold up that young man of yours. I just wanted to tell you, dinner will be ready in fifteen minutes."

Kathy leaned on the doorjamb after Mrs. C left, looking at her room: the floral carpet with its pattern of pink cabbage roses, the four-poster bed with its white chenille spread, the vanity with its stiffly starched doily centered on top. Chances were it had looked exactly the same for at least fifty years; but maybe that was why she was so attached to it.

When she'd rented the room, she planned on staying only a week or two, until she found someone to share the expense of an apartment, but five years had passed, and she was still here. She'd stayed, not only because Mrs. C was a wonderful cook and the house only a short walk to Calico Cat Books where she worked, but because she'd grown to love the Costellos who treated her like a favorite granddaughter.

She'd even chosen to remain after her engagement to Greg, despite his efforts to get her to move in with him. But really, it made no sense to add a forty-minute commute to each end of her day when Greg spent most of his nights at the hospital.

And did it make any more sense for her to leave a job and a city she loved for the short time Greg would be in San

Francisco?

Of course, staying in Denver would mean putting off the wedding, and Greg probably wouldn't be happy about that.

Still...

She closed her eyes, concentrating. *I have an idea. It's not ideal, but I know we can make it work. Why don't I stay in Denver? You'll be so busy at the hospital, you won't have all that much free time, so really it makes sense. And whenever you get a break, I'll come for a visit.*

Okay, not bad. It could use sharpening, but those were the main points.

She had a sudden vivid picture of Greg running his hands through his hair the way he did when he was tired or nervous. "But if you really loved me, you'd come with me."

Her eyes flew open. The words rang so clear, she almost expected Greg to be standing in front of her.

But was that really what he'd say?

Probably.

We'll stay close. By writing and talking, she told the phantom Greg. *Two years is nothing.* Good. His own argument used against him. *Before you know it, you'll be finished and moving back to Denver. The time will fly.*

"I need to think about all this, Kitten. I didn't expect it."

She hated being called Kitten, but it wasn't easy to point that out to someone who wasn't there.

Chapter Three

Alan stood and stretched. Time for his first one-on-one, get-acquainted meeting with his new department head, Hilary Hilstrom. Not something he was looking forward to after her unexpected visit to his class. He slipped his tie over his head, pulled the knot snug, then plucked his jacket from the back of the door and shrugged it on.

Hilstrom's assistant glanced up when he walked in. "Professor Francini. My, you're prompt. I'll tell her you're here."

As she made the call, Alan shifted until the toe-dancer in the picture hanging over the assistant's head seemed to be rising out of her tangle of gray curls. It was an amusing and curiously satisfying image; one that would have appealed to Meg.

Meg...

"...right in," the assistant said. "She's ready for you."

It happened that way sometimes. A sudden vision of Meg, bending over a wildflower maybe, or taking off her hat to let the breeze blow her hair, and the real world would fade. It was a relief when the dream released him before anybody noticed his distraction.

He stepped through the doorway into the inner office, and felt momentarily disoriented. The old chairman's filing system had consisted of proliferating stacks of paper covering every available surface, and his only concession to the gods of decoration and order had been floor to ceiling bookshelves. Now all that was gone, and a desk and computer work-station were tucked into a corner like an afterthought, while most of the space was given over to a chair, sofa, and coffee table ensemble.

Hilstrom greeted him, gesturing toward the sofa. He sat and glanced around, his gaze coming to rest on two framed prints on the opposite wall—a Picasso, its dark, slashing lines contrasting with a Monet, indefinite as fog. The juxtaposition hinted Hilstrom either had a sense of humor—something he'd begun to doubt—or she was artistically clueless.

He looked away from the pictures, trying to regain his focus as she picked up a folder from the desk and came to sit in the chair across from him.

"I thought we might start with you telling me what you consider your major accomplishment in your five years here." She sat back, ceding the floor to him.

He'd expected the question, but he took a moment to gather his thoughts before speaking briefly about the techniques he'd developed to teach grammar, after reading about the effect of music on learning.

When he stopped speaking, she waited a beat, perhaps to give him a chance to add more. When he didn't, she spoke briskly, saying the approach sounded *interesting*, her favorite word it seemed.

"I see you'll be coming up for tenure next fall. That means we need to discuss your publication record." She glanced at the file. "It appears you've been writing primarily for education journals." She peered at him over the top of her glasses. "What I want to know is whether you have any plans to write fiction."

"Is that an issue?" He'd heard rumors about Hilstrom's single-minded approach to publication; he just hadn't believed them. Had chosen to label them an *interesting* but unlikely approach.

She pulled off her glasses and looked him in the eye. "Fiction is our future, Alan, and I don't intend to support anyone for appointment, reappointment, tenure, or promotion who isn't writing it."

The shock froze him, until a welcome spurt of annoyance thawed the sudden cold. Good God, the woman ought to be writing ad copy somewhere, not directing a large, complex department at a major university. What had the search committee and the dean been thinking? He sat back, adding distance between them.

23

"There's entirely too much deadwood writing non-fiction in our tenured ranks already," she added.

So what was deadwood using to write its non-fiction with these days? Pen? Typewriter? Computer? He pictured a row of bare tree branches holding pens and leaning over sheets of paper and almost smiled.

She paused, apparently to allow him an opportunity to respond, but he had nothing to say, at least to her.

"You're not much of a talker." She cocked her head and twirled her glasses examining him.

"Better to be thought a fool..." He kept his tone calm and neutral, something he'd discovered was useful whether he was dealing with an agitated student, a frightened animal, or an academic administrator.

"Than to open your mouth and remove all doubt," Hilstrom finished when he didn't. "Yes. I do realize I'm changing the rules on you late in the game, but you have six months to make adjustments before you turn in your dossier." She tapped the glasses on her teeth. "I know you'll need time to think about all this. Then if you have questions or concerns, simply ask to see me." She set his file and her peripatetic glasses on the table. "After all, that's what I'm here for."

With a professional smile and a brief, hard handclasp, she dismissed him.

Juggling beers and hot dogs, Alan and Charles Larimore settled into their seats at Coors Field. Charles, who hated to miss even a single hamstring stretch, focused immediately on the players who were warming up.

Alan took a gulp of beer. "So how goes the fight against the forces of evil?"

Charles spoke without turning his head. "Another week, another fifteen drug dealers, two robbers and a rapist out on bond."

"You could always give up the frustration and go for the big corporate bucks."

Charles grimaced at Alan over the rim of his beer.

"Somebody's got to be stemming the tide. Besides, most corporate law's as dull as a machete used to chop rocks."

"Ever think maybe there's a good reason 'stemming' rhymes with 'lemming'?"

"You're no better. Stemming the tide of illiterate lemmings at DSU."

They stood to let a group into the row, then sat back down.

"I met with Hilstrom last week." Alan's gut tightened as he recalled the meeting. The woman was a menace.

"How's she settling in?"

"Fine. She's sure not someone I'd choose to be marooned with, though."

"And let me guess who that might be. I'd have to say your horse. What's his name again?"

"I'll give you a personal introduction anytime you say."

"No way." Charles shook his head emphatically. "Urban cowboy through and through, that's me. Four on the floor means a gearshift, not hooves. You do realize horses are large, dangerous animals."

It was a well-established position. Although Charles was a regular visitor to the ranch, he politely and pointedly declined any opportunity to get near a horse.

The sharp plop and crack of balls hitting gloves and bats began to punctuate their conversation.

"You need to jolly the lady along a bit," Charles said, returning to the original subject. "Tell her she's looking fine. Soften her up."

A picture popped into Alan's head of Hilstrom sliding off her chair and melting into a small colorful puddle with her glasses floating on top. Rather like the Wicked Witch of the West who, come to think of it, Hilstrom resembled.

It was one of the things Alan liked best about Charles, that the other man always said something that brought an amusing image to mind.

The amusement was short-lived, however, as Alan told Charles the rest. "She won't support me for tenure unless I'm writing fiction." Not that there was anything wrong with Hilstrom's ambition. Except, she acted like writing fiction was as easy as turning on a tap.

Charles gave him the gimlet look he no doubt used to good effect on reluctant witnesses. "What about your novel? Hell, it's got to be a thousand pages by now."

"Not finished." And never going to be. A fact he had no intention of sharing with Charles. Or anyone else. The familiar, hollow feeling kicked in, and he tried to smother it with more beer and the last bite of hot dog.

"About this focus on fiction. Is this the first time it's come up?"

"Yeah."

Charles shrugged. "Well then, you can surely put their asses in a sling with a suit."

"A suit would be as hard on me as them." No way was he suing, and Charles knew it.

"You can always try dangling the possibility of a suit. Ask the lady to document where writing fiction was a requirement for tenure. If it wasn't mentioned before, she has to know she doesn't have a legal leg to stand on."

Charles stopped to take a swallow of beer, but Alan saw the wheels were still turning.

"Partly she may be trying it out to see how you react."

"It's also politics."

"Yeah. Not your strong suit. You don't need to fawn. Just suck up a little."

Alan shook his head, grimacing. "You put things so elegantly."

"Hey, I was an English major, too."

"Then threw your lot in with obfuscators."

"Legal language is renowned for its unambiguous, articulate, erudite phraseology."

Alan snorted, and Charles laughed before he turned serious again. "I know you fight only when it's important to you, but you can't let them screw you on this."

Charles had that right.

They stood for the national anthem, and when it ended, Charles lifted his cup to signal the beer vendor. Once the fresh beers arrived, Charles took a drink, then spoke, obviously trying to sound casual. "A friend of Tiffany's is coming for a visit. I've seen a picture. She's hot. How about I set something up for the four of us next weekend?"

"I'm going to the ranch."

"Lame, Francini."

Alan clamped down on his irritation. This was the part of spending time with Charles he could do without. He tolerated it only because, with the exception of the one flaw, Charles was a good friend. "You're right. But it's what I'm doing." Over the years, Alan had found partial agreement more effective than giving Charles an opening to start a debate.

"I miss her, too." Charles treated the catch in his voice with a gulp of beer. "She'd want you to go out, you know."

The remark was all the more startling, because Charles rarely mentioned Meg anymore.

"I am out." Alan had been enjoying himself, with the sun warming his bare arms and the beer cooling his throat.

Until Charles reminded him Meg was gone.

And everything went flat.

Chapter Four

Kathy's heart was pounding with excitement by the time she reached the end of the jetway where Greg waited for her. Finally. They'd be able to talk about...everything. All the uncertainty, the discomfort, would go away. She knew it would. They just needed to be together. She and Greg. The man she loved. The man she was going to marry one year and ten months from today.

"Kitten, it's great to see you."

She dropped her carry-on and threw herself into his arms. He kissed her, then stepped back. Too soon for Kathy. It had, after all, been three long months since she'd last been kissed or held.

Still, they were in a public place. She took a steadying breath and squeezed his hands, enjoying the solidity of touch after the months of disembodied phone and e-mail conversations.

"Let me look at you," he said. "You are so beautiful."

She'd missed that as well—Greg telling her she was beautiful. An exaggeration, but he always said it as if he believed it.

He twined a lock of coppery hair around a large finger, pulling gently to bring her close, then bent his head and kissed her again.

She settled into the kiss. That was more like it. "You're not bad, yourself," she murmured against his lips. In his case, an understatement. He was take-your-breath-away gorgeous, and right now, smiling into the deep, clear blue of his eyes, it was hard to recall why staying in Denver had ever seemed like a good idea.

When they reached Greg's apartment, he set her bag down inside the door and pulled her into his arms. She'd been impatient for this moment all the way from the airport. They kissed, undressing with clumsy haste, running their hands all over each other. Reconnecting after the long weeks apart.

Afterwards, Kathy sighed with happiness as she curled against Greg. He stroked her hip with a fingertip, the motion slowing as his breathing deepened and he drifted off to sleep. Kathy dozed as well, her excitement easing into satiety and peacefulness.

When she awoke, Greg was still asleep. Knowing he slept whenever and wherever he could, she slipped out of bed and went to the bathroom to get dressed. Then, while she waited for Greg to wake up, she toured the apartment.

Greg had taken over the lease along with the haphazard furnishings from the previous toxicology fellow. Those furnishings, a mix of obvious cast-offs, were, nonetheless, oddly charming. And she could easily make it more charming: some pillows, an afghan throw for the sofa, curtains.

She wandered into the kitchen. Galley-size but adequate, with a small gas stove and an avocado-colored fridge. Greg's additions were a microwave and coffee pot. Maybe the apartment's owner would let her paint the cabinets. Currently they were a dirty beige, but painted white, with bright colored doors—red or green or...

So. She was considering it, was she? Moving to San Francisco.

She went back to the living room and sat on the sofa, curling her legs under her. From this angle a slice of Golden Gate Bridge was visible. She'd miss the mountains of course. Still, this view might grow on her. Besides, it would be for only two—no less than two years now. A year and nine months. Actually, the move would take her at least a month. So make that a year and eight months.

She rolled the idea around like a toffee, tasting it.

When Greg walked into the living room, yawning and rubbing his head, she was still staring out the window, trying to decide.

"Hey, Kit. Deep thoughts?"

She smiled at him. "Just resting. Flying always makes me tired. Must be all the energy I put into keeping the plane in the air."

"Nope, it's the noise. Get yourself a pair of earplugs. Fix you right up."

She'd forgotten that—how often Greg took something she said in jest and treated it as if it were serious. Well, earplugs probably were a good idea.

"If you're hungry, we can walk over to Chinatown," he said.

"I'd like that. Besides, I can use the exercise." She sat up and slipped on her shoes.

"Hey, I thought we already took care of that." He twitched his eyebrows in a fake leer, and laughing, she stood on tiptoe to kiss him.

After dinner, as they opened their fortune cookies, Greg's phone rang. He checked the number, frowning. "Damn. It's the hospital. And after Walton promised no calls tonight." He half-turned away from her. "Yeah. What's up?"

Kathy unfolded her fortune: *You will be lucky in love.* She looked across at Greg, her heart lifting. She already was. Her decision to move to San Francisco solidified.

While Greg talked on the phone, her attention drifted to a Chinese family seated nearby. The man and woman were helping their three young children to the dishes sitting on the lazy Susan in the middle of the table.

The children, all boys, with solemn, dark eyes and quick, shy smiles, were neatly dressed. Children. Three was a perfect number. Two blonds and one redhead. Two boys and a girl, or two girls and a boy, Greg and herself...

"I thought we agreed" Greg's voice dropped abruptly. A moment later he ended the conversation, closed the phone, and turned back to her.

"Sorry, Kit. An acetaminophen overdose came in. Walton thinks I need to see it. We'll have to take a cab back so I can pick up the car."

She swallowed a spurt of irritation. Why didn't people overdose between nine and five? Well, they did, of course. It just seemed like more of them chose to do it at night. She sighed, letting the irritation go. She'd already learned it was a waste of time to get upset.

Greg came in late, after she was already asleep, but he got up with her the next morning. After breakfast, he drove her by the medical center and pointed out the emergency entrance. "I bet I can drive this route in my sleep. As a matter of fact, it's highly probable I have."

"Aren't we going in? I'd love to meet Walton."

"When we have a late case, he doesn't come in until noon."

"We can stop by later, then."

"Sure." Greg reached over to fiddle with the radio button, while Kathy tried to decide if he was twitchier than normal this morning. Or maybe it only seemed that way because she hadn't been with him for a while. He never did sit still, incessantly jiggling a foot or tapping a finger. She'd found the only way to deal with it was to ignore it.

"So what do you want to do today?" he said.

They decided on the Alcatraz tour, a visit to the Japanese Tea Garden in Golden Gate Park, and a ride on a cable car. Greg said that would be more than enough.

Kathy found Alcatraz haunting, but in the bright sun and brisk chop of the boat ride back to the mainland, her slight melancholy dissipated. And as it did, she realized San Francisco was beguiling her. Like Greg predicted it would in one of their first conversations after he moved. *Guaranteed, Kit. Love at first sight. Like us.*

A cool breeze brushed her cheek and made her shiver. Greg draped an arm on her shoulder and she shrugged off her unease.

After lunch, they wandered, sedate as fifty-year marrieds,

through the Japanese Tea Garden, then reverting to childhood, they raced each other across a stretch of grass in Golden Gate Park. Greg built up a lead, then turned, caught her hands and swung her around and around in dizzying circles until they both collapsed to the ground laughing and exhilarated.

In the late afternoon, they returned to the apartment, made love, and afterwards they caught a cable car to the waterfront for dinner.

After dinner, Kathy curled up on the couch with a book while Greg worked on a case presentation for the following week. When his phone rang, he checked the number. Saying it was the hospital, he went to the bedroom, closed the door, and for the next twenty minutes, only the intermittent murmur of his voice was audible.

When he came out, she looked up. "An emergency?"

"Yeah." His hair was standing up at odd angles as if he'd spent the entire call pulling on it.

Noticing his strained tone, she set her book down. "You need to go in?" She didn't even mind too much if he had to spend the night at the hospital after having him to herself all day.

"Yes...no."

"You don't have to go in?"

"It wasn't a case." He sat in the chair next to the couch, rubbing his hands on his thighs.

She sat up, put her feet on the floor and leaned toward him. "But it was a problem."

"Yeah. You could call it that."

"You want to talk about it?"

He closed his eyes, then opened them and turned away. "I need to tell you something."

He was scaring her, the way he looked and the tone of his voice. Her heart began thudding in a dull, heavy rhythm, and her stomach swooped as if she were in a free-falling elevator.

"...didn't plan it, Kit. Julie and me. We, well we just...clicked."

She shook her head. The words he'd spoken rattled around inside, like a handful of pebbles that needed to be sorted out and lined up before they made any sense.

"I don't understand." Her mouth was almost too dry to form the words.

He gave her an anguished glance and started wringing his hands. "I know. I know. I should have told you right away. No excuse. Stupid. Julie told me to."

The elevator jarred to a halt as the words made sudden, awful sense. *No! You can't possibly love someone else. We're engaged. You're marrying me!* The words piled up, broke free. "Why didn't you tell me not to come?" Not what she thought she was going to say. Surprising her even more was the calm, detached manner in which she said it.

"I thought it would be easier. Better. If I told you in person."

"You slept with me!" Her control slipped as the words lurched from her mouth.

He sat back abruptly, as if he'd been slapped.

Now there was an idea. Although she didn't believe in violence, right this minute, she understood why it happened— could almost feel the relief a hard physical connection between her hand and his face would bring. Except. She didn't want to touch him. Ever again. Or let him touch her.

She wrapped her arms around herself, holding on tight as he shifted around like a man with ants in his pants. Nasty, stinging, fire ants if the choice were up to her.

"I still have...feelings for you." He gave her a pleading look. "I wasn't sure. It's been confusing, you know?"

No, she didn't know.

"I had to see if what we had... If it's over."

"And is it?" She almost choked on the words, overwhelmed by the sudden, vivid memory of him swinging her around this afternoon, the two of them laughing with the sheer joy of being together. Or so she'd thought.

He nodded.

She clamped her lips shut to keep the whimper clogging her throat from emerging. A sudden pain made her realize she was digging her fingernails into her arms. Fingernails she'd splurged to have manicured for this trip. Probably he hadn't even noticed.

She pushed back against the sofa cushions to get further away from him, fighting the temptation to leap up and rake her perfectly shaped nails across his beautiful, deceitful face. Carefully, she loosened her grip, slid her hands together in her lap, and took a breath. When she tried to speak, she found she had to stop to clear her throat. "I expect you'll want your ring back."

"That's okay. You can keep it."

And let him think he'd bought her off? No way. "Here. I've no use for it." She slid the ring off her finger and laid it on the end table next to him, then re-clenched her hands in her lap.

She didn't know how she was managing to sit on the couch as prim and composed as if she were at a tea party. Shock maybe. But whatever its cause, she was grateful for it. She would *not* cry in front of him.

"Look, Kitten. I didn't do it to—"

"Don't. Call. Me. Kitten." The words ground out, surprising her as much as they seemed to surprise him. But then she'd never used that tone with him before. Quite possibly she'd never used that tone with anyone before.

"Sorry. Sorry." He stood and backed carefully away from her, as if she were a rattlesnake coiled to strike. "I'll get some things. Leave. You can stay here until you go back."

"Just a minute." She unclenched her jaw, but kept her tone firm. "I'm not through here."

He froze.

"I want to get this straight. You're in love with another woman, but you still slept with me."

His eyes appeared glazed, and a feeling of power swept through her, momentarily pushing aside any possibility she might cry.

"Do you have any idea what that makes you?"

His body bowed slightly, as if he were folding in on himself.

She thought of all the names she could call him. Delicious, colorful, awful names. "You're...despicable. Dishonest. And dishonorable." Good strong spitting words, and she made the most of them. She eased her hands apart and took a breath, but she was finished. Less is more, she told herself. Too many words would dilute her contempt. Besides, if she kept talking, she might not be able to stop. Might start weeping. And she *would not cry* in front of him. Damn him.

After a stunned moment, he escaped into the bedroom, and she took a deep breath and closed her eyes against the pain beginning to spread inside her chest. *A few minutes more, Kathleen Hope Jamison. Two minutes, three at the most. Then you can fall apart.*

When Greg came out of the bedroom, he'd recovered his composure. "I'm really, really sorry about this."

As if that would erase what he'd done.

"We can talk more if you want. Tomorrow. And here, this will help pay for your ticket. It's all I've got on me."

Kathy stared in disbelief at the hand holding money out to her. When she didn't move to take it, he set the clutch of bills on the table.

For a moment their eyes met before his skittered away. He cleared his throat as if to say something more then, apparently thinking better of it, he picked up his bag and left.

She sagged in relief, taking several deep breaths, then glanced at the table. The money was where he'd placed it, but the ring was gone. She stared at the empty place where the ring had been, realizing abruptly how much she'd hated it. Hated it for what it represented. The excess and carelessness she hadn't let herself think about, the lack of concern for her point of view she'd refused to acknowledge.

The large emerald-cut diamond had been Greg's choice. "Hell, Kit, what's more debt?" he'd said, when she protested it made more sense to pick a less expensive ring. "Only a couple of years before we hit the big time. Besides, you'll have it forever."

Right.

So why hadn't she thrown it at him? It was the least she could have done, and probably what he expected her to do. But no. She'd let him off with words.

He'd taken her future and, with one sharp twist, skewed it into an unknowable shape. Then he walked out. Going to...what did he say her name was, Jeannie, Jennie? No Julie, that was it. No longer Kathy and Greg. Now it was Greg and Julie. Julie and Greg.

So why wasn't she crying? Or yelling? Or something?

Instead she felt hollowed out, as if Greg had walked out taking with him not only a change of underwear but her emotions.

After a time, she managed to stand, her movements labored and stiff, like someone bruised all over from a terrible fall.

*Falling in love. Right. More like floating in love. But this...this...*Angrily she gave up trying to find the right word. *This other thing* that just happened. *That* was falling.

She searched until she found a phone book, called Continental Airlines and reserved a seat on the six a.m. flight to Denver. *One step at a time.* Then she went to the bedroom, and averting her eyes from the bed, re-packed. *One step at a time.* She called a cab and, without looking back, left the apartment.

Continental's ticket counter was closed for the night, and only a few people were scattered around the terminal. A janitor pushed a mop to the rhythms of whatever played in his headphones, and a young man slept on the floor with his backpack under his head, both of them blissfully unaware of their surroundings. Envy of their oblivion flared, faded.

She chose a seat away from everyone else. The unreality that set in after Greg left the apartment lasted through the remainder of the night. She knew it would eventually desert her, but as long as it lasted, she accepted it with relief.

In the morning, as the clerk did the ticket rewrite, Kathy handed over her credit card, letting herself neither think about the additional cost nor question her decision to leave Greg's money, torn into hundreds of tiny pieces, on the table. Shredding it had been a totally mad, but completely satisfying thing to do.

Still numb, she boarded the flight. Halfway back to Denver, without warning, the numbness wore off, and pain and anger surged through her in a huge, swamping wave. She bit her lip, hard, to stop a howl and pressed her forehead against the window. Tears ran into her fingers, as six miles below, the landscape crept past, mostly a lifeless brown but here and there marked with the gaping red wounds of canyons.

Words. She'd let him off with words. Not enough. Never again would she not fight back when someone hurt her.

By the time they landed in Denver, the tears had stopped, and she was relieved to discover she no longer felt like crying. Instead she was so exhausted, she could barely keep her eyes open.

But then maybe that was just because she'd forgotten the earplugs.

Chapter Five

Kathy stood in the doorway, imagining the room filled with women in graceful gowns and men in formal dress. Instead she faced a chaos of tables, desks, and file cabinets with every flat surface supporting at least one lopsided pile of paper. Yesteryear's ballroom, today's publishing company. Calico Cat Books. What she'd traded Greg for.

She thought about the work. The excitement of the new find. The daily conversations, jokes and laughter. The feeling of accomplishment when a book came out.

And she thought about the people. Calico's co-owners— Polly Lewis and Columba Whitlow. Polly with her quirky sense of humor and careless clothes and Columba, with her dry wit and Jackie Kennedy elegance. And Jade Mizoguchi, her fellow editor. Jade, whose serenity kept the rest of them sane.

So, would she have made the same choice had she known from the beginning Greg would forget her almost as soon as she disappeared from his rearview mirror? But then it was a different question now. Because now she knew Greg was the kind of man who would sleep with a woman as if he were checking out a pair of shoes or test-driving a car.

Remembering that part of it, she felt as dumb as a pet rock.

But maybe the whole miserable sequence of events had to play out before she could see through the dazzle that Greg wasn't the man she thought he was. And that was the important point. The point she needed to focus on whenever the anger and grief choked her. He wasn't the man she thought he was.

"Kathy?"

With a start, she turned to find Jade, face full of concern, staring at her.

"I didn't think you were coming back until next week."

"Yeah, that *was* the plan." Kathy held up her bare left hand.

Jade took Kathy's hand and folded it between hers. "Oh, Kathy. What happened?"

"Someone named Julie."

"Oh, honey, I'm so sorry. Are you okay?"

Kathy took a deep breath and looked around Calico and then back at Jade. She wasn't ready to smile yet, but at least she no longer felt like crying. She had been saved, after all, from becoming Greg's wife, something she now knew would have eventually made her miserable. "You know, I think I am, actually." Or she would be soon.

§

Hilary Hilstrom peered at Alan over her glasses. "I'm negotiating to bring in an editor from a local press to teach the writing seminar in the spring."

This was worse than their last meeting with its fiction-is-our-future declaration.

"It's a wonderful opportunity for our students," she added.

Probably she was expecting him to be ecstatic at having his teaching load reduced. Any normal faculty member would be. But for him, the students were a welcome distraction, and he particularly enjoyed teaching the seminar.

"I also need a favor." Hilstrom pulled off her glasses and twirled them. "Ms. Jamison will need office space. The adjunct area is simply unacceptable. I thought perhaps the second desk in your office."

Giving up his favorite course wasn't enough, now he had to share his office? It felt like Hilstrom had picked up his life and shaken it the way a dog would a dead rabbit. Damn the woman, for her blinkered vision and oblivious ambition.

"It shouldn't inconvenience you. She'll only be there

evenings and it would help me enormously." She leaned toward him, her glasses dangling from one hand.

Knowing he had no good reason to object to the request, he nodded in acquiescence.

Hilstrom sat back, looking satisfied. "I very much appreciate your cooperation in the matter of Ms. Jamison, Alan."

Right. As if he had a choice with tenure on the line.

Charles had his usual tongue-in-cheek solution. "I know a good lawyer, you want to sue."

"Yeah. And kiss tenure goodbye." Alan struggled to keep his tone light, but the subject of tenure was anything but light. If he didn't get it, he might have to leave Denver, and if he left Denver, he might end up too far from his family's ranch to spend his weekends there.

"Tenure is an outmoded concept anyway," Charles said. "Guaranteeing someone a job for life based on six years of effort." He snorted. "Can you imagine what would happen if the Rockies operated like that?"

A swift image of a white-haired Andres Galarraga rounding third and heading for home waving a cane, made Alan smile. But while that image was amusing, nothing else about this situation was. "You're right, but I need tenure in order to keep the job."

"There is that." Charles sighed. "So the editor. Male or female?"

"What?" Alan said. "Oh, female."

"Maybe she'll fit the bill."

Yeah. Right.

About as likely as one of the women Charles wanted to set him up with knowing something about literature.

❧

Kathy wiped the last dish and put it away, then stood

looking out the window at the Costellos' backyard. Mr. Costello was out there fussing with his roses, getting them ready for winter.

It was a month since she came back from San Francisco, more than enough time for her to stop picking over her shattered dreams. It was done, over, time to let it go. She knew the drill. She'd spent her entire life doing it. Saying goodbye, letting go.

So. From now on. No more staring into space, thinking of all the things she could have said, could have done. No more trying to figure out how she'd overlooked the flaws in Greg's character. No more seeking clues to his treachery. Instead, she needed to nurture the feeling of relief that every once in a while replaced the tangle of anger and regret. After all, she'd barely avoided making a huge mistake.

And maybe eventually, she'd be able to write a heck of a good story about it.

But not yet.

Still, writing about something...it was how she'd gotten through rough times before. It was worth trying again. She could start someplace simple. Perhaps a name.

She went upstairs and got her book of names, then sat at the kitchen table and flipped through it, jotting down any name that jumped out at her. After several minutes, she sat back to look at what she had: Andrea, Andy. Nope, too tomboyish. Sofia? Too pretentious. Linette. Too feminine and kind of icky, actually, now that she considered it. Ramona, too old-fashioned. Amanda, Mandy. Not bad. She might enjoy getting acquainted with an Amanda.

Okay. So Amanda it was.

Tomorrow she would make a fresh start. In a fresh place.

Hilary Hilstrom had called today to invite her to teach a writing seminar at DSU next spring. Kathy had met Hilary at a writers' conference, but had never expected Hilary to follow up on her offhand comment about Kathy teaching a course. Even better than being invited to teach, though, was the fact Hilary had offered her the use of an office.

Kathy had hung up feeling excited and relieved. Serendipity, missing from her life the last six months, now seemed to be back in operation, bringing her the perfect opportunity at the perfect moment. She would go to DSU every night and write for at least an hour about...Amanda.

℘

"Professor Francini?"

Alan looked up from the stack of papers he was grading to find a young woman with copper-colored hair standing in his doorway.

At his acknowledgement, she stepped into the room, and he noticed other things: eyes that appeared tired or maybe sad, and cheekbones that were a touch too prominent, as if she'd lost weight recently. In spite of the brightness trapped in those strands of smooth hair, she seemed dimmed.

One of the graduate students? If so, she would have been hard to overlook. Her face not so much beautiful, but something better. Interesting. Arresting.

"I'm Kathy Jamison." She cocked her head, and her hair shifted and slid, catching the light. "Hilary Hilstrom told me to see you about a desk."

What the...? *This* was the editor Hilstrom hired? He'd expected someone considerably...well, older for one thing. Besides... "You're early, aren't you?"

She looked puzzled, and a small crease formed between her eyes. "It's five-thirty."

He shook his head. "It's September. Your seminar isn't until spring semester."

Quick comprehension dawned along with a blush that turned her face rosy. She tucked a strand of hair behind her ear, and he watched as it slid right back to brush against her cheek.

"Hilary said it was okay for me to start using the office now."

Hilary?

"I need a place to write."

So, go to the library. He didn't say it out loud, of course. Not fair to take his anger at Hilary Hilstrom out on this stranger. After all, he *had* told Hilstrom he would share his office. He just thought it would be for one night a week and for only the duration of the seminar.

"I should have called."

A call wouldn't have helped. He passed a hand across his brow, trying to figure out how to handle it. "There's been a misunderstanding."

She examined his office, taking in, no doubt, its lack of amenities, its almost fanatical neatness, a hold-over from his college days of rooming with Charles. *I say, Francini. You do realize a neat office is the sign of a sick mind,* was how one colleague put it.

Her mouth trembled, and she blinked rapidly. She looked like she was on the verge of tears, except that didn't make any sense. Her glance came to rest on the extra desk sitting in the corner. Like his, its oak top was scarred from years of service. A wad of paper folded into a thick square shimmed one of its legs.

Still staring at the desk, her chin came up, and her mouth firmed. "I understand. You didn't think you could turn Hilary down. But, really, you don't want to share." She concluded her assessment of the other desk and gave him a quick, intent look out of eyes as dark and light as shade and sunlight on a mountain stream.

He thought about how to answer her. But the plain truth? She was right. He didn't want to share.

"I'll make other arrangements, then. I certainly wouldn't want to inconvenience you." Her hands were so tightly clenched the knuckles were turning white. "Nice meeting you." Her tone, at odds with the words, was in perfect concert with the clenched hands. Without giving him a chance to respond, she whirled and walked out, pulling the door shut with a sharp click.

He stared at the closed door without moving. Too bad. All of it, because he'd liked the way she'd brightened the office with that hair. Liked as well her voice, musical, low-pitched. Would have liked a chance to...but no. Better this way.

Chasing her off was what he wanted. But he'd also made her angry. She'd probably run directly to Hilstrom to complain.

And that really would cook his tenure goose.

He ought to chase after her, apologize. Beg her to come back. Instead, he sat there, allowing the seconds to tick away until it was too late.

ℰ

Men! Kathy's racket connected with a satisfying thunk as she sent the tennis ball back at the practice wall. As if dealing with her residual anger at Greg wasn't enough. No. She had to have the additional pleasure of an encounter with the most arrogant, *whack*, insufferable, *whack*, obnoxious, *whack,* office-hogging professor she'd ever met. If she'd been a large, rabid cockroach, he couldn't have been more obviously appalled at the idea of sharing his office with her. Even worse, he'd almost made her cry.

"I think you've killed it." The masculine drawl distracted Kathy, and the ball went sailing past her racket. She glared at the man, then jogged after her ball. That was the problem with the practice walls at City Park. Some guy always figured you for a pick-up. And if she was ever not in the mood, it was now. Especially given the man so strongly resembled Greg. One blond Greek god in her life was more than sufficient, thank you very much. She suppressed a shudder.

"There's a court free, if you'd like a game," the man said as she returned with her ball.

"No thanks." She didn't look at him, not caring she was being rude, and she was hardly ever rude. In fact, whenever she was, she always regretted it afterwards. But not this time.

She tossed the ball and with a smooth stroke slammed it into the wall thinking how satisfying it would be to be aiming at Greg. Or that selfish, arrogant professor.

The return sailed past her racket, and the man loped after it like a damn golden retriever. He tossed it to her.

She turned her back on him and continued to stroke the ball at the wall, but whenever she checked, she found him still watching. It appeared the only way to get rid of him was to leave. But she was not, *whack,* going to let some man, *whack,* chase her away before she was ready to go, *whack*.

"You don't remember me, do you?" he said, when she finally stopped for a drink of water.

She didn't even glance at him. "Nope."

"Charles Larimore." He extended his hand.

She stood holding her racket, a ball, and her bottle of water staring at his hand until he lowered it, grinning at her. "You do seem a bit tied up at the moment."

"I am." She gave him a steady look she hoped he would find off-putting.

"You're single. An editor." He closed his eyes as if mentally reading a checklist. "Graduate degree. Against the death penalty."

Her eyes narrowed. Was the bastard guessing or stalking her?

"You still don't remember, do you?"

She shrugged and took another drink of water.

"Really know how to smash a guy's ego to smithereens." He shook his head in what was obviously mock sorrow. "Juror number...seven, wasn't it?"

Memory stirred. She'd been called for a panel, a murder case. But when the prosecutor asked if she opposed the death penalty and she said she did, she was excused.

With that came another memory. When they'd first taken their seats in the jury box, the woman next to her had taken one look at the prosecutor, sucked air in through her teeth, and whispered, "Sheesh. Wouldn't you like that coming home to you every night."

But Kathy had been immune to Charles Larimore. After all she *had* been dating a man every bit as attractive, professional, and intelligent as the prosecutor appeared to be.

"Look, I'm not trying to pick you up," Charles said, jerking her back to the present.

Right. As if she believed that.

"I have a girlfriend. What I need at the moment is a tennis partner. I was supposed to meet a friend for a game, but he called to say he can't make it." He gave her what he no doubt thought was a winning smile. Impossible for her to judge in her current mood.

Still, it would be more comfortable to play a set with him, rather than having him continue to stand there watching her. "Okay. You're on."

They played two sets which he won, but she made him work for it. She felt better when they finished. Hot, sweaty and exhausted, but better.

"Here's hoping you're available the next time my friend stands me up." He gave her a sunny smile and held up crossed fingers, before slipping his racket into its case. He extended his hand. "So long."

This time she shook it. "Thanks," she said, meaning, *thanks for the game and thanks for not trying to hit on me afterwards.*

Chapter Six

The head of the reappointment, promotion and tenure committee stopped by Alan's office.

"Thought we might chat about your situation," Grenville said, smoothing one hand over his thinning hair. "Professor Hilstrom has made her position quite evident." He cleared his throat with a harsh noise. "Deuced inconvenient."

Grenville's specialty was British literature, and although he didn't go as far as to assume an accent, he did cultivate the speech patterns and grooming of an upper crust Englishman of the nineteenth century.

Alan nodded. "Yeah. I know. No fiction, no tenure."

Grenville gave him a sharp look, and Alan looked blandly back, his stomach gathering in a tight knot.

"No matter what the committee does, if your dossier doesn't include fiction, she'll give you a negative recommendation." Grenville rolled the papers he was carrying into a tube and tapped them on his leg. "Given she's brand, shiny new, unlikely the dean will oppose her."

"Have you looked at my appointment letter?" Alan's tone kept his bland look company, but his calm was only a thin veneer.

"Of course."

"Then you know it says a good publication record is a must, but there's no mention of what type of publication."

Grenville's eyebrow arched. "Would you sue?"

Perfect. All the man needed was a monocle. Alan looked steadily at Grenville. "Wouldn't you?" It was as far as he was willing to take Charles's advice.

Grenville sighed. "I'm glad it's not an issue for me. But Hilstrom appears to be committed to her position."

"And the lady does like getting her way." Alan felt a brief pang of sympathy for Hilstrom's husband.

Grenville harrumphed. "Deuced woman is even putting the screws to those of us with tenure. Says we're resting on our laurels. Has absolutely no comprehension of current market conditions."

Grenville had published a single novel, a tedious tribute to Jane Austen, shortly before he was granted tenure. As far as Alan knew, he hadn't tested market conditions since.

Grenville continued to tap the rolled papers against his leg. "You may win a battle or two, old chap. But, if I were you, I'd be prepared to lose the war."

It was what kept Alan awake nights—that possibility. And now Grenville's words had added weight and menace to Alan's fears.

Alan opened his closet and pushed his clothes out of the way in order to get at the box in the back corner. Reluctantly, he pulled it out and opened it. Inside lay the manuscript pages, computer disks, and research material he hadn't looked at since packing it away after Meg's death.

As he lifted out a portion of manuscript, the pages slipped from his hands onto the floor. He stared at the mess as Hilstrom's words played over in his head: *"Fiction is our future."*

Yeah. At one time that was what he'd thought. That fiction was his future. Along with Meg. The two of them chasing their dreams. Together. Hers to paint, his to write. Nothing impossible.

And now...?

There was music in words. Music he no longer heard. But he could fake it, couldn't he? Take Charles's advice. Look at all the pages he'd written. All he needed to do was find the right disk, pop it in his computer, and print a fresh copy to attach to his dossier. Highly unlikely anybody on the committee would even look at it. They'd just check the heft.

He stared at the jumble of pages, knowing he couldn't manage it.

Not even to get tenure.

As Alan and Charles left the restaurant after lunch, they were just in time to see a car streak toward them, followed by the screech of locked tires and a thump. In the aftermath, a border collie lay shrieking in pain by the curb. Alan's heart kicked into a gallop, even though he knew the dog couldn't possibly be his Cormac.

A woman bent over the dog, her voice melding with the animal's cries of pain. "*Ay Dios mío.* Blackie."

Charles rushed to the woman's side, leaving Alan standing alone, the scene freezing in front of him. Then Charles was back. "Alan. You have to help. You're the one who knows about animals." And everything began to move again as he followed Charles into the street.

He bent over the dog and automatically began to murmur. "That's okay. Take it easy, boy. We'll take care of you." He smoothed his hand over the long fur on the animal's neck, and after a moment, the dog stopped struggling and subsided into whimpers. The woman continued crying, her words a mixture of Spanish and English.

The dog's left hind leg was gashed, but more worrisome was the fact the animal couldn't get up. Alan swallowed, clamping down on sudden nausea. "He needs a vet. You have a car?"

"*Sí.* At home. I live on Albion."

Too far. He turned to see Charles talking to the man who had hit the dog. "Get my car, will you?" Alan handed his keys to Charles and pointed. "It's around the corner."

"Damn dog came out of nowhere." The man who spoke was dressed like Charles, in a dark suit, white shirt, and conservative tie. He drummed his fingers on the hood of the silver Lexus angled into the curb near the dog. "Ran right in front of me."

You were speeding, and besides, if you had a heart, you

wouldn't blame the dog. Alan bit down on the words before they escaped, turning away in disgust as the man leaned over, apparently checking for damage to the front of his car.

"You seem to have this under control." The man cleared his throat. "I, ah, have an appointment." When Alan continued to ignore him, the man climbed into his car and backed away. A moment later, Charles pulled Alan's Forester into position.

While Charles cleared a space in back, Alan worked his coat under Blackie to make a sling. Then Charles helped him lift the dog into the car.

Charles put his hand on Alan's shoulder. "I have to be in court in half an hour, or I'd hang with you."

That was Charles for you. Damn Tom Sawyer. Suck you into helping, then leave you holding the bag, not to mention the dog.

With his other hand, Charles handed Alan a thick wad of bills.

"What the—?"

"Vet bill. Courtesy the asshole in the Lexus. He insisted."

Right. And Alan didn't need a crystal ball to know how Charles had managed that. No doubt words like district attorney, legal suit, and accident report had been bandied about, obviously to good effect. Alan stuffed the money in his pocket and got into his car.

The woman climbed into the backseat and leaned over it to calm her dog. She gave Alan directions to the vet's, and he drove, taking care with corners and avoiding bumps. He pulled into the curb in front of the vet's and slid out, saying he'd get someone.

As Blackie was carried inside, Alan realized his hands and shirt were sticky with blood. The thick metallic scent of it overpowered the waiting-room odors of urine and disinfectant. He was directed to the bathroom and cleaned up. When he returned to the waiting room, he found Blackie's owner rocking back and forth, her arms clutched around herself.

He'd seen the look on the vet's face, and he knew it would be a lie to tell her Blackie was going to be okay. "Your dog's in good hands," he said instead.

"*Es mi culpa.* I wasn't paying attention." The woman's voice was thick with tears. She looked up at him, wiping her eyes.

He tried to find words to ease his exit. He'd done enough. More than Charles had. Or the asshole in the Lexus. She could handle it from here. It was her dog after all.

"Accidents happen. You mustn't blame yourself. *Está bien.*" He clamped his mouth shut to cut off the flow of platitudes. They'd never done him any good, why inflict them on her? He took a breath to tell her he was leaving, but just then the vet's assistant appeared and beckoned the woman into the examining room. She stood and touched his arm. "*Por favor.* Please. Can you come with me?"

He tried to say, *I'd like to, but I have a class.* A lie. Two lies, actually. Maybe that was why he couldn't force the words out. *"If you're in for an inch, might as well go the mile."* One of his father's favorite sayings. He must have inherited the gene.

In the examining room, Blackie lay on a stainless steel table. When the woman touched the dog's head and spoke softly in Spanish, it opened an eye and tried to lick her hand, but its tail lay limp and motionless.

"I'm sorry," the vet said. "Blackie has extensive internal injuries, and his spinal cord has been severed."

"No. *No es posible.*" The woman's voice wobbled, and a sob escaped. "You can't. You just can't. Please. Delia loves him." As if Delia's love should make all the difference.

If she thought that, she didn't have a clue how things really worked.

The vet spoke firmly. "You know it's the kindest thing."

The woman trembled. Feeling awkward, Alan laid a hand on her shoulder.

"*Está bien,* it's okay." Alan patted. "Blackie knows you love him."

It must have been the right thing to say, because after a moment, the woman stopped weeping and smoothed Blackie's head with a small hand. The dog sighed and closed its eyes.

The assistant came in carrying a syringe, and the woman gave the vet a small nod. While she continued to stroke the soft fur and murmur in Spanish, the doctor injected the contents of the syringe.

Enough already. Alan turned abruptly and walked out. What had he been thinking to let Charles pull him into this?

And once pulled in, why hadn't he simply called the police to help the woman?

When he reached the waiting room, the receptionist motioned him over, handed him a plastic bag containing his jacket and told him he better move his car to the back parking lot before he got a ticket. Almost out the door, he remembered the money. He pulled it out and handed it to her. "Appreciate it if you'd use this for Blackie's expenses."

The girl took the money and flipped through it quickly.

"Will it be enough?"

"There's over four hundred here. That will more than cover it."

Alan nodded. "Good. Just give the lady any change."

He walked out, relieved it was over. The woman could take a bus home. It wasn't far.

Then he remembered those small shoulders shaking in grief and, instead of leaving, he pulled in behind the building, parked and walked back into the clinic.

After a while, the woman returned to the waiting area, looking calmer, cried out perhaps. When the receptionist handed over the extra money, saying the bill had been paid, the woman turned wide, dark eyes on Alan. "*Ay bendito.* It's too much. I can't let you do it." She held out the money to him.

He shook his head. "It's from the ass—the man who hit Blackie. He insisted."

She closed her eyes, taking a deep breath. "I'm so sorry for all the trouble I've caused you." Her voice caught as her eyes focused on his shirt. "And your clothes. *Lo siento.*"

He shrugged. "I've been looking for an excuse to get rid of the jacket. Actually, I'm not crazy about this shirt either." But he was even less crazy about shopping.

She gave him a watery smile, holding out the money. "Please. Take this. To replace your clothes."

He shook his head, refusing again. "Figured you could use a ride home."

"*Gracias.*" She held out a slim hand. "I'm Grace Garcia de Garibaldi."

"Alan Francini." He shook her hand briefly, then opened

the door and ushered her out of the clinic. "You live on Albion, you said?"

"*Sí.* Near the medical center." Her voice was still uneven.

He kept the conversation going with simple questions as he drove her home. He learned she was Puerto Rican and an ICU nurse who wrote children's books in her spare time. In turn, he talked about his border collie and told her he was a professor at Denver State.

He turned on Albion. "Which house?"

"The white one on the left," she said, pointing. "I appreciate so much what you did today. For me and Blackie. My daughter." Her voice caught. "Delia. She's only six. I don't know how I'm going to tell her."

He pulled the car to a stop, and she turned toward him, biting her lip and holding out her hand. "*Muchas gracias*, Alan."

He shook her hand gently. "*De nada*, Grace." Sometimes he thought that would be a relief, to live his life in a foreign language using words that held no memories.

Grace slid out of the car and walked quickly toward the small house, turning as she reached the front stoop to wave at him. He acknowledged the wave, then drove away trying not to picture an unknown little girl named Delia who would shortly learn her dog was dead.

Charles called Alan that evening. "So what happened with the dog?"

"It had to be put down."

"Too bad. Cute dog. Looked a lot like Cormac. And the owner, she was cute too."

"Was she? I didn't notice." Alan stood and walked over to lean against the balcony door.

"You never do. You get her name or anything?"

"Grace Garcia de Garibaldi. Puerto Rican. Nurse at the med center. Lives on Albion. Writes children's books." He rubbed his forehead, trying to forget the rest of the details of his meeting with Grace and Blackie. "I miss anything you want to know?"

"She a *señora* or a *señorita*?"

"I'd guess *señora.*"

"Guess. Hell, I don't understand how you can get into a cultural, literary, and career discussion with a woman and fail to get the basic stats."

"She just lost her dog. Besides, she has a little girl."

That should effectively end it. Since Charles had an inflexible rule about dating women who had children, he could hardly insist Alan do it.

"Grace Garcia de Garibaldi. Nice alliteration. That's a literary term, you know. Well, got to prepare for court. Catch you later." As usual, Charles stopped right before he tipped Alan into saying something he'd regret.

Alan disconnected the call and stood staring out at the darkness.

Damn Charles and his eternal nudging.

∽

Kathy located the library carrel she'd reserved after her encounter with Alan Francini and got out paper and pens. She sat for a time, letting her mind drift before she began writing.

"So, Amanda, tell me about yourself."

"I loves 'orses, you ken. Love 'em."

Amanda was dropping her "h's" all over the place.

"When everything else goes to pot, I can always count on Sukie, my black stallion. He can pull me out of the worst funk. You cannot imagine."

Kathy stopped writing abruptly and stared at the words. Who did Amanda think she was, Eliza Doolittle? And a black stallion named Sukie—where did that come from?

Horses. What had made her come up with a character who wanted to drag horses into the story, when Kathy was scared to death of them? Well, she'd liked them once, before she made the personal acquaintance of a fat, scruffy one named Peaches. At a summer camp when she was ten.

The first time Peaches began to trot, Kathy had bounced off, and everybody laughed. She'd climbed back on and promptly bounced off again. Peaches was so fat, Kathy couldn't get a grip.

She'd brushed off her clothes, determined to try yet again, when Peaches swung around and nipped her arm. Granted it was more pinch than bite, but enough was enough. Kathy had stomped away, trying not to cry, and for the rest of her time at camp, she gave the stables a wide berth.

So if Amanda insisted on dragging horses into the story, Kathy was going to have to make peace with the equine world and possibly do some personal research. Or, better, she could just get rid of Amanda, who, at any rate, sounded like a ditz. But then again, if Kathy didn't follow up on this nudge, her muse might sulk, and she could end up sitting here night after night with nothing to write about. It had happened before.

Surely she could manage one riding lesson. She lived in Colorado, after all. She'd insist on a skinny, geriatric horse that would be perfectly happy to plod along. And maybe it wouldn't be all bad. Facing an old fear might serve as a distraction from the new fear she'd been struggling to suppress.

She closed her eyes, took a deep breath, and there it was, the dark panic that came to keep her company whenever she wasn't busy. The fear, still faint but growing more distinct, that she might never find a man she could trust completely and love with all her heart. Because even if such a man existed, she no longer trusted herself to recognize him.

Chapter Seven

Alan answered the phone to find Grace Garcia de Garibaldi on the other end.

"*Mira*, Alan," Grace said. "I'm calling to invite you to dinner. Delia and Frank want to meet you. To thank you for helping with Blackie."

Frank? Son or husband? "You already thanked me." In fact, the large plant she'd sent, accompanied by an Overland Traders' gift certificate, was still alive, although a few leaves had turned an ominous yellow.

"Can you possibly come this Saturday?"

Since he spent all his weekends at the ranch, he didn't need to consult a calendar. Still he hesitated, worrying the small mystery of Frank.

"Frank told me it was too short notice. But I thought it was worth a try," Grace continued, sounding hopeful.

Okay. Frank had to be a husband. Which meant this was exactly what it seemed: a friendly invitation for dinner. "As a matter of fact, I can come." He'd have to drive in from the ranch, but that was no biggie.

"And bring a guest, of course," Grace said, clinching the Frank-as-husband hypothesis.

"No. No guest."

"Can you... This is going to seem silly, but can you possibly bring your dog? Delia asked me to invite him."

"I think Cormac would enjoy a night out."

And Cormac wasn't the only one. Alan was surprised at how pleased he was with the invitation. Still, he was glad he had the dog with him to help ease those first, awkward moments when he arrived at the Garibaldis'.

Grace greeted him at the door, and then a little girl came skipping down the hall, right up to Cormac. She knelt and extended her hand for the dog to sniff, and when he gave it a lick, she giggled. Cormac hadn't been around children much, so Alan bent down to supervise the interaction, but clearly he didn't need to worry. The collie's tail started wagging furiously, and he wiggled with pleasure as Delia hugged him.

"Traitor," Alan muttered.

Grace laughed. "*Mira.* She does have a way with animals."

Then Grace introduced her husband. At first glance, Frank Garibaldi, who seemed as imperturbable as an old dog sleeping in the sun, seemed an odd choice for Grace, who was as quick and vivid as a hummingbird. But it seemed to be a happy union. And Delia was a delight, as sunny and good-natured as a puppy.

After that first dinner, Alan went with Frank to the animal shelter to help pick out a new dog for Delia.

"If Delia came, we'd end up with not only a dog, but a brace of kittens and the miscellaneous gerbil or two," Frank said, as he and Alan moved from cage to cage, assessing the available animals. They settled on a collie mix with a sweet temperament that looked enough like Blackie to satisfy the little girl.

Delia christened her new dog Blackie-two and begged Alan to help her train it. He began stopping by the Garibaldis' a couple of afternoons a week to work with Delia and her dog. Afterwards, Grace always insisted he stay for dinner.

"It's the least I can do, *verdad?* It's so good of you to help, Alan."

"It's my pleasure, Grace. Delia and I are pals." He smiled at the little girl, who grinned back at him.

The only downside of becoming a regular part of the Garibaldi family was that it made him more aware of how alone he was the rest of the time.

&

Kathy glanced from the instructions to the dirt road coming up on her right. This had to be it—exactly three point six miles from the last turn. Then she saw the sign confirming it. TapDancer Ranch.

The minivan she'd been following since leaving the highway turned under the TapDancer sign as well. Someone else arriving for a riding lesson, no doubt.

After another quarter mile, the road topped a rise, and there in front of Kathy lay a valley cupped within the curve of the foothills.

She stopped the car to look. A large, weathered barn the color of brushed pewter was surrounded by newer structures, and the fenced-in pastures were golden with grass and dotted with grazing horses. A house of wood and glass perched on a hill overlooking it all.

It was...beautiful was too insipid a word. Beyond beauty, there was strength in the up-curving lineaments of the land forming the valley's boundaries and peace in the slow movements of the horses. She wondered if the people who lived here realized how lucky they were.

She drove slowly down the hill and parked next to the minivan. As she got out of her car, a dog came rushing from the barn to greet the woman and little girl who had arrived in the van. The girl gathered the dog in her arms.

Kathy looked away from the child and delirious dog, to see a man coming toward them from the barn. She took in the scuffed boots, faded jeans, and worn shirt. The Virginian in the flesh, although this man was shorter and lighter-haired than her mental picture of The Virginian. Charmed, she watched him approach.

"Hi, Grace," he said, hugging the woman. "Welcome to TapDancer."

No. It couldn't be.

The little girl bounced over to him, and he scooped her up.

"Hi, Alan."

But it was. The "Alan" clinched it. Not The Virginian or a

close facsimile thereof, but the arrogant, obnoxious professor. She'd done nothing to deserve this, really she hadn't. *Pretending* to slam a tennis ball at someone didn't count, did it?

"Delia. How's my best girl?"

"Ter-ri-fic." Delia bobbed her head with each syllable, then gave the man a smacking kiss before he set her down.

Kathy edged back toward her car, planning to open the door, slide in and drive away, as if she'd turned in here by mistake—the truth, actually.

But before she reached safety, Alan looked over at her, frowning. "Ms....Jamison isn't it?"

"I-I was just—I mean, there's been a mistake." She reached out a shaking hand to open the car door, but found she'd locked it. She fumbled in her pocket for her keys, then dropped them from fingers gone numb. As she bent to pick them up, she saw that man, woman and child were all staring at her.

Standing, she flipped the keys to get at the one to her elderly Toyota. "Umm. That is, I talked to Stella Francini, to schedule a riding lesson." She blew out a breath to dislodge the strands of hair that had blown across her face, remembering that Stella had said her husband did the teaching. But who knew her husband would be this man? Odd, though, that he didn't seem to know Kathy was coming. Didn't they talk to each other? "You weren't expecting me, I can just..." The car key had gotten caught in the keychain. She shook the keys, trying to dislodge it.

"The folks rushed off to be with my sister," Alan said. "She's having a baby. Guess they were so excited, they forgot to mention you were coming."

His folks? So that meant Stella was...his mother? And this Grace, whom he'd greeted so affectionately, she was what? His date?

"That's okay." Kathy fumbled the key free and tried to fit it in the lock. "I can come back another time." As if that were going to happen.

"*Ay Dios mío,*" Grace said. "You must stay. It's a long drive, *sí?*"

What was the woman, nuts? Two horses and a pony were saddled and standing tethered to the side of the barn waiting for the three of them. And Kathy had no intention of making it a foursome. "No. Really. It's okay. I'll reschedule." *Not.*

"Nonsense," Grace said. "I'm only here for Delia's sake. I don't need to ride."

"I can always saddle another horse," Alan said, but he didn't make it sound like that was an appealing idea. "It's up to you, but there's no reason for you to leave."

"*Por favor.* You must stay. I'll feel terrible if you leave." Grace looked both concerned and sincere. "I'm Grace Garcia de Garibaldi, by the way, and this is my daughter, Delia." Grace stepped toward Kathy, extending her hand.

"Kathy Jamison." Kathy tried to smile, but she doubted it was a success. Peachy. Just peachy. She'd finally decided to try to conquer her fear of horses, and this is what she got. Fourth wheel on a date with a man she'd hoped never to see again.

She shook Grace's hand and smiled a hello at Delia, who gave her a sunny grin.

"You must stay," Grace said.

"Okay. Thanks." So where was the ability to click her heels and wish herself away when she needed it?

"*Mira.* You don't need to saddle another horse, Alan."

Alan shrugged. "It's no trouble."

Grace shook her head.

"Let's get started, then." Alan took Delia's hand in his and led the way to the side of the barn where the horses and pony stood waiting.

The pony whickered softly and rubbed its head against Alan's arm. "Her name is Arriba," he told Delia. "She's a Galiceno, from Mexico. These other two are Paso Finos from Puerto Rico."

"Like my *mami*," Delia said.

Alan pulled a carrot from his back pocket and handed it to Delia. "Hold your hand out flat. Like this. Let her take it from you. Don't worry, she won't bite."

"Oh, she wouldn't bite me. She knows I'm her friend." Delia sounded as serious as an elderly schoolmarm. Then she giggled. "Ooh, she's tickling me." She gave her mother a luminous smile, a smile that caught at Kathy's heart, causing a sharp pain. It was her biggest regret—not her broken engagement—but the loss of possibility, of children, a family.

"You ready to ride?" Alan asked Delia, his words pulling Kathy from dark thoughts back to the sunny day.

Delia nodded, her whole body joining in. She was obviously so filled with happiness, there was simply no room for words.

As Alan lifted the little girl onto the pony's back, Kathy turned to Grace. "I'm really sorry to have barged in like this."

"*Ay bendito.* Not your fault Alan's sister picked today to have her baby. Besides, to tell you the truth, I was looking for an excuse not to ride. *Entonces,* I'm glad you're here."

Grace *did* look relieved.

"Here, Grace." Alan handed Grace the lead he'd attached to the pony's bridle. "You can lead Arriba around the ring, while I get Ms. Jamison started."

Ms. Jamison indeed. Kathy wondered if she was supposed to call him *Mr.* Francini, or *Professor* Francini, or perhaps something more casual, like *Your Almighty Professorial Majesty*? And couldn't he be a little friendlier instead of acting like he'd just been told he had an unpleasant disease?

As Alan approached the remaining two horses, the chocolate-colored one leaned into him, lipping his pockets. Obviously kids and animals loved this man, although Kathy failed to see the attraction herself.

"This greedy gut is Sonoro." He pushed Sonoro's head firmly out of the way in order to untie the other horse, which he led over to Kathy. "And this is Siesta. She's a real sweetheart."

Right. Kathy gave Siesta a tentative pat.

Alan gave her a speculative look. "You've ridden before?"

"Once or twice. With a western saddle." *And got tossed on my butt for my trouble.* Damn Amanda. She was out of the story—if Kathy survived long enough to delete her.

Alan's eyes narrowed. "These are Spanish saddles. Don't worry, you'll be fine."

If he was trying to be reassuring, his tone, brisk and business-like, ruined the effect.

"Here's your get-acquainted carrot. You know how to hold it?"

She nodded and held her hand flat trying not to think about how large Siesta's teeth were. If a small child could do this, so could she.

Siesta blew a warm breath across her palm before delicately lifting the carrot and crunching down on it, and Kathy couldn't help but smile. It *did* tickle. But when Siesta butted her, Kathy couldn't help that reaction either. She jumped back.

"She's just hoping for another carrot." Alan's cool tone clearly indicated his opinion of Kathy's instinctive recoil. He patted the filly, which, thankfully, switched its attentions to him.

At least Siesta was acceptably skinny. Kathy winced at the thought of Alan's reaction if she insisted on a different horse.

Alan motioned Kathy to move closer. "Best way to mount is to face the back. Put your hand up here on her neck, turn the stirrup, put your foot in, then swing up and around."

Siesta wasn't a tall horse, but the swing up was more difficult than it looked, and Kathy was relieved to manage it with reasonable grace. She didn't want to appear clumsy when she was working so hard to look down on this man.

Alan adjusted her stirrups, took the reins, tied them in a knot and handed them to her. "Hold them up a bit, right at the knot. That will make her arch her neck. Give you a better ride. Sit up nice and straight with your heels down." He smoothed his hand over the filly's neck. "She has a real soft mouth. She starts backing up, means you're pulling."

"Heels down, reins up, don't pull," Kathy chanted under her breath as Alan went over to the other horse and swung gracefully into the saddle. Damn him.

"Okay. We'll begin with a slow walk around the ring. Relax. Siesta knows what she's doing." *Which you obviously do not* was clearly implied by his tone and the look on his face.

As the two horses walked side by side, Alan showed Kathy how to signal the filly to turn to the right or to the left. Then he had her walk Siesta through a large figure eight while he watched.

"You ready to try something faster?"

I don't do faster. Then why was she nodding, dammit?

Because she couldn't stand the thought of seeing another one of his cool, superior looks? But that look certainly wasn't going to be any easier to take from a prone position in the dirt, which was where she was headed if she let Siesta do anything but walk.

Alan's horse moved into a fast gait, and before Kathy could react, Siesta joined in. Kathy's heart hammered against her ribs as she clutched at the edge of the saddle with her hands and gripped Siesta with her legs. She squeezed her eyes shut.

One breath, two, and she realized she was still sitting on Siesta, and instead of bouncing, she was moving in an easy side-to-side motion. She opened her eyes, and after several more careful breaths, she unclenched her legs and let go of her death grip on the saddle. She lifted the reins the way Alan had told her to, and after she did, she began to notice other things. Like how the world looked from the back of a horse, as if there were more of it, somehow. The way it had looked when as a small child she'd been lifted onto her father's shoulders in order to see better.

The autumn air brushed her cheeks, lifting her hair and cooling her neck. In an instant, delight replaced fear. She was riding, and not only that, she understood for the first time why people actually did it for fun.

After several circuits, Alan slowed his horse back to a walk, and Kathy's horse quickly followed suit.

"How was it?" he said.

It was. Wow! She couldn't tell him that, of course. Their relationship was much too cool and distant for that kind of sharing. "She's so smooth. I didn't bounce at all."

"That's a Paso Fino for you. Do you know any Spanish?"

"Fine passage?" Kathy hazarded.

"Close. Fine step or fine gait. Let me show you something. Stay here."

Kathy tightened her reins slightly, and Siesta stopped and stood quietly. It made Kathy feel in control, safe.

Alan, meanwhile, rode over to Grace and Delia and spoke to them briefly before turning Sonoro toward the center of the ring, where Kathy had noticed a wooden platform embedded in the dirt. At an invisible signal from Alan, Sonoro's legs began moving in a quick step that, given his forward progress, was rather like jogging in place. Reaching the wooden platform, Sonoro danced slowly across, rapping out a staccato rhythm.

Delia clapped her hands in delight, and Kathy felt the same delight as the little girl. It was magic. Enchantment.

When Sonoro's dance ended near Grace and Delia, Alan leaned over to say something to Grace before riding back to Kathy.

"I see why you call this TapDancer Ranch," Kathy said.

They began walking around the ring again, and Alan cleared his throat before speaking. "I've been trying to figure out how to apologize."

Kathy, still feeling exhilarated from having faced her fear, was abruptly reminded she didn't like this man. "Oh." She tightened her legs, and Siesta danced sideways.

"Easy."

Kathy didn't know if he was speaking to her or to the horse. She relaxed her muscles, and Siesta instantly responded with a return to a slow walk.

"You surprised me at the tail end of a bad day, and I acted like an ass," he continued. "No excuse. But well. Anyway. If you still want to use the office in the evenings, it would be fine."

"I'm using a carrel in the library." Okay, now she was the one sounding like the recipient of a bad diagnosis. "Thank you, though. It's kind of you to offer." Better, but still not award-winning.

"I also want to thank you for not complaining to Hilstrom."

"How do you know I didn't?" Kathy said, feeling a sudden urge to tease him.

He glanced at her quickly, looking glum, and Kathy remembered her first impression of Hilary Hilstrom—that the woman wasn't someone she'd want to cross.

"I'm not a snitch. And I fight my battles myself."

He met her eyes briefly, looking relieved, then he signaled Grace to lead the pony over. "Time we call it quits for today."

When they reached the barn, Kathy dismounted. Not smoothly like Alan, but awkwardly. Her leg muscles were already letting her know they would be reminding her of the ride for several days to come. She held Siesta's reins until Alan came and took them from her.

"Thank you for the lesson."

"You're welcome." He glanced at her briefly before turning to Grace. "You and Ms. Jamison ought to talk," he said. "She's an editor." Then he turned to Kathy. "Grace writes children's books."

"Oh. How nice." Kathy's face felt stiff as she smiled at Grace. But after all, it wasn't Grace's fault she was being foisted on Kathy.

Alan and Delia started for the barn, leading the pony, and he spoke over his shoulder. "We'll just get the horses unsaddled while you two chat."

To Kathy, it sounded like an order, and that sundered the tentative truce he'd achieved with his apology.

She turned toward Grace, wondering what the other woman's relationship was with Alan, then decided they had to be dating. After all, Grace was wearing more makeup for a horseback ride than Kathy would wear to the opera. Although on Grace it looked good, enhancing her already vivid eyes and lips. The truth was, Grace made Kathy feel drab.

"You and Alan." Grace glanced at her. "Do you know each other well?" An echo of what Kathy had been thinking.

"Not exactly."

"*Mira.* You should work on that."

"Excuse me." Kathy examined Grace, trying to make sense of what she'd said. Maybe there was something in the Spanish sprinkled among Grace's words that Kathy wasn't getting. What she did get was that Grace seemed determined to drag Alan into the conversation while Kathy was equally determined to ban him.

There was only one way to move the subject to safer ground, and Kathy took it. "So, what kind of children's books do you write?"

She'd tried to make her tone interested, but Grace tensed, and her face took on a defensive look. "Short chapter books for middle readers. I've been told they're good stories, but they rhyme, and they mix English and Spanish together. And everybody who knows anything about publishing tells me

65

nobody is going to take a chance on a book like that."

"It's an interesting concept." Kathy's comment was sincere. Grace's book might well fit into Calico Cat's bilingual book line. "I'd be happy to take a look and tell you what I think."

Grace gave her a searching look before beginning to smile.

"I'll get you my card," Kathy said. "I have one in the car."

As Kathy turned to hand the card to Grace, she found the other woman watching Alan and Delia lead the last horse into the barn.

"*Ay bendito.* Those two. *Son amigos.* It's a good thing I'm crazy about Frank or I would be sorely tempted by that man."

Once again, Kathy found herself shuffling through Grace's words looking for the meaning. "Frank?"

"My husband."

Husband? Grace was married? "You're not Professor...I mean Alan...his date?" And there was absolutely no reason to feel like giggling.

"*Ay Dios mío.* Is that what you thought?" Grace chuckled. "That's why you looked so shocked when I suggested you get to know him better."

"Maybe." Kathy narrowed her eyes to stare at Grace.

Grace laughed again. Then her expression turned serious. "You act like you don't like him much, *querida.*"

Kathy shrugged.

"I met Alan when our dog was hit by a car." Grace turned away, continuing to speak in a pensive tone. "Blackie. He was hurt really bad. Alan and his friend helped me, while everyone else, including the man who hit him, just stood around or walked away." Grace took a deep breath. "He's a good man. But lonely, I think."

Kathy could see no reason why she should be concerned about Alan's loneliness. "Yes. Well. I need to get going. You send in your manuscript. I'll take a look."

She was halfway back to Denver before she realized she'd forgotten to pay for the lesson.

Chapter Eight

When there wasn't room for them to run, the horses learned to dance. Kathy lifted her hands from the keyboard, frowning at what she'd written. Clearly, she must still be under the spell of yesterday's trip to TapDancer Ranch.

She closed her eyes, trying to summon Amanda, but what came instead was a vision of Sonoro, legs flashing, neck arched, dancing across the wooden platform, looking as if he knew full well how beautiful he was.

And Alan Francini? Was she remembering him as well? Not gorgeous like Greg or the man she'd met in the park. But with an appeal that trumped the polished glitter of men like that. Or maybe it was seeing him on horseback. The romance of the Old West. If she hadn't first seen him at DSU, she'd now find it impossible to imagine him in any setting other than a ranch.

Odd to realize, if she'd gone with her instincts and ditched Amanda and her "'orses", she would never have known riding a horse could be so marvelous. And she wouldn't have the memory of Sonoro's dancing.

So all in all, maybe Amanda did have her uses.

Kathy looked back at the computer screen, but she knew she wasn't going to be able to write anymore today. She had all the signs. That feeling of restlessness and tension when she looked at the screen. The silence in her head. No voices, Amanda's or anyone else's, clamoring to be heard. No "what ifs" niggling at her.

Better then to go over to City Park and spend some time hitting balls against the practice wall. At least she'd get some exercise, and the afternoon wouldn't be a complete waste. With quick resolution, she shut off the computer and gathered her things together.

But in spite of spending an hour practicing her serve, followed by a long run, dinner and an evening of television shared with the Costellos, Kathy still felt out of sorts—an uncomfortable jostling mix of irritability and sadness that had to be more than simple frustration over being unable to write this weekend.

Maybe it was seeing that little girl yesterday. Delia. An unexpected reminder that when she lost Greg she'd also lost the possibility of family, at least anytime soon.

Kathy shook her head, trying to banish Greg. She didn't miss him. She knew she'd had a lucky escape. But still, there were times when she felt an emptiness that was more than simply his absence from her life.

She said goodnight to the Costellos and since she wasn't sleepy, she went through the stack of books in her reading pile. None quite fit her mood. In desperation, she fell back on her old standby: Emily's diaries.

Funny now to think how disappointed she'd been the day she'd unfolded that piece of paper and discovered the interviewee she'd chosen for her twentieth century history class was a ninety-year-old housewife named Emily Kowalski.

But it had turned out to be one of the best things that ever happened to her, because Emily was the one who gave her the courage to follow a riskier path. "Life is full of uncertainties, my dear, no matter what you choose," Emily had said, pushing a plate of chocolate chip cookies toward Kathy. "Better then to choose what you love."

Kathy, a computer science major the day she met Emily, had always wanted to be a writer. "If I follow my dreams, it will be really difficult." Kathy stared at the pink and lavender blossoms of Emily's African violets lifting in the breeze from the kitchen window.

"But if you give up your dreams, Kathleen, nothing else will matter very much," Emily said.

When they finally got around to discussing Emily's choice of historical event for the term paper Kathy was to write, she had expected Emily to choose something dramatic, like the bombing of Hiroshima or men landing on the moon. Instead, Emily had talked about the discovery of penicillin by Alexander Fleming.

"A miracle. But not soon enough to help our dear Bobby." Emily's eyes misted. "Only five when he had the meningitis."

After Emily told Kathy the story of Bobby's illness and its aftermath—years spent caring for an invalid son—what Kathy most wanted to know was how Emily managed to have a happy life, because there was no question in her mind, Emily and her husband, Jess, were happy. Kathy planned to ask about that when she took her finished paper to show Emily.

That day, Jess, looking more stooped than Kathy remembered from her last visit, had answered the door.

"Hi, Jess. I'm here to see Emily. To show her my paper."

The house framed Jess with dark and quiet, and no smell of fresh baking floated in the air. He'd stared at her, his silence stretching like a cobweb pulling against her hair. "Emily." He stopped, cleared his throat. "She died. A week ago."

Kathy didn't really need the ordinary words Jess used to confirm what she already suspected, but the pain she felt on hearing them was sudden and extraordinary.

"What happened?" The words seemed to come from a distance, as if someone else were speaking.

"Heart just gave out." Jess stopped, then went on, his voice wavering, his throat working. "Nearly killed me, too."

Kathy reached out to touch his arm, before she remembered. Jess didn't seem to like to be touched. Emily was the hugger. "Oh, Jess, I'm so sorry."

He motioned her to come in, leading her slowly back to the kitchen, Emily's kitchen, where he fixed tea.

Kathy sat, fighting the tears that were making her throat tight and her head ache. Finally, she gave in and let the tears run down her face. After Jess poured the tea, Kathy warmed her hands on the cup, and she and Jess sat in silence until Jess cleared his throat. "Emily left something for you." His hand trembled as he lowered the cup onto the saucer with a click. "I'll get it."

Kathy waited in the quiet of Emily's kitchen. The ticking clock and an occasional drip from the faucet were the only sounds, until Jess returned, that new uncertainty altering his step. He carried a large shoebox. "It's Em's diaries. I came across them the other day when I cleared out her desk. She wanted you to have them. Took a real shine to you, Em did."

Later, when Kathy opened the box, she found a number of small books with a note, written in a neat, clear hand, lying on top.

November 12, 1990

My dearest Kathleen,

I know from our talks, you worry about making the right choices in your life. I cannot, nor should anyone, tell you what to do. For that, my dear, you must listen to your own heart. And, never fear, it is speaking to you.

Perhaps I can help a little though, by showing you how I found my way. There is no one I would rather share that with.

I also want you to know, Kathleen, your visits brought this old woman so much pleasure.

Love, Emily

After she read Emily's note, Kathy started to cry again, which was strange. After all, Emily wasn't family. Only, that's what Kathy's sorrow felt like. Like she was mourning a death in her family. Of someone precious to her.

Eventually, Kathy came to realize that choosing the piece of paper with Emily's name on it was the fulcrum on which her entire future tipped. Just like the nursery rhyme, the one that went...for want of a nail the shoe was lost, for want of a shoe the horse was lost, all the way to the end with the country being lost, if she hadn't met Emily and learned to trust her dreams, her life would have been something else altogether.

And tonight, she needed Emily again.

Kathy sorted through the box of small leather-bound books, looking for the beginning of Emily's story. When she located the right book, she curled up in her easy chair and opened it to the first page.

ℬ

Excerpt from the diaries of Emily Kowalski
1925...

Here I am, starting a diary of all things. When I told Jess I didn't have any idea how to do that, he said I ought to start by telling where I came from and how I came to be Mrs. Jess Kowalski, living in Cincinnati, Ohio.

I guess that's as good a way as any.

I grew up on a farm near Red Oak, Iowa, never expecting to do anything different than live out my life as a farmer's daughter and a farmer's wife, until I had that talk with my brother, Bill, the autumn I turned sixteen.

Funny, we spend our whole lives talking, and we don't remember most of it for two minutes, but every once in a while someone says something, and everything afterward is changed because of it.

Bill was just back from the war. He went away my strong, funny, eldest brother and came home a thin, quiet stranger, recovering from German nerve gas and a shrapnel wound. In the evenings after supper, he took to walking to the other end of the pasture. He always went by himself, except for one of the farm dogs that followed him everywhere.

One evening, I went out to join him. When I reached the fence, neither Bill nor the dog paid any attention to me, so I just stood next to them and looked at the sky.

That night was one of those orange sunsets that deepen into red that come mostly right before winter sets in. The bare limbs of the trees made dark patterns against the sky color, and I started in to thinking how to make a picture of it.

Finally, I asked Bill if that was why he came here every night, for the sunset, and he replied he came to pray.

Well that surprised me some. I don't believe anyone else in the family ever thought to go out at sunset to stand in the pasture and pray.

I couldn't think of a thing to say in response, but that must have been okay, because after a bit, Bill started talking again, although he sounded sort of dreamy-like, as if he were talking to himself and not to me at all.

"When you're in a war, maybe it's the knowing you could die anytime, but just seems like you notice things more. Like these little pink flowers, used to grow in the ruts along the road. And you start in to looking for those kinds of signs, because it's the only thing gives you hope. If something that fragile can survive, maybe you can too." He leaned over and patted the dog for a while, before he went on speaking in that dreamy voice. "And you pray. Mostly it's not much of a prayer. Just a, 'Please, God, keep me safe today. Please, God, let me see my family again. Please, God, let me live so I can get married and have a child.'"

His voice trailed off, he straightened and for a time he continued to gaze at the sky. Then he shrugged and spoke more matter-of-factly. "Finally, one day, you add thanks you've made it through another day, and after a while longer, you find it's come to be a habit."

It was the most talking Bill had done since he got home. Actually the most talking he'd ever done to me, and what he said surprised me some. I stood beside him, picturing those pink flowers, and thinking how they were like the violets in the muddy pasture in the spring.

Then I remembered the part about him getting married and having a child. "Are you going to marry Doris Goodwin?"

"No. Leastways not right now. I've been thinking on what to do about it."

But it was simple really, and I told him so. "It'll hurt Doris a lot more to be married to someone who doesn't want to marry her than to be told you've changed your mind."

Bill looked startled, then he nodded. "Little Emmie. Seems you grew up while I was away." He smiled and, for the first time since he got home, looked like himself. "I figure on owing you some advice in return." The smile faded, and his expression turned serious, almost fierce. "Don't you go getting yourself trapped on the farm before you know what living is all about, you hear? And promise me. You'll let me know if you want my help to go take a look at what else is out there."

When I nodded my agreement, he went back to watching the sky, and we didn't talk any more. I hugged tight everything he'd said though, figuring to pull it out and think about it later.

Shortly after that, Bill and Doris, who were unofficially engaged when Bill went off to the war, were officially unengaged. Then Bill left the farm for good, to go off to Omaha to get settled before starting classes at Creighton University in January.

When I finished my schooling the following summer, I knew I was expected to pick one of the eligible young men in the area, marry him and start a farm and a family of my own. But although I didn't feel any particular opposition to the idea, I just didn't seem to actually be doing it.

Mother asked me about it when we were spring cleaning, washing windows with vinegar water. "Emily Margaret, you be sure you get that spot, right there, girl, and what about the Moriarity boy? He comes from a big farm and only the two boys."

I don't recall exactly how I answered her, but it was right then I knew what I wanted to do was take Bill's advice. I had no idea how to do it though, not until my best friend said I ought to be a teacher. I decided that surely sounded more interesting than marrying the Moriarity boy.

Once I made that decision, I discovered I had a whole raft of dreams that would never come true in Red Oak, Iowa. Dreams of travel. And of meeting people who did other things for a living besides farm. Dreams of hearing music played by a hundred instruments instead of the single rickety piano in our parlor. And dreams of seeing paintings, full of color, hanging on cool white walls.

Getting on that train to go to Omaha for the teachers' certification course was the most thrilling thing I'd done in my whole life. After the course, I taught in Ames for five years, saving every penny I could, because I finally knew what I wanted to do next. Study art.

Lucky for me, when Bill finished at Creighton, he moved to Chicago. The day I arrived there for my art studies, he met me at the train. He had a young woman with him. She had curly black hair and dark eyes. Her name was Kiara Sullivan.

I saw the way Bill's face changed when he looked at Kiara, and I knew right away they were more than friends. Then that evening, when Bill and Kiara came to take me to dinner, Bill brought along one of the other teachers to be my escort. His name was Jess Kowalski.

I went to bed that night thinking what an amazing day it had been. There was the excitement of arriving in Chicago and seeing Bill again, of course. But even more exciting, was meeting Kiara and Jess. From the very first, I knew they were going to be an important part of my life.

And so they were.

Bill and Kiara married in late summer, and Jess escorted me to the wedding. Then, after we'd already made it past the darkest, coldest part of the following winter, Kiara fell ill. It was right after she discovered she and Bill were expecting a baby.

At first we all thought she had a bad cold overlaid with morning sickness. The doctor came out of Bill and Kiara's room looking grave. She had pneumonia.

We took her to the hospital, and I kept telling myself and Bill she was going to be fine.

Only she wasn't.

I had to stop writing yesterday to have a good cry. I miss Kiara something fierce. She was the best sister a girl could ever hope to have. Being happy with Jess, well sometimes I feel so terrible sad for Bill.

After Kiara died, it was a hard time, even though Jess and I had fallen in love and had begun to plan our life together. We got married that next summer, and shortly after that, Jess came home to say we were moving to Cincinnati.

My biggest concern was leaving Bill, but it was such a wonderful opportunity for Jess to teach at Xavier University. We just couldn't turn it down.

I surely do miss Bill, though, and I worry about him.

Here in Cincinnati, we have a big house, bigger than I ever dreamed I would have, and a huge yard. On the weekends, Jess puts up fencing and clears out the woods while I put in a vegetable garden and plant flowers.

It is the perfect home for all the children we plan to have.

ɞ

Kathy shut the small book and placed it on her bedside table, wiping moisture from her eyes. Emily's joy at the thought of the children she hoped to have always made Kathy want to cry.

But maybe that was exactly what she needed from Emily tonight. Permission to cry.

Chapter Nine

Grace, with manuscript in hand, arrived at Calico Cat Books at ten o'clock Monday morning. When Kathy opened the door, Grace, wearing as much makeup as she had on Saturday, pulled her into a hug, then stepped back, grinning. "*Mira.* I thought this would be better than putting it in the mail."

Most of the people who came to Calico's door were deliverymen, and if one of them had tried to hug her, Kathy would have been tempted to deck him. But it was hard to take offense at someone as spontaneous and affectionate as Grace. Kathy stifled her instinctive response, an *oh, good grief,* as her good manners reasserted themselves.

She gestured for Grace to come in. "Would you like a cup of coffee?"

"No, no. *Gracias.* I don't want to take any more of your time." Grace handed Kathy the large envelope, then backed toward the door.

Since she was in the middle of an edit with a deadline looming, Kathy didn't argue with Grace. "I don't know exactly when I'll have time to look at it. So don't worry if you don't hear for a while."

"*Esta bien.* Take your time." Grace grabbed Kathy's hand and shook it. "*Gracias.* Thank you. So much."

Kathy ushered Grace out, then returned to her desk and set the envelope containing Grace's manuscript to one side. She hadn't been happy when Alan maneuvered her into talking to Grace in the first place, and the personal delivery of the offending manuscript simply compounded that sin.

Jade looked over from the desk next to Kathy's. "What's up?"

Kathy grimaced. "An aspiring author."

"Well that much, I figured."

"I met her this weekend at my riding lesson. I told her to send me something. I just didn't expect her to hand deliver it."

"At least she didn't stay long," Jade said.

Kathy went back to work, but the envelope kept catching her eye. *It rhymes, and it's a mix of English and Spanish.* So it could be the worst thing she'd ever read. Or...it could be just the kind of book Calico was seeking.

By lunch, the envelope had taken on the character of a present, wrapped and waiting under a Christmas tree. And the suspense was killing Kathy. Eventually she could no longer deny the urge to take a look.

She pulled the pages out, and setting aside the cover letter, began to read.

High in the Andes, in the *verde* folds
of valleys mid *montañas*
La familia Tocado lived peacefully raising
chickens, children *y llamas*

She stopped and went back to the beginning, this time reading out loud. With growing excitement she finished the first page and then the first chapter. There were thirty pages of manuscript, and she flew through them. When she finished, she sat back, her face stretched in a wide grin.

It was wonderful.

Jade's eyebrows rose in twin arcs. "You know, some places would call in the guys in the white coats for a person who mutters to herself and then smiles at nothing."

Kathy doused the grin. "Take a look at something for me?"

"Sure."

"Right now?"

Jade shrugged. "Why not? It's a slow day."

Kathy knew Jade was busy, but she was too anxious to get Jade's response to feel guilty about it. She handed over the pages.

"This the hand-delivered manuscript?"

"The very one."

Jade took the pages and swiveled her chair so her back was to Kathy. Kathy watched that back as Jade started reading. After the first two pages, Jade straightened abruptly and turned to look at Kathy. "Is it all like this?"

"Actually, it gets better."

Jade's lips twitched. "I think you've got a hot one, kid. But you already know that."

Kathy let the feeling of delight grow and spread. She knew Grace's story was good, but having Jade say it made it real. "Yeah. I almost blew her off, you know."

Jade gave her a questioning look.

"I don't like the person who introduced us." And thank God she hadn't let that dislike push Grace away.

Jade laughed. "I'd say it's a good thing you let your good manners get the better of you."

Kathy had meant to mail the payment for the riding lesson to Alan Francini on the way to work, but she was out of stamps. And now she faced a dilemma, because she no longer owed him a simple payment for a riding lesson. She owed him a thank-you for referring Grace and *Verde Mountains* to her.

Polly and Columba had looked at the manuscript and quickly agreed it was precisely the kind of book they were looking for to add to Calico's list. By the end of the day, Kathy had the go-ahead to contact Grace and make an offer.

That was the easy part, although all she'd gotten when she called Grace was an answering machine. More difficult was deciding what to do about the thank-you she owed Alan. That uncertainty nudged at her all afternoon. She finally decided she'd stop by his office on her way to the library. If he was still there, she'd thank him. If he wasn't—which was the more likely scenario—she'd write a note, append it to the check, and leave it under his door.

Once she made that decision, the nudgy voice shut up, and she was able to get back to work.

She didn't arrive at DSU until nearly six, but she found Alan's light still on and his door ajar. Darn. She'd been so sure she wouldn't have to actually face him, she'd already written the note. She hesitated, trying to decide what to do.

Coward. Wuss.

No she wasn't. She could do this. No biggie. Just a few words, hand over the check and leave. Then she'd make sure she never encountered him again.

She lifted her hand and hesitated before forcing herself to knock. At his "come in", she pulled the door open, her heart beating quickly, her palms beginning to sweat.

He was sitting tipped back in his chair, reading a manuscript, a fierce scowl on his face.

"That bad, huh?" she said.

He looked up, his feet came off the desk with a thump, and he set the papers down. "Student essays." He cocked his head in question.

"I forgot to pay you Saturday. For the riding lesson." She stepped closer and held the check out to him.

He stared at her hand for a moment, as if he couldn't quite understand she meant for him to take it. Then he waved it away. "Keep it. You got only a partial lesson, anyway."

"I still got a full complement of sore muscles." She let the hand holding the check drop to her side. She'd slide it on his desk when he wasn't looking.

He shrugged, giving her a slight smile. "You have to ride regularly before you get over that."

"Yes. Well. I only planned on one lesson."

"Why?" He looked as if it were inconceivable anyone could possibly be satisfied riding only once. But then, as far as he was concerned, likely it was.

"It was research."

"Research?"

"I'm writing a novel. One of the characters pushed me into

it."

"Oh. Well, that explains it."

She thought his look was patronizing, and it annoyed her. "Hasn't one of your characters ever pushed you into anything?"

"Not lately." His voice was suddenly flat, his face blank.

Feeling uneasy, she spoke quickly. "Speaking of writing, I owe you for sending Grace our way. Her book is wonderful. We're going to publish it."

He raised his eyebrows in apparent astonishment. "That was fast."

She found herself meeting his eyes. Deep brown but with a sadness in their depths that pulled at her. She shook off the feeling. Definitely an over-interpretation. Likely it was a result of Grace saying she thought he was lonely.

"She hand delivered the manuscript this morning."

"Sounds like Grace." He smiled, then breaking eye contact, fiddled with a pencil.

She liked the smile. She wondered if she could get him to do it again. "You know, Calico doesn't pay finders fees, but I think they'd spring for dinner. How about it? A dinner, to thank you for referring Grace." Now where had that come from, the invitation tumbling out before she could stop it. Not attraction. No way. More like desperation. She *really* didn't like the feeling of being in debt to this man.

He sat back and examined her over steepled hands. "You afraid of horses?"

Was this the latest way to let a person down easy? Ignore the invitation? Annoyed, she spoke crisply. "Let's just say I had an unhappy experience with one, and it skewed my opinion of the entire species."

"Must be one gem of a character to have pushed you into another encounter, then."

"Actually, Amanda's an idiot. I'm deleting her."

He shook his head, looking serious, but his eyes gleamed with humor. "Not going to work."

Was he laughing at her? "How do you know that?"

He gave her a knowing, superior look. "If a character's got the *cojones* to push his creator into doing something the creator would never do otherwise, he's got the *cojones* to hang on."

She shook her head, her mouth twitching without her permission into a smile, surprised to realize she was enjoying the interaction. "As far as I know, *cojones* are not part of Amanda's equipment."

"Make you a deal," he said, outwardly serious again. "I'll go to dinner with you, if you come back for another riding lesson. I think you're going to need it to handle Amanda."

She thought about it as she looked around his office, noticing how bare it was, as if he were only a temporary tenant. She remembered once again Grace's diagnosis. Pushed that thought away. A riding lesson to go along with dinner. What would it hurt? And he was probably right, another lesson might help. Besides, she'd enjoyed that first lesson. Had even thought she might enjoy doing it again...only not at TapDancer.

"Okay. Deal." She bit her lip in concentration. "I don't suppose you like Indian food, do you? Or Chinese. Or maybe Italian?" Really, it would have been so much better if she'd given this whole thing more thought. Spontaneity. Not all it was cracked up to be. But she'd opened her mouth. Twice. Once to invite him and a second time to accept his offer. So now she had to deal with the consequences.

"Indian would be fine."

"You're sure? A lot of people don't like it. It's okay. It doesn't have to be Indian." And why couldn't she stop babbling?

He, if anything, was looking more relaxed. He leaned back, his hands lying loose in his lap, watching her. "Indian's fine."

"The Tandoor, then. You know it?"

He nodded.

"Good. I'll meet you there. How about Friday at...seven?"

He nodded again, and she escaped. When she got to the library, she found she was still gripping the envelope containing his check.

And she was smiling.

80

Damn. Talk about your ill-conceived impulses.

Alan ordered a beer and drank it in quick nervous gulps, fighting the urge to walk out of The Tandoor. He still couldn't figure out why he'd accepted Kathy's invitation. And not only that. He'd elevated the entire interaction beyond dinner. Forcing her to agree to come for another lesson. He ought to pretend he'd gotten a call then tell the waitress there was an emergency. The only thing stopping him was the knowledge it would make him feel like a coward.

What the hell, he could handle dinner. No big deal. People ate dinner all the time. Including him. Every day.

Then Kathy walked in, and as he stood to greet her, he caught the edge of the tablecloth, spilling what was left of the beer down his pant leg.

Hell of a way to break the ice, Francini.

Kathy's eyes widened, then she walked toward him, shaking her head, with a grin on her face that made her look about twelve. "You sure know how to make a girl feel comfortable. I'm always knocking over drinks, but now you've beat me to it, I can relax."

"Happy to help out. But I'm going to smell like a brewery."

"I like beer."

He'd felt clumsy and out of sorts when the beer spilled, but here he was moments later almost laughing. A surprise she could affect him that way, especially given the constraint in their interactions up to now.

The waitress directed them to another table, and Alan excused himself to clean up. When he returned, Kathy was sipping a beer, and a new, full glass sat at his place.

"You're trusting me with another one?"

"Not me. The waitress. She insisted. Said she'd never had anyone spill two."

"What about you. You planning to spill that?"

"Don't have to plan. It just happens." She spoke matter-of-factly but her eyes were filled with merriment.

"I know you're trying to make me feel better."

"It's working, isn't it?"

Pleasure curled through him like a cup of hot coffee after

chores on a cold morning. "As a matter of fact, it is." Odd, that spilling a beer was turning out to be the best thing to happen to him in a while.

They negotiated what to order, but once they made their selections and the waitress left, silence fell between them. Kathy was the one who eased it by asking him about the horses.

In his relief, he probably told her more than she ever wanted to know, starting with the fact Columbus brought the first Paso Finos to the New World on his second voyage, and ending with a description of the trip he and his father took to Puerto Rico where they bought several of the TapDancer horses.

The food arrived and, as they served themselves, Kathy continued to ask questions about the horses and the ranch. Finally, he held up a hand. "It's your turn to answer some questions."

She tore off a piece of flat bread and cocked her head at him. "Okay. What do you want to know?"

"All I know so far is you're an editor, you're working on a novel with a character named Amanda, and you don't like horses, even though you've been listening with apparent fascination while I went on and on about them."

Kathy shook her head slightly. "You were right about Amanda. I can't seem to shake her. So the horse talk is all...fodder, so to speak."

The delicate pun made him smile until he noticed the forlorn look on her face. She started to take a bite of food. Then she set her fork down, and reached for her beer without picking it up. "The only problem is she keeps clamming up on me. It's discouraging." She looked down, her fingers making restless patterns in the moisture on the glass.

"Most writers have trouble at one time or another. Maybe you need to take a break. Then try again." He didn't know why he was giving her advice that hadn't worked for him, except he wanted so badly to banish that lost look.

"Do you write?" she asked.

He was pretty sure she was asking about his writing only as a way to distract herself. At least he hoped so. "Sure. Memos, handouts, exams."

She gave him a rueful smile that barely moved her lips and

didn't make it as far as her eyes. Then she gave herself a little shake. "Sorry. Didn't mean to interject a dreary note in the proceedings. So was the baby a boy or a girl?"

The switch was so abrupt and unexpected, he had no idea what she was talking about. He raised his eyebrows in question.

"Your sister's baby," she prompted, looking amused.

"Oh. I forgot you knew about that. She had a boy."

"So you're an uncle."

"That I am." That topic exhausted, he cast about for the next one. Then he remembered their deal. "About your riding lesson. Grace and Delia are coming again tomorrow. You can join us if you like." He hoped she would. Much better that way. His folks were less likely to misinterpret, get their hopes up.

She smiled. "Why not. A twofer. I get to know Grace better and work on my Amanda research at the same time."

When she arrived at TapDancer on Saturday, Kathy discovered Grace had been called at the last minute to fill in for a sick co-worker, so she and Delia weren't coming after all.

But that was okay. Kathy was much more relaxed this time. She didn't even flinch when Siesta greeted her with a nose rub. And with her fear mostly gone, the ride was even more delightful than the first time. Afterward, Alan showed her how to unsaddle and groom Siesta, then he led her to the tack room and began explaining the various bits of harness and their functions.

"I'll never remember it all," Kathy said as he held up a tangle of straps. "That's the nightingale. Like Florence, right?"

He shook his head reproving her. "Martingale. A true horsewoman would never make a mistake like that."

"I'm beginning to suspect Amanda's a dilettante."

"I can take a hint. Enough for one day, right? How about a hot drink before you drive back?"

She nodded, then watched him replace the martingale on its hook, marveling at how different he was from their first meeting. Gone completely the closed, superior look that had sent her away to take out her frustration on some poor, innocent tennis balls. Gone as well any impression of arrogance. This new, improved Alan Francini not only knew how to laugh, he could make her laugh.

And when something amused him, she liked the way his face rearranged itself, smile lines fanning from his eyes and bracketing his mouth, and his eyes shining. She found it impossible not to smile back, a thoroughly unexpected and pleasant surprise.

Alan walked her to the house and ushered her into the kitchen, where a brown-haired woman was mixing something in a bowl. The woman looked up with a smile when they came in.

Alan cleared his throat. "Mom, this is Kathy Jamison. Kathy, my mom, Stella."

"Oh, my goodness," Stella said, putting her spoon down and extending a hand to Kathy. "You're the one we forgot about when Elaine called from the hospital. I'm so glad to see you've forgiven us."

Kathy shook Stella's outstretched hand. "Nothing to forgive. Congratulations, by the way."

"Yes. Our first grandchild." Stella's voice sounded normal, but her face was pensive. She turned away and started stirring again.

A man walked into the kitchen. "Well, well, this the young lady I was watching put Siesta through her paces?" The voice was a slightly deeper version of Alan's.

"Dad, this is Kathy Jamison." Alan set a mug of hot water and a tin full of tea bags in front of her. "Kathy, my dad, Robert."

"My, those hands are a dite chilly," Robert said, clasping her hand in greeting. "You should have told Alan you were getting cold."

"I didn't want to stop."

Alan's eyebrows shot up at that, and Kathy swallowed a giggle.

"She's the one we rushed off and forgot last week," Stella said.

"I do apologize for that," Robert said.

"No need. I think a baby trumps a riding lesson any day."

Robert made an indeterminate sound in response, as he turned to accept the mug of tea Alan held out to him.

Given Stella and Robert's muted reactions, Kathy wondered if the baby was all right, but it wasn't something she could very well ask. Instead, she changed the subject, hoping to smooth over the sudden discomfort she was feeling. "You have the most beautiful house. I bet your view is amazing."

"Come check it out," Robert said. "You're about ready to join us, aren't you, dear?"

"In a minute," Stella said.

Kathy followed Robert into the living room. "It must be marvelous when it snows."

Robert chuckled. "Until we have to go out to shovel a path to the barn, it is."

"Oh my..." Her voice trailed off as she looked out the window.

Meadows of golden grass bounded by foothills speckled with the black of ponderosa and lodgepole pine stretched out before her. The foothills rose against the navy blue flanks of the Rampart Range and, behind that, Pike's Peak gleamed white and silver with the first snow of the season.

Kathy moved slowly into the room, still looking at the view. She chose a swivel chair and sat down, only then noticing the room itself: the warm honey tones of the pine floor and exposed ceiling beams; chairs and sofas set in two comfortable groupings; Navajo rugs on the floor and bright quilts folded on the backs of several of the chairs. All of it overlaid with a faint aroma of wood smoke and pine. A room in synchrony with the grandeur framed by its windows.

"What a wonderful room." Awe made her voice slightly hoarse. "Do you ever get enough of it or this view?"

"We've only been here ten years," Robert said. "But we're not tired of it yet."

"But..." Kathy stopped because what she'd been about to say—that it was odd for someone to start ranching when they were middle-aged—would have been rude.

"Oh, we had a ranch before," Stella said, joining them and accurately interpreting Kathy's hesitation.

"Yep. Out east of Denver," Robert said. "Likely you've been there. They call it Denver International now."

Kathy cocked her head, thinking about it. "That must have been difficult."

"Yep." Robert chuckled. "Real hard leaving a thousand acres of dry scrub to come here."

Stella sat next to Robert, and Kathy found herself the focus of the senior Francinis' friendly attention. But that was okay. They were pleasant people and, unlike Alan, she'd warmed to them both immediately. Well she'd warmed to Alan, too. It had just taken longer.

"Have you been riding long?" Stella asked.

Kathy shook her head. "This is only my third time." If falling off Peaches twice counted as one time.

"Oh my. Well you should feel real honored, then. Alan doesn't allow just anyone on that filly. She's his pride and joy."

Kathy glanced at Alan, who leaned over to pet Cormac. Parents. They seemed to have an ingrained universal ability to embarrass their children without even trying. But then Alan threw the assumption he was embarrassed into question by glancing up at Kathy and winking.

Completely unexpected, and if he only knew it, devastating.

"I forgot to ask when you called. Who recommended us?" Stella said.

With a start, Kathy refocused. "Oh, my pencil did." She grinned at the look on Stella's face. "You know, I opened the phone book, closed my eyes and..."

Stella's face cleared. "See, Rob. I told you a big ad would pay off."

"What made you decide to take riding lessons?" Robert asked.

Kathy glanced at Alan, trying to catch his eye, tempted to wink if she did. "I needed to know something about horses for a novel I'm working on."

"Oh, you're a writer," Stella said. "Did you know Alan is an English professor?"

"As a matter of fact, I did know that. I'll be teaching a course at DSU in the spring."

87

"You're a professor, too?" Robert asked.

"Actually, I'm an editor. At Calico Cat Books."

Stella frowned with her finger over her lips. "That name. It seems familiar. Oh, I know. That's the publisher that does those bilingual books. We bought our grandson one."

"Which one did you get?" Kathy was puzzled. Didn't Stella say the baby born a week ago was their first grandchild?

"The story about the little boy and girl rescuing the grasshopper with the help of the dragonfly."

"That's one of my favorites." Kathy pictured Jade working the Japanese characters for danger, courage, and sanctuary into the illustrations. "But then I love all our IchiMichis."

"IchiMichi. What language is that?" Alan asked.

"Japanese. Actually, IchiMichi is our pet name for them. They're stories about a brother and sister, Ichiro and Michiko."

"And they're beautifully done," Stella said, turning to Alan. "You'll have to ask Elaine to show it to you the next time you're over there. They're mostly in English, but they have Japanese characters and Japanese words." She turned back to Kathy. "Alan has quite a collection of children's books. We should have guessed he was going to be an English teacher, what with all the reading he did when he was growing up."

"And look who's buying a one-week-old baby books already." Alan was obviously teasing his mother.

Kathy was relieved. She must have completely misread the situation in the kitchen.

"So, does your family live here in Denver, Kathy?" Robert said, swinging his legs onto the ottoman and leaning back.

"They're in Ohio. Dayton. My dad's in the Air Force. But I was born in Denver. That's why I decided to move here, to see what it's like."

"And what do you think?" Stella said.

"I love it." *So much, I traded a fiancé for it.* Not that she'd say that out loud of course, although it would be interesting to see their reaction. And what did it say about her? That the thought amused her.

Later, when Alan walked her back to the kitchen to retrieve her coat, she handed him a check.

He frowned. "What's this?"

"For the lesson."

"I coerced you into it. I can't require you to pay for it as well." He handed the check back.

She refused to take it. "I don't feel right about it."

He shrugged, tore the check in two. "So take me out to dinner again. Friday would work for me."

This was getting to be more than she'd bargained for. Riding *and* dining. Time to call a halt.

"All right," she said.

ॐ

"You better explain one more time." Jade hooked a length of black silky hair behind her ear. "You need me to help you pick out a special dress, because the character in your novel needs a dress. And then you bring me here?"

Kathy frowned in concentration as she sorted through the rack of dresses in the vintage dress shop she'd picked out of the yellow pages. Amanda again. First she'd pushed Kathy to learn to ride. But was that enough? Not for Amanda, who then decided she needed a fancy dress for...something, and it couldn't be just any fancy dress.

Darn Amanda, anyway. But then what was Kathy, an author or a mouse? She could just say no. Tell Amanda, *no dress. Deal with it.* Instead, here she and Jade were, giving up their lunch hour to stir up rose-scented, hundred-year-old dust.

"Kathy, these aren't dresses." Jade flipped through a second rack. "They're rags." She sneezed, and Kathy's nose tickled.

"No they're not. They're living history. Well at least some of them are." And working to repair and alter the right dress might be kind of fun at that.

She turned back to her rack and pulled out the burgundy dress that had caught her eye. "Look at this one." She held it against her waist, smoothing her hand across the soft velvet.

Jade frowned, then nodded. "I like the color. It shouldn't work with your hair, but somehow it does." She reached out and fingered the torn lace collar. "But it has a problem."

"It might look even better without the collar." Kathy already knew if the fit was even close, she was going to buy it, even though it was an extravagance, and she was never extravagant. The sensuous feel of the heavy, wine-colored velvet made the decision easy for her. It was simply too wonderful to walk away from.

"What if you can't fix it? Then you've wasted your money," Jade said, striking an uncharacteristic frugal note.

But regardless of Amanda instigating it, if Kathy didn't buy the dress, she'd regret it, and that was one of the things she'd decided since getting back from San Francisco. She was going to do everything she could to limit her regrets.

≈

In the six weeks since Kathy's first visit to TapDancer, Grace, finally acceding to pressure from Delia and Kathy, had begun riding, and Kathy and Grace now took turns driving to the ranch for their weekly ride. Today since it was Grace's turn to drive, Kathy parked her car in front of the Garibaldis' house and joined Grace and Delia in the minivan.

As Grace navigated through the Denver traffic, Kathy chatted with Delia, asking her about kindergarten and getting a detailed report. Once they were on the highway, Kathy told Grace her news. "We got some illustrations for *Verde Mountains* back. If you stop by sometime this week, you can see them."

Grace's mouth widened in a huge grin. She gave Kathy a quick glance. "Are they okay, do you think?"

"More than okay. We were lucky with the illustrator we picked. We got someone just starting out, but I think she's terrific."

"Just like me. I mean, just starting out."

"And terrific. Don't forget that part," Kathy said, laughing at Grace's transparent glee.

"It's all so exciting. You can't imagine. Sometimes I have to pinch myself to believe it. Don't I, *niñita*?" Grace looked at Delia in the rearview mirror, and Delia nodded her head vigorously.

Kathy knew if Grace hadn't been driving, she and Delia would have been doing a happy dance—Grace's excitement was that obvious.

"Even though the illustrator is working fast, we don't think we can get it out by Christmas, but in the spring for sure."

Grace took a deep breath and let it out, shaking her head. "Can you believe it, *querida*? If I hadn't met Alan, and you hadn't decided to take riding lessons and picked TapDancer, none of this would be happening."

"But, don't forget. When Alan pushed us together and ordered us to talk, I didn't want to, because I was in a snit over how he acted the first time we met."

Kathy, Grace and Delia laughed together.

"And if you'd done that, we wouldn't be *amigas*. *Interesante*. Life. Strange how things happen. All those little *cosas* having to come together perfectly and then everything works out."

"Yep. We've been victims of one of the mysteries of the universe," Kathy said. "By the way, you don't happen to have any more stories just lying around?"

"As a matter of fact, I think I have one or two. What do you think, *nene*?" Grace asked Delia. "The one about the coquis and the coffee plantation or the one about the lizards that live on the beach?"

Delia clapped her hands. "The lizards."

"Coquis?" Kathy said.

"Tiny Puerto Rican frogs."

"Why not bring along copies of both when you come to look at the illustrations?"

Grace nodded her head solemnly. "I can do that."

Kathy pushed her chair back, feeling satisfied at how well the evening's writing session had gone. Actually, lately they were all going well. She'd finished a short story about the dancing horses, and she was steadily adding to her novel—at least four pages a night was her goal. And she'd met that goal easily for the past—well, pretty much ever since she started spending time with Alan Francini.

Not that there was any cause and effect to that.

෫ා

Right before Christmas, Grenville delivered a copy of the departmental committee's decision on Alan's request for promotion and tenure. "A real sticky wicket for us, old chap," Grenville said, rolling and tapping the letter on the desk. "These decisions often are, but this was one of the most difficult I've been involved in."

Alan sat back, putting his hands behind his head, pretending a calm he was far from feeling.

"No sense leaving you hanging. We approved your request for tenure but without promotion." Grenville handed over the letter. "Hilstrom might dig her heels in, but given the fact your initial appointment didn't make writing fiction a requirement, I expect she'll send this up the chain with a positive recommendation."

It was a blow, not being recommended for promotion, but Alan could see it was a compromise position on the part of the committee. He still couldn't count on getting tenure, of course, but for the first time since the meeting with Hilstrom, he felt optimistic about his chances.

Chapter Ten

As Kathy exited the jetway in Dayton, her parents were waiting for her.

"Oh, Kathy. Oh, it's so good to see you." Her mother pulled Kathy into a long hug, then stood back, still holding Kathy by the arms. "Just look at you." She shook her head, smiling. "You look wonderful."

"Hey, it's my turn," her dad said, throwing his arms around her.

They walked to baggage claim, and Kathy and her mom waited to collect the luggage while her dad went to get the car.

"I know one of these days, you're not going to be able to come home for Christmas, but I'm so glad you made it this year."

Kathy felt a spurt of alarm at her mother's somber tone. "Is something wrong?"

"No. No. Of course not. It's just... I really wanted to see you, to know for sure you're okay. You are okay, aren't you?"

Kathy nodded and met her mother's worried eyes. "He wasn't the right one, Mom. Better I found out before I married him instead of after."

Her mother gave her a steady look which Kathy had no difficulty returning.

"Oh, I'm so glad to hear it. I hated to know you were hurting." Her mother blinked rapidly, then swiped at her eyes.

"It's okay. Really. I'm fine. It did hurt for a while. Maybe my pride is still a little sore. But I'm fine." It wasn't completely true, but it was what her mother needed to hear.

Her mom knew all about the pain of loss after her first husband was killed in an accident when Kathy was two. It wasn't until Kathy was five that her mom met and married Colonel Matthew Jamison. Matt was also widowed and raising a son, Matt Jr. In one fell swoop, Kathy had gained a father and an older brother. Matt Jr. was now married, and this year he was spending the holidays with his in-laws. Likely that was another reason her mother was so thrilled to have her home.

"What is all this about you taking riding lessons?" her dad said at dinner that first evening.

"I thought you didn't like horses," her mother added. "Didn't something happen?"

"Yeah. At Y camp. I kept falling off, and then the horse bit me. But the TapDancer horses are completely different. They're really easy to ride."

"And the son of the owners is the one teaching you?" her mom said.

Kathy knew where that was going. "Yes. And yes, he's early thirties, single and good-looking."

"Ranching's a rough life," her dad said, shaking his head.

Kathy ate her dinner, smiling to herself, while her parents debated the point. No way was she adding fuel to that particular fire by telling them Alan was a college professor.

"Maybe we shouldn't get too hasty here about pairing her up with this guy," her dad finally said. "She may have no interest in him." He gave Kathy an interrogatory look that she ignored.

"Do I get any say in all this?" she asked.

"Prefer you didn't," he growled. "Better to let your mom and me pick someone. I've got a couple of decent prospects we could start with while you're here."

Kathy rolled her eyes, and they all laughed.

It was lovely to sink into the warmth and comfort of her parents' love, and she enjoyed their gentle teasing. It helped take her mind off the fact that not all that long ago, she and Greg had talked about the possibility of getting married this Christmas. Before Greg took the San Francisco residency. Before he met Julie.

On Christmas Eve, Kathy and her parents went to Mass. As the beautiful hymns soared, Kathy found herself blinking back tears, but then she always choked up on Christmas Eve. After Mass, the family exchanged gifts. Kathy smiled as her dad handed her the first package, remembering the year Matt discovered their parents always opened their gifts to each other after Mass while he and Kathy had to wait until the next morning. Now that she was older, she could see it had been their special time together as a couple, but she wasn't sorry Matt had insisted he and Kathy be included.

As she had every year since taking the job at Calico, she gave her parents a signed copy of one of the books she had worked on that year. Next year it would be Grace's book, but this year it was a Russian fairytale.

Her mother opened the package then looked at her. "Have you ever thought of writing your own book, dear? Dad and I were talking about the stories you sent us when you were studying at Iowa, and we thought they were wonderful."

"Maybe I will, someday." She didn't want to tell them about Amanda. Not yet. Knowing Amanda, she would jinx it.

"As long as you think about it, hon."

On Christmas Day, they had a big dinner with a number of her father's command filling out the places at the table. This year the invitees were five men and two women. It was a Jamison family tradition, that her dad invite any singles unable to go home for Christmas to have dinner with them. When Kathy was in high school, she'd flirted outrageously with the young men, safe in the knowledge none of them would dare ask her out.

Today, in the midst of the gaiety, she felt suddenly out of place, as somber thoughts of canceled weddings and uncertain plans for the future cast a pall. She tried to focus on talking to the young man her father had maneuvered into the seat next to her. He was good-looking, obviously intelligent, and she had absolutely no interest in him.

She hadn't lied to her mother. She *was* doing better. Just not quite well enough to be ready to let something get started with someone new.

☙

Alan was sitting in the living room on Christmas Eve, waiting for Charles to arrive, when Elaine came in and without ceremony deposited her son in his arms.

"Here, little brother," she said. "About time you and your nephew got better acquainted."

Alan considered himself already acquainted. Hadn't he gone to the hospital when Mark was born? And he'd visited Elaine and Ted at home, well, at least a couple of times since.

Before he could hand the baby back, or even protest, Elaine was already across the room. "He's just been fed, so all you have to worry about is a little spit-up. If you get desperate, I'll be in the kitchen helping Mom."

Alan looked down at the baby and found Mark looking considerably better than he had three months ago. His skin was now a smooth pale ivory instead of being wrinkled and red, and he opened dark blue eyes to give Alan a wise look. Alan put out a tentative finger, and Mark grasped it with a tiny hand, and pulled it toward his mouth.

"I don't think that's such a good idea, buddy," Alan said, pulling the finger away. He always washed thoroughly after chores, but still. Mark's arms flailed for a moment, then he settled on sucking his fist and examining Alan with those solemn eyes.

Alan looked over at the Christmas tree and the pile of presents they'd be opening in the morning. Christmas was always the hardest day of the year for him because of Meg. Meg, the brightness in his life. Brighter than the Christmas lights, tinsel or sun on the snow.

He looked back at the baby, now asleep, finding it easier than usual to distract himself from the old pain. That had no doubt been Elaine's intention. She could annoy him more easily than anyone he knew, but this time he felt a reluctant gratitude.

When Elaine came back a few minutes later, Alan shook his head at her. "He's asleep," he said softly.

Elaine smiled a contented smile and went back to the kitchen. Alan continued to sit, holding the sleeping baby, feeling more peaceful than he had in a long time.

"So how're the riding lessons going?" Elaine asked as they were eating dinner.

"Not too good," Robert answered. "Only had a couple of takers, but since they're friends of Alan's, we don't charge them."

"Surely not Charles?" Elaine gave Charles an amused look.

"Absolutely not," Alan said. "You know he hyperventilates whenever he gets within twenty feet of a horse."

Charles simply raised his eyebrows and continued eating.

"We're not going to put the ad back in next year," Stella said.

"Nope," Robert said. "Found we've got enough on our hands working to get the yearlings trained so we can sell them. More money in that."

"Pass the rolls down here, would you," Stella said, and Alan breathed in relief that the subject of exactly who Alan's "friends" were had been cut off before it could be fully explored. With any luck, Elaine, fighting the fatigue of new motherhood, would forget about it. And hopefully, Charles would as well.

Chapter Eleven

Jade handed Kathy a mug of hot chocolate. "So did you ever get that dress altered?"

Kathy set the mug down, moved the galleys she was working on out of the way, and sat back stretching her arms over her head. "You mean the velvet?"

"Umm." Jade sipped her hot chocolate.

"It turned out really nice. I changed it a bit, got rid of the collar."

Jade raised eyebrows above the rim of the cup. "Have you worn it yet?"

Kathy shook her head. "I'm saving it for a special occasion." She'd taken it home at Christmas, but then decided not to wear it.

"And the riding lessons?"

"Good. I don't even get sore anymore." In spite of the fact occasional blasts of winter weather had kept her from riding every week like she had through the fall.

"And Alan? You seem to have changed your mind about him."

"Naw." Kathy picked up the mug and grinned at Jade. "I'm just using him to get access to his horses."

Jade snorted. "No way I believe that. Whenever you mention him, you get a look."

"What look?"

Jade demonstrated, gazing off in the distance with a sappy expression. "That look," she said.

Kathy was pretty sure she was blushing. At any rate, she felt awfully warm all of a sudden, and it wasn't because of the hot chocolate. "Well, I no longer despise him, if that's what you mean." She attempted nonchalance, but Jade wasn't buying.

"Yeah, I kind of gathered that."

After Jade went back to her own desk, Kathy sipped her hot chocolate, thinking about Alan. She'd stopped being angry at him after that first visit to TapDancer, and she'd begun to enjoy his company at that first dinner. It turned out he was easy to be with, strange as that seemed after the way they'd begun. As a companion, he was undemanding, pleasant, interesting and occasionally funny.

But beyond that lay mystery.

Or not.

Alan had, after all, made it crystal clear all he wanted from her was...companionship, she supposed. He treated her almost exactly the way he treated Grace and Delia when the three of them came out for their weekly ride. Except, he never gave her a hug like he did Grace and Delia. Never touched her at all if he could help it.

She frowned. Was that true, or something she was making up?

True, she decided. Sure he helped her with her coat, and occasionally his knuckles brushed her neck. But he never followed up on it.

And in spite of her decision, after what happened with Greg, to take a good long break from men, Kathy was ready for him to touch her. Not by accident or because he was being gallant, but just to touch her.

Because she wanted to touch him.

∞

Alan nodded at the plate of spaghetti sitting in front of Charles. "If I ate all that, I'd spend the afternoon in a coma."

"Brain needs lots of calories to function optimally when faced with the cunning genus *Defenses lawyerensis*."

"It's still a good thing you run ten miles a day."

Ignoring the jab, Charles picked up a piece of bread and dipped it in olive oil. A moment later he took the last drink from his glass, and it was no surprise to Alan when the server came over immediately, carrying a refill. Alan continued to eat peacefully, waiting for Charles and the girl to finish flirting with each other.

The waitress left, and Charles looked back at Alan. "By the way, the roommate ever show up?"

"Roommate?"

"The editor who was supposed to share your office."

"Oh yeah. Showed up, decided the office didn't meet her specifications and left." Always best to stick as close to the truth as possible with Charles, whose ability to remember details was disconcerting at times. Besides, if he told Charles he had been giving Kathy riding lessons and having dinner with her on a regular basis, Charles would assume something was going on he needed to know more about.

Charles took another bite and squinted at Alan. "Varicose veins, coke bottle glasses and a lisp?"

"Psychic," Alan said.

"Colored contacts," Meg said the first time she met Charles. "Nobody's eyes are that blue."

"His eyes are no bluer than yours." Alan ran a finger down her cheek. "And you don't wear contacts."

"He hit on me, you know."

"You hit back?" Alan knew from the spark of humor in her eyes she was teasing.

"Of course not. He's too blond, too tall, too Greek god-ish."

"He likes you."

"Yeah. I like him too, actually. Just tell him he needs to chip a tooth or something. All that perfection." She shook her head in mock sorrow.

Alan blinked, refocusing on Charles before the other man noticed his distraction.

If Charles did find out about Kathy, he'd ruin it by asking questions, not believing it was simply a casual friendship. Charles, always pushing at him. To go out with someone. To move on. Watching for signs of how Alan was doing, whether he asked the questions out loud or not.

But although Alan wasn't yet ready to tell Charles, he *had* taken a partial step—spending time with Kathy, allowing a relationship to develop. As long as he kept his distance and continued to make it clear all he was looking for was companionship, it could work. No harm done. A win-win situation for them both. Clearly, Kathy loved spending time at the ranch with the horses. And he liked being with her. She helped him forget for a time.

If he was careful, nobody would get hurt.

Chapter Twelve

It was the first warm weekend in spring. When Alan called to say Grace wasn't coming and suggested Kathy come early and make a day of it, she agreed.

After an hour on a narrow trail, they emerged from the shadow of lodgepole pines into a sunny meadow edged in the distance by the silver glimmer of water.

"Oh. What a perfect place," Kathy said, feeling a quick burst of pleasure.

Cormac flushed a rabbit and bounded across the meadow after it, while the horses ambled behind. At the intersection of a stream with the lake, Alan helped her dismount.

"Does the lake have a name?" she said.

"Nothing official." His tone was oddly curt, but maybe that was because he was bent over loosening Sonoro's girth. Then he loosened Siesta's saddle and led the two horses to the stream for a drink.

The water, clear as air, purled over boulders and stones, polishing them into opaque crystal. Kathy glanced from the stream to Alan, still puzzling over his reaction to her question about the lake's name.

"We can hike to the top of that hill," he said, pointing. "There's a nice view."

"Sounds good."

"You wading across, or do you want to be carried?"

"Oh. I can wade." Then she was immediately sorry she'd turned him down. The offer to carry her presented definite possibilities, although she did wonder why he'd suggested it.

Leaving the horses to graze in the meadow, they sat on adjacent boulders to remove their shoes and socks for the stream crossing. Kathy rolled up her jeans, then took her first step into the water. She jumped back out with a yelp. "Yikes, that's cold. You could've warned me."

His eyes crinkled with amusement. "Why do you think I offered to carry you?"

"It did seem odd."

He laughed, and it made him look ten years younger. "Change your mind?"

"No, I can manage." It had become a point of honor, but one she'd just as soon concede.

Cormac splashed across the stream behind them, then shook out his wet fur, sprinkling them with cool droplets before they jumped out of range, laughing. After they dried their feet and put their socks and shoes back on, Alan led the way up a steep, barely visible trail.

Man and dog were equally adept at negotiating the rough terrain, Cormac scrambling up by himself and Alan climbing, then reaching back a hand to help Kathy or to point out something.

Once it was a lavender flower that looked like a crocus, blooming in the shade of a fallen log. "We know spring has officially arrived when we see one of these." It was an anemone, he added when she asked.

At the top of the hill, Kathy stood on a shelf of granite catching her breath. While they'd climbed, the day had turned into a typical blue Colorado day—crystal sky, indigo mountains, amethystine peaks. The kind of day when she could no longer imagine ever living anywhere else.

Taking in deep draughts of the cool, clean air with its hint of pine spills and melting snow, she realized that for the first time in months, she felt really okay. Gone the holiday funk, fueled by memories of how happy and excited she'd been in the first throes of love last year. Gone as well that heavy weight of uncertainty that had replaced her anger and grief over her broken engagement.

She didn't know when it had lifted. Knew only that this was the first time she'd noticed its absence. It was such a relief, she wanted to fling her arms into the air and spin in a mad choreography of joy.

Alan sat back on his heels rubbing Cormac's ears, while she looked her fill.

She turned in a slow circle, trying to imprint it all on her memory. "'Nice view' was an understatement."

"Didn't want to oversell," he said.

"It's so...complete."

He stood and stretched. "You a misanthrope, Kathy Jamison?"

Taken off guard by his teasing tone, she stopped turning to look at him. She wasn't altogether certain, but she thought a smile lurked around his eyes.

"Why do you ask?"

"All that completeness." He gestured at the view. "No people as far as the eye can see."

"You're here." And it would be perfect if he'd walk over and tip her face up to his and...

He stayed where he was. "So what we have is a case of semi-misanthropy."

"Easier to cure. Requires only semi-biotics."

A flock of crows chose that moment to land noisily in a nearby tree, breaking off the delicate strand of connection she and Alan had forged with their bantering. But a feeling of ease stayed with Kathy all the way down the mountain. And humming underneath in counterpoint was a growing desire to be more to this man than a friend.

When they got back to the creek, Kathy was warm from sun and exertion, and the water felt good for the first two steps. But by the time she waded across, her feet were cramping from the cold.

Alan pulled the towel from his backpack, crouched down and dried her feet. The sunlight glanced off his head, picking up glints of warm gold among the darker strands. Kathy reached out to smooth the cowlick that had sprung up when he took off his hat, but before her hand reached him, Alan sat back and looked up at her. "There, that should feel better."

Smiling, she used the errant hand to hook her own hair

behind her ear. "It does. Thanks."

She took a deep breath, trying to remember if that had ever happened before—an urge to smooth her hand over the head of a man she barely knew, or for that matter, one she knew well.

Alan dried his own feet and put his boots back on, then walked over to Sonoro and unstrapped a blanket from the back of the saddle. While Kathy spread it in a patch of shade, he unpacked the saddlebags, handing her packages containing pretzels, apples, and sandwiches made with thick slices of homemade bread. Then he walked over to the stream and fished out the beer and water he'd left there to cool.

"You thought of everything," she said.

"I'd love to take the credit, but Mom helped."

She watched him unwrap a sandwich, noticing, as she had before, the oddly bent finger on his right hand. She fought the urge to reach out and take his hand and measure that bent finger against one of hers. "What happened?"

"Oh. This you mean?" He glanced at his finger, then away. "Umm. Fat calf, narrow chute."

"You have cows?"

"Not here. The old ranch. A long time ago."

"So what happened? To the calf?"

"Oh we branded him, then turned him loose." He held up a sandwich. "We have ham and turkey. Which do you prefer? Or would you rather share?"

"Sharing works for me."

It was a mark in his favor that he was willing to share, not a characteristic she'd encountered in many men.

Funny, though, that quick change of subject from his finger. She wondered if he'd done it on purpose, but decided that made no sense.

When they finished eating, Alan walked over to Sonoro and returned carrying a fishing rod and a small plastic box. She raised her brows in question.

"Thought if you've never seen a trout up close and personal, I'd show you one."

He led her along the stream until they reached a spot where it widened, forming a small pool, then he dropped to one knee, looking at the water.

"What are you doing?"

"Checking for fish. And see those flies?" He pointed to a bunch of dry grasses hanging over the edge of the stream that had a halo of insects circling their bent tips. "I'm trying to figure out what to use, and they give me a clue." He opened the plastic box and selected a gray and brown tuft.

"But that doesn't look anything like those bugs."

He glanced up at her raising an admonitory eyebrow. "You mean flies. And it may not look the same to you, but it will to the trout."

"So it's all a matter of having a fishy perspective."

"Are you calling the trout's viewpoint dubious?" His eyes were amused.

A laugh tickled her throat. "Indubitably fishy."

He chuckled as he tied the tiny gray tuft—not a bug, a *fly*—to the end of his line. While he did that, Kathy watched his hands, long-fingered and capable in spite of the bent finger. Panting, Cormac came over and flopped down next to her, and she patted him.

"Come here, let me show you." Alan held the rod, demonstrating the proper movements, then placed it in her hands.

She attempted a cast, but it was too tentative, and the fly landed at the edge of the stream near her feet. Alan moved behind her, and placing his hands over hers, once again demonstrated the proper motions.

He stepped away, and she tried another cast, still feeling the imprint of his hands on hers. This time the fly almost caught in the rocks lining the far shore. The third time, though, she began to get the idea, and the fly landed with a small plop in the middle of the pool. She was wondering what to do next when it disappeared, leaving behind a patch of ruffled water.

As the rod tip bent sharply, Alan stepped closer and placed his hand over hers giving the rod a quick jerk. "There," he said. "The hook's set. Now keep enough tension so you can feel him, but don't try to overpower him. Slow and easy is better."

The fish partially surfaced looking much too large to be

held by the tiny hook and its gossamer lead. But then she forgot about that as she focused on Alan's directions and the tug of the trout on the line. When the fish moved away, Alan told her to let out line. When the fish turned toward her, she retrieved line, only to have the trout dance away yet again. As if the two of them were involved in a delicate minuet.

Then, with a suddenness that surprised her, it ended, and Alan was bending down, reaching into the water. "Come take a look."

Reluctantly, because she didn't want to see the part where he killed it, she bent over the fish. Cormac came trotting over as well, but at a word from Alan, sat quietly. The fish, beautiful and sleek, fluttered its gills as if panting from its efforts. She looked away while Alan removed the hook.

"See the white edges on his fins? He's a brookie."

"Brookie?"

"Brook trout. Here, you can touch him if you want. He needs to rest a minute before I turn him loose."

"You're not keeping him?" A relief. She didn't want to see or hear him kill the fish.

"Nope." Alan took her hand, dipped it into the water, then guided it gently over the satin flank of the fish. "Feel that?"

The fish felt as soft and smooth as the old velvet of the dress Amanda had insisted Kathy buy.

"They have a mucous covering that protects them. Always wet your hand before you touch one."

"*Glory be to God for dappled things—*" Kathy spoke softly. "*For skies of couple-colour as a brinded cow; For rose-moles all in stipple upon trout that swim.*" She paused, looking at the fish, at its speckled side with its faint rosy glow. "You know, I've always loved that poem, but I never understood that last line until now."

Alan moved the fish gently back and forth in the water before loosing his hold on it. The fish lay motionless for a moment, then moved away, gathering speed as it realized it was free.

Kathy watched the swirl of water behind the fish, but she was thinking about Alan's reaction to the poem. For an instant, his face had held a look of such anguish, she began to reach out to touch him, to ask what was wrong. But then he'd shifted, his face had smoothed out and her hand had stilled.

For an instant longer, the spell cast by the trout and the poem lingered, then Alan stood and helped her up. "You ready for dessert?"

Matching his tone, she set aside his odd reaction for later reflection. "There can't be any more food in those saddlebags."

"We could stay out a week." He gathered up the fishing equipment and they walked back to the horses. When he re-stowed the rod, he took a small tin out of the saddlebag and offered her a cookie. Sitting in the early spring sun, her stomach full and her body pleasantly tired, she yawned.

"You sleepy?"

She nodded. "I better get up and move around."

"I have a better idea. Stay there."

She watched as he pulled the saddle off Siesta, brought it over, and set it down near her.

"What are you going to do?"

"Same thing."

He unsaddled Sonoro, placed the saddle on the opposite side of the blanket and lay down. After a moment, she lay down as well. The chitter of a squirrel and the chuckle of the stream wove together with Alan's quiet breathing.

Into that peace, the memory of the look on his face when she'd recited the poem intruded. It wasn't the first time she'd sensed a melancholy in him. Grace had seen it as well and labeled it loneliness. But that seemed unlikely to Kathy. After all, the stories he told about his students indicated he was a popular and well-liked professor, and he had his family and friends.

Maybe, like her, he was recovering from a failed relationship. He never mentioned anyone, but then she'd not told him about Greg, either. And that was odd, come to think of it. That given all the time they'd spent together this winter, their conversations continued to be...well, almost impersonal, really.

In some ways it was a relief. To spend time with someone who simply let her be. Lord knew, she had no interest in revisiting her engagement.

But wouldn't the pain of a failed relationship have faded by now? Certainly hers had. And yet there was no denying the darkness that had stilled his body and stretched the skin of his face into that fleeting mask of agony today.

How he must have loved her.

If that was what it was.

And even if it wasn't, how much longer could they continue the way they were, spending time with each other, but refusing to share more of themselves. And what did that say about her that she still preferred this to her relationship with Greg?

Greg, an open book. Early reader level. Not a deep thought to be found. Had they stayed together, likely she would have been bored inside a year. But Alan. He had a supple, curious mind and a quick wit that made exchanging opinions with him fun. Unlike Greg, he even "got" her sense of humor.

A man like Alan would infuse the lives of those around him with surprise and delight. Although Greg had managed to surprise her, come to think of it.

So where did she and Alan go from here? And why did their relationship still feel distant? A distance demonstrated clearly by their relative positions at this very moment. He, lying propped on a saddle on the far edge of the blanket, and she on the opposite side. Did he make sure he brought a large blanket in case this very thing happened?

She glanced over at him. He had his hat tipped over his face, and his breathing was deep and regular. Even his dog seemed to know his role was to lie between Alan and anyone who might think about trying to move closer.

Her thoughts trailed off, and her eyes drifted shut. Breathing in the scent of sun-warmed pine, her breaths began to match Alan's. Slow and deep.

The next thing she knew, she was waking up, and Alan was no longer lying propped on the other saddle.

Momentarily disoriented, she sat up, running fingers through her hair. Then she saw Alan and Cormac walking toward her, the sunlight glowing around them. The man lean and graceful, his face in partial shadow. The dog dancing at his side.

Her breath caught at the sight.

"You should have awakened me."

"You looked too peaceful to disturb. Besides, there's no rush."

She looked away, her heart startled into a quicker rhythm at the thought of him watching her sleep. But she'd done the same to him, after all.

"I'm going to get the horses saddled. You want privacy, that clump of bushes over there would work." He pointed.

It was a second before she realized what he was suggesting. "Thanks."

Afterwards she walked over to the stream and rinsed her hands and face with the icy water, washing away the last vestiges of drowsiness. Then she watched Alan as, with smooth, easy movements, he saddled the two horses.

Riding back, she knew no matter how long she lived she would never completely forget this day. Knew as well, friendship with Alan was no longer enough for her.

But Alan gave no indication it wasn't enough for him.

౸

He should have known better than to take Kathy to Meg's special place.

It had started out all right. He'd managed Kathy's ordinary everyday questions about the lake's name and his finger, the one that got broken defending Meg, with only brief glitches of pain. But then she quoted the Gerard Manley Hopkins poem, and it all came crashing over him.

Meg had loved that poem. The last time he heard those words...a bright, warm day, very like today. His head in Meg's lap, his eyes closed as he savored the sound of her voice and the images painted by the words.

Then, the poem finished, she tickled him with a blade of grass, and he opened his eyes to see her looking down at him.

"I've decided on a name for the lake," she said.

When he raised his eyebrows in question, she said, "*Lago de Lágrimas*. Lake of Tears."

"Why tears?"

She looked away, a small frown creasing her brow. "I think...

"What?"

"That's supposed to be its name. You know, like naming a foal, or a dog or...I suppose, a child. If you wait awhile, you just know what the name should be, and after that nothing else will quite do."

Then she'd smiled and kissed him, and there had been neither tears nor talking for a time.

In loving Meg there were no doubts, no shadows, only joy. They were each other's safe harbors. Soul mates. How many of those do you get in one lifetime?

Still, he'd had high hopes when he and Kathy started out this morning. Going to the lake with someone else was the kind of step Charles kept urging him to take.

But Kathy's words had brought the memories swirling around him. Thank God she hadn't noticed. Thank God she'd agreed to the nap.

He had lain there, breathing slowly and deeply until she fell asleep. Then he stood and, careful not to disturb her, had looked down at her. She looked peaceful and sweet, and his heart clenched with pain because she wasn't Meg.

Everyone told him it took time. That eventually he'd feel better. Not that he'd ever forget Meg, but that it would gradually get easier, until someday he'd wake up and realize his memories had lost their sharp edge of sorrow.

There was a time when he didn't believe it.

But these last months—sharing them with Kathy, Grace and Delia—they had been easier somehow.

Until today, which reinforced what he already knew.

He couldn't let anyone get too close or matter too much.

Chapter Thirteen

"You've been mighty pensive the last two days." Jade looked across at Kathy who was picking green peppers off a piece of pizza. "You know, we could always order it without green peppers."

"You like them, and I don't mind," Kathy said.

"So what gives?"

"Alan."

"Hmm. Thought so. Has something happened?"

"We went on a picnic Saturday. It was..." Kathy propped her head on her hand, remembering. "We caught a trout."

"The former cold fish gives you a fish." Jade grinned at her. "There has to be something deeply meaningful in that, but beats me what it is."

"Does anyone have a clue what they're doing when they fall in love?" Kathy passed the last piece of green pepper over to Jade.

"Stop. That's quite a leap you just took. Do you think you're falling in love with him?"

"It's just. Well. I like him. Rather a lot, actually. And Amanda is definitely smitten."

Jade grinned then shook her head. "Amanda, huh. And what about Kathy?"

Kathy concentrated on her pizza.

Jade touched her wrist. "Do you know what made you think you were in love with Greg?" Her voice was no longer playful.

Kathy bit her lip in concentration. Sometimes, the way Jade asked questions reminded her of Emily.

"Let's see. He was fun to be with. Bright. Good-looking. Settled. Knew what he wanted from life. Had a good career picked out."

"I like your list. Especially that bit about him being settled. But by those criteria our postman comes close to qualifying."

Kathy pictured their middle-aged, slightly pudgy postman and smiled.

"So what made Greg special?" Jade persisted.

Kathy shook her head. "Darned if I know, now that I think about it. But being single. Dating. It's not all it's cracked up to be." Years and years of kissing frogs, hoping she wasn't missing the one who might turn out to be the prince. Then thinking Greg was a prince, only he'd turned out to be the biggest, ugliest toad of all. It made her tired to even think about starting again.

"Yeah. I'm glad I'm done with all that," Jade said.

"So how did you know Dennis was the one?"

Jade put her pizza down, looking thoughtful. "Before I met Dennis, I was engaged to someone else. I took him home and asked Mom what she thought. She said what mattered was what I thought, and if I had to consult her to figure that out, he wasn't the one for me. Then I met Dennis, and I didn't need to ask Mom or anyone else their opinion." Jade smiled a secret, inward smile.

"You make it sound so simple." And it couldn't be. It was the most difficult thing in the world, making the right decision about whom to marry, wasn't it? After all, look at how many people got it wrong.

"Actually, it is simple, once you know how it feels." Jade sighed. "Relationships. The good ones, well, you just know. Whenever you have to work hard on one, though. Chances are there's something wrong with it you're trying to beat into submission."

It was a moment before Kathy remembered the piece of pizza she was holding. She took a bite, thinking about what Jade had said.

It was suddenly so clear how hard she'd had to work to

113

convince herself she was in love with Greg.

"Excuse me."

Kathy looked up to find three of the students from the senior seminar standing in the doorway. They had the look of a delegation.

"Yes?"

"We just wondered. That is—"

One of the girls gave the boy who was speaking a poke, then took over. "We want to know why you're teaching this class instead of Professor Francini?"

There was enough hostility in the question, Kathy hesitated before answering. "I'm afraid I don't know the answer to that. You'll have to ask Professor Hilstrom. I believe she's responsible for teaching assignments."

"Oh," The girl who'd spoken tossed her head before leading her two cohorts to their seats. The three of them whispered furiously until the other students arrived, but once class started they were attentive and pleasant. Kathy was relieved about that, but their question left her with a slight unease.

"I always eat way too much when we come here." Kathy took another bite of Tandoori chicken, then looked across at Alan, trying to decide. But why not? Nothing ventured, nothing gained. "You know what I'd like to do after dinner?"

Usually they parted outside the restaurant, Kathy to drive home to the Costello's and Alan to drive out to the ranch for the weekend.

"What's that?" Alan asked as he helped himself to more rice.

"It's such a beautiful evening. Perfect for a walk. We could go over to Cheesman or to City Park."

"Your choice."

She'd take that as a yes. "City Park then. There should be ducklings."

Only a few people were scattered around the park—a family having a picnic, a young man lying on a blanket with a book open over his face, a couple curled together kissing. Kathy looked away from the couple, feeling a momentary stab of envy.

"I'd forgotten there were tennis courts," Alan said, getting out of his car.

"Do you play?"

"I haven't for a while."

"I have a couple of rackets in my trunk." She raised her eyebrows in question.

He shook his head. "You weren't the only one eating too much."

"Excuses, Professor Francini?" She threaded a challenge into her voice. "There's a practice wall. If it looks like you can give me a game, we can come back some evening before we stuff ourselves."

He looked at her a moment before nodding. "You're on."

She opened her trunk and got out a can of balls and two rackets, handing him the one her folks had given her for Christmas.

They stood about six feet apart, taking turns hitting the ball. As she might have guessed, Alan had a fluid, easy stroke. Not only was he going to be able to give her a game, she would have to be in top form to give him one.

After several minutes, she went over and sat on one of the benches, lifting the hair off the back of her neck to cool it. Alan continued hitting the ball, switching between forehand and backhand, not even working up a sweat. He finally caught the ball and walked over to her.

"One can only hope your serve sucks."

"Yep. Not only weak, but erratic."

As if she would believe either of those things. "You a tennis hustler?"

"It's only a hustle if money's involved." He sat down next to her. "So, how's Amanda doing these days?"

"Good. Over two hundred pages." She twirled the racket, glancing over at him. He looked perfectly relaxed, his long legs stretched out in front of him. She was tempted to reach over and tickle him. Would that lead to something, or would he just move away?

Before she could decide whether or not to do it, he spoke again. "And the class?"

"I think it's going well. They've been very patient with me."

"It's one of our more talented groups of grad students."

"You were supposed to teach it, weren't you."

Tipping his head, he glanced over at her. "I taught it the last couple of years."

"Was it your choice not to teach it this year?"

"Why do you ask?" His tone was wary.

"At Iowa, the faculty liked teaching the advanced seminars." She glanced at him. He hadn't moved, but he didn't seem as relaxed somehow. "I just wanted to apologize, if I got crammed down your throat."

He shrugged, then stood. "About that walk. Didn't you say something about ducklings?"

So she had been forced on him. And not only had Hilary taken his course away, she'd made him share his office with the usurper. No wonder he hadn't been very friendly in the beginning. But what about now?

He offered his hand to pull her to her feet, but as usual, he let go once she was up. They wandered over to the lake where they found a brood of ducklings being shepherded by their doting mother. Intensely aware of Alan standing beside her, Kathy pondered their relationship as she watched the ducklings.

Usually it was the man who pushed too quickly for physical intimacy, but Alan seemed to be doing everything he could to avoid it. Given her experience with Greg, that had been a relief in the beginning. But not anymore.

She was ready for...something. So was it up to her to make a move? But what if she did, and he rejected her? Better maybe to leave things as they were, at least for the time being.

And if things continued the same way?

Well, she could make a decision about that later.

8&

Even though it was a dangerous escalation, Alan suggested a walk after dinner the following week.

They settled on the botanical gardens. When they arrived, Kathy pulled out her membership card. "My treat. I live only a couple of blocks from here. Seemed silly not to be able to come whenever I want."

Strange that after all these months, he still had no idea where she lived. He nodded toward the two apartment buildings rising above the trees on the northern edge of the gardens. "Over there?"

"Not in an apartment. I live with this wonderful old couple, the Costellos. Over there." She pointed in the opposite direction.

The information surprised him, and yet he could picture it easily. "In order to help them out?"

"More the other way around." Her expression was serious, but her eyes were alight with humor. "Mrs. Costello is a wonderful cook. And Mr. C fusses over me. You know, he makes sure I wear my boots when it snows and take an umbrella when it rains. Whenever I think about moving into an apartment, I realize how lonely it would be."

She had that right.

She picked up a brochure and handed it to him. "So what would you like to see first?"

"You're the expert." He tucked the brochure in his pocket. "Why don't you give me a guided tour?"

She cocked her head, obviously thinking. "Since you're a professor of literature, we'd better start with the Secret Garden."

"Like the children's book?"

She nodded, turning to lead the way. "You know, it's been adapted into a musical. I went to see it with Grace last week when Frank didn't make it back from Kansas City in time."

Alan frowned, trying to bring up the details of the story.

"Frances Hodgson Burnett, isn't it?"

"Uh huh."

"I don't remember the story."

"An orphaned girl is sent to live with her only relative, an uncle by marriage. He's a humpback who lives on the moor and is grieving for his wife who died years—"

"I remember now." He didn't remember, not really. But he didn't need to hear any more. Not about a man who had lost a wife. He spoke carefully. "Rather a peculiar story to base a musical on."

"I thought so, too. But it works. I think the book would face a hard time getting published today, though."

"Why?"

Kathy frowned. "If a story like that came in with a character who had been holding onto his grief for so long, I'd probably ask the writer to reconsider."

But surely it was the other way around. You didn't hold onto grief. Grief held onto you.

He turned away. The careful arrangement of walkways and flowers blurred. "You must not have lost someone essential." Oh, God, where had that come from. His body shuddered, fighting off the anguish. He wanted to be free of grief, wanted to live. He hadn't chosen this...this. He took in a deep breath, unclenching his hands, trying to steady his vision.

He moved away from Kathy and bent blindly over the flowers at the side of the path, trying to come up with something that would ease them away from the abyss.

"It was Hemingway, wasn't it?" Kathy sounded pensive. "Didn't he say something about if sorrow is cured by anything short of death, it isn't real sorrow?"

Islands in the Stream. When Alan read the book, he'd thought it made for a pretty quote. He hadn't believed it. Now, he knew it was true.

He had to do something to get this conversation stopped. If they continued this way... He straightened and took a careful breath.

The brochure dropped out of his pocket. He bent to pick it up, then glanced at the list of garden names, picking the first one he managed to bring into focus. "What about the Japanese Garden?"

Kathy gave him an odd look before leading the way.

He looked around at the Japanese garden, finding relief for his rioting emotions in the lack of bright colors. Gray stones and black water were interwoven with the varied greens of grass, juniper, cypress and rushes. The most delicate green of all was the willow, bent over the small pond. The water shimmered slightly, and the reflection of the willow moved as if touched by a breeze.

Kathy led the way to a bench on a small pavilion built out over the water.

"This is my favorite part of the gardens." Her voice sounded hoarse.

He glanced at her and was surprised by the look on her face. The sort of look he'd been trying to hide from her in the Secret Garden. He spoke gently. "You don't seem very happy about it."

"It's ridiculous really."

"It can't be ridiculous if it's making you unhappy." It was a relief to let go of his discomfort by focusing on hers.

"I got engaged here. Then he broke it off."

Alan remembered how she'd looked the first time he met her, as if she hadn't been sleeping or eating enough. She'd lost that strained expression some time ago, but right now he could see traces of it, and he felt a spurt of anger at the unknown man who had caused it.

Her hands twisted together in her lap. "I don't miss him. It turned out he wasn't a very nice person. But being here, I remember the beginning. The beginning was good."

He reached over and took one of those restless hands in his. As he rubbed his thumb gently across the silky skin of her wrist, he realized how much he struggled not to touch her every time he was with her. "You could have said something. We didn't have to come here."

"Yes. Yes I did, actually. I love this garden. I've missed it." She raised her head and looked at him with a rueful smile. "I thought... Well, I'm glad you're here."

Her eyes were still troubled, and he wanted to banish that look, make her smile again, but he had no idea how. He put his arm around her and sat quietly holding her, rubbing his cheek in the softness of her hair, wishing he had the courage to be more than her friend.

After a time, she shifted against him and lifted her head from his shoulder. For a silent moment, they gazed at each other. Then, still meeting his eyes, she leaned closer and kissed him.

The touch of her lips did it. A tipping point, freeing the emotions he'd tried to hold in check, not just this evening, but whenever he'd been with her these last weeks. He wanted her. God, he wanted her. Was tired of forbidding himself this comfort.

He tightened his arm around her and bent his head, his lips seeking hers, wonder coursing through him at the touch of her mouth. Why had he waited so long to do this? It felt inevitable. Right.

Except. The last time he kissed a woman. Meg.

When Kathy's lips moved against his, for the space of a heartbeat, it was Meg in his arms.

There was a sudden commotion as the garden was invaded by two small boys chasing each other, their mother following behind, pushing a stroller and yelling at them to stop running.

Kathy pulled away, and he sat, unmoving, shaken by the strength of the feelings coursing through him.

When the intruders moved on, Kathy took a breath. "We need to go. The gardens close soon."

Her voice was husky, and it wobbled, but he didn't think his voice would work at all. And he needed to say something casual, meaningless, to ease them back from what the last moments had shown. That she was becoming too important to him.

He couldn't let that happen. Not fair to either one of them.

He never should have kissed her, and yet, right now, he didn't regret it. Wanted only to repeat it, again and again. And hold her. Just that.

But from his reaction, he knew kissing was a step he didn't have the courage to go beyond.

She tucked her hand in his, and they walked slowly toward the entrance. Maybe it was only lust, the hunger humming in his veins. But if it were only that, it would be easy. Lust was the least of it.

He wanted so much more.

But to have it, he had to risk the pain.

Chapter Fourteen

Alan snapped awake, shaking and sweating.

He hadn't had the nightmare in over a year, but it was still as bright and clear as the day it happened. He lay still, breathing carefully, waiting for his heart rate to slow down and the discomfort in his throat and chest to ease.

So what was the proper term for a man who kisses a woman then dreams of his dead wife? Conflicted, peculiar, bizarre, pathetic?

No doubt, Elaine could come up with several more esoteric terms.

He turned his head to look at the clock. A large, red 3:14 glowed back at him. Then he gazed at the wall at the end of the bed. In the dim light, all he could make out was the outline of Meg's picture.

He turned on the lamp and lay there looking at Meg. In the picture, she was leaning against the corral, her thumbs hooked in the pockets of her jeans, the tiny diamond on the fourth finger of her left hand catching a spark from the sun.

Meg. She was woven so tightly into his memories, if he rooted her out there would be nothing left. And yet what he wanted to remember often seemed to slide beyond his grasp, like a dream he could still sense but couldn't quite put into words, while what he wanted to forget swirled through his thoughts like the howling of a blizzard.

The memories ambushed him when he least expected it—in a flash of golden hair on a woman walking down the street, in the sound of a merry laugh, in the clean smell of rain.

And more than that. Meg had made him aware. Taught him to see. And now he couldn't turn it off.

How many times in all those years had she taken his hand, and said, "Quick, Alan, you have to come." The first wildflower in the spring—she was always the one who found it. Snow beginning to outline the branches of the cottonwood tree growing in the dry creek bed at the old ranch. A new foal falling back on its haunches with a surprised look on its face, and Meg's voice saying, "Oh, Alan, isn't he a beauty?"

Without Meg...his life, a moonscape. Not somewhere anyone would want to stay for long.

It wasn't right to get involved with a woman and take whatever she was willing to give when he had nothing to give in return.

He had to end it.

მ

It was Kathy's turn to drive to TapDancer for the weekly riding lesson. She listened to Delia and Grace's chatter with only partial attention as her mind chewed over the events of the previous evening.

Alan had kissed her. So why wasn't she over the moon? Why instead of a happy fizz, did she feel a shiver of unease?

Maybe because of what preceded it, not to mention how it had ended. First there was that odd conversation when she'd taken him to see the Secret Garden. They'd talked about the book, and Alan's reactions had been so... peculiar.

Who was the someone *essential* he'd lost? There had to be someone, because she was certain he hadn't been speaking theoretically. He'd turned away from her, but she'd been able to tell from his posture and the slight hoarseness of his words, he was struggling to control his emotions.

And what had she done? She'd blundered in with that Hemingway quote. Alan hadn't even bothered to respond. And it had made her feel...shut out. Maybe that was why seeing the Japanese Garden again had affected her the way it did. The strong emotions had been a surprise—a mix of sorrow over what might have been and relief it hadn't. Making no sense really.

And Alan. In spite of whatever had made him withdraw from their conversation earlier, he'd been so kind. Not trying to jolly her out of her mood. Just holding her, waiting until she was ready to let it go.

She'd kissed him. Because in that moment, she couldn't not kiss him.

And he'd kissed her back.

How *right* it had felt. As if, when his lips touched hers, her world had shifted and, with a satisfying click, moved into proper alignment. *So this is how it feels to want someone to the exclusion of all others.*

Would it have ended differently? If they hadn't been interrupted, forced to pull apart before either of them was ready?

The walk back to the parking lot had been silent. That was all right, though. She hadn't wanted to dilute what she was feeling with talk. Had wanted simply to hug tight the wonder and not let it slip away.

But when she turned to him before getting in her car, she saw he had that troubled expression on his face. The one he'd had the day at the lake after she quoted the poem. She'd touched his arm, asking him what was the matter, and he'd blinked without answering. And then, as if a switch had been flipped, the look disappeared and when he spoke, the calm everydayness of his words denied all that had been wordless in the touching of their lips. And those ordinary words pushed her away more effectively than any physical force.

Where had he gone? The man who had kissed her.

As always, Cormac was on hand to welcome them to the ranch. His bark summoned Alan from the barn, and Delia ran to get a hug.

Alan also greeted Grace with a hug. Or maybe it was fairer to say Grace hugged him. Like she did everybody. Kathy's heart, skipping into a quick beat as she waited for a special look, settled into a slow, heavy rhythm when he barely glanced at her.

Feeling like crying, Kathy brushed then saddled Siesta and led the filly outside.

Alan's father was in the ring working another horse, and he rode over to her. "You're doing real fine, my dear. It looks like you've been riding all your life."

She managed a smile. "Thanks. I'm still having trouble getting Siesta to do exactly what I want every time, though."

"It's all in the body language. That Siesta horse, now she's real sensitive. If you like I'll take a look, see if there's anything I can suggest."

Kathy rode around the ring, following Robert's suggestions, her thoughts stilling, her pain easing, as she concentrated on his calm voice both correcting and praising her.

"Don't she and that filly look real nice together?"

Kathy, glancing over, saw that Alan had ridden Sonoro into the ring, and Robert's last remark was aimed at his son, not her. She reined Siesta in and walked her over to the two men. "Where are Delia and Grace?"

"They're riding in the meadow today." Alan glanced at her then looked away.

"Arista's had her workout. Time for you to take over, Son." Robert touched his hat to Kathy and rode over to the barn, leaving her to face Alan.

"Dad giving you some good tips?" Alan adjusted effortlessly as Sonoro danced and pulled at the bit.

"Yes." She waited for Alan to look at her, but all his attention seemed to be on Sonoro, who continued to fidget.

"He's the best."

"Yes." Tears gathered in her throat.

"Okay, let's see what he showed you." Alan's tone was the one from last night—calm, detached.

Quickly, she turned Siesta and gave her the signal to move into her fastest gait, the *paso largo*, running away from that bland look on Alan's face. Running from the knowledge that Alan's disinterest hurt more than Greg's betrayal.

For the remainder of the lesson, she kept her eyes focused between Siesta's ears, and her thoughts blank.

125

By the time they led the horses into the barn for unsaddling, Grace and Delia had already taken care of their horses and had walked over to the mares' pasture to visit the foals.

In the dim quiet of the barn, Alan spoke in an unhurried voice. "Grace said she needed to get back early today, so I'd be happy to finish up Siesta for you."

"Thanks. I'm sure Grace will appreciate it." Kathy forced the words out of a throat that was tight and aching. She put Siesta in her stall and started to leave.

But, no. She had to face this head on. Now. Before she got in too deep. Because there was no longer any doubt in her mind where this was going. There would be no floating into love. Not this time. Not with this man. The two of them in this moment, poised on the brink of—something. One small step—toward him or away—and the future would be irrevocably changed,

She turned back. Alan was lifting Sonoro's saddle off. "Tell me something," she said, grateful her voice was working all right, even if the rest of her felt tight and frozen.

"What?"

"About last evening."

There was a slight hitch in his movements as he set the saddle down. Then he picked up a brush and began to groom Sonoro with long smooth strokes. "What about it?"

She walked over and stood near Sonoro who leaned into her, snuffling at her pockets. Only a short time ago she would have jumped away, certain he was going to nip her.

"I'm confused. Last night you kissed me, but now you're acting as if we're barely acquainted." She ran her hand over the soft velvet of Sonoro's muzzle, taking comfort in that touch. "I'm okay with the idea of going slow, but..."

Alan lifted his head. Although he didn't meet her gaze, she saw his face tighten, making the dark circles under his eyes more noticeable.

"It's best if we're just friends." He moved to Sonoro's other side and resumed brushing.

"If that's all you want, you shouldn't have kissed me." Well, she'd kissed him first. But she was in no mood to be fair. It was all she could do to keep her lips from trembling.

"I'm sorry." He continued to brush Sonoro.

Then he straightened, and for an instant, his eyes met hers. His looked tired, sad. Silently he seemed to be begging her, *please don't do this*. Then he turned away, and spoke in that impersonal tone she was beginning to hate. "I won't be able to have dinner with you next Friday, but I'll see you as usual on Saturday."

It defeated her. His calm. His insistence they could act as if none of it had happened...the kiss, this conversation.

She dropped her hands away from Sonoro and walked blindly out of the barn, away from Alan, sucking in deep breaths, trying to clamp down on the sudden onslaught of grief.

❧

The Galiceno mare was late foaling. It was her first, and Alan knew his dad was worried. Since the only thing on his schedule Monday was an afternoon meeting with Hilstrom, he decided to spend Sunday night at the ranch. Better by far to sit up with the mare than to lie awake a second night thinking about that scene with Kathy. He'd hurt her, when his intention had been to keep her from being hurt.

He hadn't even realized she'd left until he looked up from brushing Sonoro and discovered she was gone. He'd dropped the brush and gone to the barn door, then stood in its shadow watching as Grace, Delia and Kathy got into Kathy's car and drove away.

When he let her walk away the first time they met, he'd risked only his standing with his department head, not that that was a small matter. But this time, as he watched the car roll out of sight, he knew the stakes were so much higher. His peace of mind...and his heart.

When he returned after dinner to check on the mare, he found her lying down and lightly sheened with sweat. He called his father, and the two of them kept watch. At three in the morning, after an uncomplicated labor, the foal slipped out into the clean straw. The mare stood and began cleaning it off with strong sweeps of her tongue.

It was perfect, from the tiny hooves to the small head that

was the image in miniature of its sire. But as Alan moved forward to get a better look, he realized the foal wasn't moving. And then he saw it. The cord, twisted around the foal's neck and with a sharp bend in it, like a garden hose folded over to stop the flow of water. Only this bend had restricted the foal's lifeblood.

For a moment, Alan stood frozen, staring at the dead foal, until the soft sound of his father's distress nudged him into action. He stepped forward and lifted the foal, turning away from the mare who whickered in uncertainty. Behind him, his father, voice rough with sorrow, tried to comfort the mare.

Death. Inevitable. Especially on a ranch. Calves born too early in the spring. Injured animals that had to be put down. The horse he'd had since he was eight that died of old age when he was twenty. The two dogs that preceded Cormac.

He hated it, but he'd accepted it. Until Meg. Losing her had knocked him asunder, erased all the messages he'd used in the past to comfort himself. "...a long, happy life...better off out of pain."

Meg. She'd had a happy life, he was certain of it, because he had been there for most of it.

But not a long life.

It wasn't supposed to be that way.

His arms tightened around the dead foal as the memory of holding Meg that last time engulfed him, the pain for a moment as overwhelming and unendurable as the day Meg died.

Monday afternoon, Alan arrived for his meeting with Hilstrom, his eyes gritty from lack of sleep, his stomach raw from too much coffee and too little food.

Hilstrom's assistant looked up when he walked in. "Let me tell her you're here."

As she made the call, Alan stared at the picture hanging behind the woman—a ballerina who could be made to appear to be balancing on the assistant's head. With a start, he remembered noticing the same thing the first time he met with Hilstrom. Damn, had it been a year already? He shook his head, realizing as he did, he was half looped with weariness. He should have rescheduled, but it was too late now.

"Go on in," the assistant said.

He stepped through the doorway and took a seat on the sofa.

Hilstrom sat across from him. "I expect you know what this meeting is about." She spoke briskly, glancing from the file on her lap to him.

He struggled to keep his eyes open and focused.

"As you know, the RPT committee has recommended you for tenure. I'm sorry, Alan, but I've decided not to support that." She looked up and met his eyes briefly before looking back at the file.

He started to lift a hand to rub his aching head, then let it subside in his lap.

So that was that.

"You still have next year with us, of course, and I'll be happy to write you a positive letter of recommendation. You're a fine teacher, dedicated and creative, and I expect you'll have no difficulty finding a position more aligned with your interests."

Her words echoed, as if coming at him in a cave. He tried to rouse himself to the proper reaction: contempt at a system that focused on publication records to the exclusion of everything else, derision for Hilstrom, whose narrow-minded approach had already forced out several good people, resolution to follow Charles's advice after all and sue. But all he could manage was a vague disinterest in the whole proceeding. It was taking every bit of his energy just to stay upright and keep his eyes open.

He took a breath and spoke carefully. "Thank you for meeting with me and making your position clear." Then he stood, taking the initiative for ending the meeting away from her. Not caring that he'd broken protocol. Not caring about any of it. "Now if you'll excuse me." Without waiting for her response, he walked through the door, closed it softly behind him, nodded at the assistant, then kept walking until he was outside.

His feet carried him to the parking lot, where he got into his car. On automatic pilot, he drove to his apartment. When he arrived, he dropped onto the bed without undressing and fell into a blessedly deep sleep.

Chapter Fifteen

Her heart sinking, Kathy went over her last meeting with Alan: Sonoro's restlessness, when she had never seen Sonoro other than perfectly under control when Alan was riding him, and the way Alan wouldn't look at her. But it was the interaction in the barn that left her most perplexed. That ravaged look on his face when he said he was sorry he'd kissed her. How did that fit with the way he'd kissed her...as if he were starving and she were food and drink.

None of it made sense. And all of it hurt.

Saturday. She'd ask Grace to give her a chance to talk to Alan privately. And this time, she'd stick it out. Not leave until he explained why they couldn't be more than friends.

Kathy had just arrived home from work Friday evening when Mrs. Costello called up the stairs to tell her Grace was on the phone.

"Kathy. *Mira*. We can't go to the ranch tomorrow. Delia has a fever. Could you let Alan know?"

Kathy was sorry Delia was sick, but it was going to make it easier to have that talk with Alan.

Saturday, as she was leaving for the ranch, Kathy called Grace to check on Delia.

Frank answered the phone. "Oh, God, Kathy. She's in the hospital. We almost lost her last night."

Kathy's breath caught in her throat, and all she could manage was an incoherent sound. It couldn't be. Not Delia. Sweet, laughing, lovable Delia with her bright eyes and cloud of curls. So sick they'd almost lost her? It wasn't possible.

When Kathy arrived at Children's Hospital, she found Grace sitting in the corner of the intensive care waiting room, staring out the window. As Grace turned a tear-stained face toward her, Kathy pulled her into her arms.

Grace held on tight, sobbing. "*Ay Dios mío*, I'm so scared. She's so sick. She's in septic shock."

"I don't know what that is." Kathy took Grace's hands in hers. "Septic shock."

"It's a bad infection. In her blood. Then her body tries to fight it, and just makes it worse."

Although Kathy didn't totally understand Grace's explanation, the other woman's fear made her stomach clench with dread.

"But how could it happen so fast?"

"It just does." Grace wiped her eyes.

"When do you get to see her?"

"In a couple of minutes."

As if Grace's words conjured her, a young woman in surgical scrubs decorated with Mickey and Minnie Mouses appeared. "Mrs. Garibaldi? You can come on back now."

"Kathy, *por favor*. Come with me."

They walked over to a door that Grace pulled open when the lock release sounded. After they washed their hands, they put on gowns, gloves, shoe coverings and face masks, then Grace led the way to Delia's room, accompanied by the clicking, beeping and soft whooshing of medical equipment.

Delia lay motionless in a tangle of wires and tubing, looking tiny, and so incredibly fragile. Tears welled out of Kathy's eyes and ran down into the mask.

Grace touched one of Delia's hands with her finger, and spoke softly. "Delia, *Mami* is here. And so is *Tía* Kathy." Grace glanced at Kathy. "It's good to talk to her. Sometimes patients remember when they wake up."

Kathy moved to the other side of the bed and took Delia's

131

hand in hers. The tips of Delia's fingers were white, and her hand felt cool. She glanced at Grace.

"It's the infection," Grace said. "It acts like frostbite."

Her throat aching, Kathy spoke to the little girl. "Delia, Arriba will be disappointed you didn't show up to ride her this week. She'll be real sad to hear you're sick. I'm sad too. I love you, baby."

Delia didn't react.

Kathy looked over at Grace, who was crying silently. Grace's desperation frightened Kathy even more than Frank's had. After all, Grace was a nurse. Nobody was going to be able to fob her off with false hope.

Kathy continued to hold Delia's hand, but instead of speaking to the child, she began to pray—asking, imploring God to help the little girl—while Grace, murmuring in a mixture of Spanish and English, smoothed Delia's hair.

After a time, a nurse came to check on Delia, and Grace and Kathy took a break. When they returned to the waiting room, Frank was there. He gave Grace a hopeful look.

Grace shook her head. "How is Blackie-two?"

"Fine. She did make a mess in the basement, though. Not her fault. That's why I didn't get back right away."

"Poor Blackie-two," Grace said. "We forgot all about her."

"I can take care of her for you," Kathy said. "Then you won't have to worry."

When Frank and Grace went back to sit with Delia, Kathy borrowed Grace's key and drove to the Garibaldis' house to pick up Blackie-two along with her bed, dishes, and food.

It wasn't until she got Blackie-two settled at the Costellos' that Kathy remembered what she'd been doing when she heard the news about Delia—getting ready to go to TapDancer. After Frank told her about Delia, she hadn't even thought to call Alan to say they wouldn't be coming.

She looked up the number for the ranch and dialed. A female voice said hello.

"Stella?"

"No. Sorry. This is Elaine. Did you want to speak to my mother?"

"No, no. Actually, I need to speak to Alan."

"He's not here. Can I take a message?"

Kathy heard the sudden piercing howl of an infant in the background.

"Oh shoot," Elaine said, sounding harassed. "Could you call back later?"

"Sure," Kathy said, but Elaine had already disconnected.

Kathy almost called again after dinner, but then remembering Alan's sister was visiting, decided it might be better to wait until Sunday night when he would be back in Denver. But Sunday night there was no answer at his apartment. She thought about leaving a message, but decided against it. It wasn't something she'd want to find on her answering machine—news that someone she loved was in intensive care in critical condition.

After that weekend, Kathy's sense of urgency to speak with Alan was pushed to the background by her worry over Delia. Even the fleeting thought that Alan needed to be told, failed to move Kathy to actually pick up the phone and dial his number. She was simply too emotionally exhausted after a day at work followed by an evening at the hospital to deal with anything more.

Her major comfort during days and nights filled with worry about Delia and grief over the ending of her relationship with Alan, were the few minutes every evening she spent re-reading Emily's diaries.

They reminded her that Emily had made it through a time every bit as dark and difficult.

ℰℭ

Excerpt from the diaries of Emily Kowalski
1930...

I sure haven't been very good about this diary business, but it seemed like once I got the history part done, I just couldn't get the knack of writing about things as they were actually happening. But I aim to try again. Jess thought I'd filled up the book he gave me, so he bought me another one.

This last year has been awful hard, although not for us so much. But everyone is learning to do with less and not to waste a single thing, like half a diary.

Jess and I have been lucky. Jess is teaching, and I was as well, up until a few weeks ago. Then I had to stop, because we are going to have a baby, at last.

I'd about given up hope it was ever going to happen, although I never said so to Jess. But maybe he felt that way, too, because when I told him I was expecting, he was even more excited than I was.

It feels like all my dreams have come true. I know, I still haven't done everything I planned. But the most important thing is I met Jess, we fell in love and now we are going to have a baby.

I think it will be easy to write every day, now. I will have so much to write about. I want to remember every moment.

1933...

When Bobby was born, the doctor told me I would be risking my life if I had another child before I recovered fully. I was so excited about Bobby arriving safe and sound, I paid him no heed. It was only later, when he repeated the warning, that I noticed how serious he looked. He also insisted on speaking to Jess.

I thought a year or two would be sufficient time, and I didn't let it worry me. But today he told me I must continue to avoid pregnancy at all costs. When I tasked him about it, he said it would be best if I never had another child.

It is a difficult thing to hear.

I take comfort in Bobby, who is growing like a weed and is so quick and intelligent. Not to mention handsome. He and Jess are the lights of my life.

1936...

It's been such a long time since I felt like picking up a pen and recording my thoughts or the events of my life. In truth, this last year is one I don't want to remember, but I doubt I shall ever forget.

I don't know if I'm ready even now to write again, but I'm going to try with this new year to make a new beginning.

The last time I wrote anything was March 20, 1935. The day before our dear Bobby fell ill with the meningitis. He was only five. A baby still.

I wonder, will I ever be able to go back and read those journals for the years passed, now that everything has changed. Even my handwriting is different. It hurts so much to think of that younger me who had no idea dreams were so fragile.

This time has seemed darker even than when Kiara died, although our Bobby lived. And now I must find a way to cope with it. If I don't, dear Bobby will have no one. And Jess needs me as well, to help him heal and live again.

But who will help me heal?

It was all I thought to ask for. That Bobby would live. But nothing is the same.

Before the meningitis, the house was full of sounds. Bobby's feet running, Bobby banging my pots and pans, Bobby chattering to himself like a squirrel in his own language, then surprising me with words in my language.

Now, I cannot tell if he understands me or, indeed, if he feels anything. He lies so quiet, I can hear the clock ticking in the other room.

I am suspended in time. Jess goes out into the world each day, and returns each night, but the boundaries of my world are this house and yard. It's as if Bobby and I are under a spell and are waiting for a fairy godmother to touch us with her magic wand so he will be able to run and talk and I will be able to feel once more.

ℰↃ

"What do you think?" Charles asked. "We got a shot at the division title this year?"

Alan hadn't been in the mood for a baseball game, but Charles had insisted. "Classic definition of 'hopeful' is a baseball fan in the spring."

"In other words?"

"Not a prayer."

"That optimistic, huh?" Charles waved the beer vendor over. "You ready for another?"

"No. I'm good." Not true. Only eight days since he learned he wasn't getting tenure and four days since Grace, Delia and Kathy had failed to come for their weekly ride. At first, he worried they had been in an accident, but the highway patrol said there had been no accidents on any of the roads leading to the ranch.

He'd called Grace, several times, but there was no answer. He didn't know what to think. Were they away, or were they choosing not to speak to him?

He knew he'd handled the situation with Kathy badly, but he hadn't expected Grace to cut him off as well. Delia loved the horses, so it was cruel of Grace to let his problems with Kathy interfere with that. It really was taking feminine solidarity entirely too far.

"You never mentioned what happened with your tenure decision," Charles said, paying the vendor and taking a sip of his fresh beer.

It was a relief for Alan to change the direction of his thoughts, even though this subject was almost as painful. "Committee approved it. Hilstrom didn't."

"That's a tie. What happens next?"

"Dean, then the board of trustees." Alan took a sip of beer and, finding it lukewarm, set it down.

Charles glanced at him. "Next time I'm trying to teach a witness to answer just the question and not give details, remind me to give you a call."

"Dean and Board are all for show, not go. I'm out."

There was a sudden flurry of activity as the batter hit a high fly to left field. After the Rockies' player caught the ball, Charles sat back down. "You're not going to fight it?" he asked, picking up the thread of conversation along with his beer.

Alan shrugged. "I followed your advice. Gave the impression I might sue. Obviously, it didn't work."

Taking a sip of beer, Charles examined him. "Hell, how did I miss it? You're not writing anymore." He set his beer down. "It's Meg, isn't it."

"You think everything is Meg." Alan looked away, his gut tightening.

"Yeah. Matter of fact, I do."

The sudden surge of anger shocked Alan. Then the anger ebbed, as swiftly as it had come, leaving him exhausted. "Could be you're right."

"Then do something, man. See a shrink. Talk it out." Charles sounded as ragged as Alan felt.

Alan closed his eyes and turned his head away. Talk. Elaine had been pushing it as well. As if that were the magic formula. But if they couldn't understand how impossible it was for him, there was no way he could explain.

Charles was silent for the rest of the inning. Then he sat back, stretched slightly, and spoke without looking at Alan. "You got a plan?"

"I still have a year. Contract runs through next May."

"You think they'll change their minds?"

"Nope."

"So what happens next May?"

Unable to speak, Alan shrugged.

"And you don't want to discuss it."

"You got it."

As always, Charles seemed to know when he'd pushed far enough.

Alan had just walked into the house Saturday morning,

filthy and exhausted from spending the night with a colicky mare, when the phone rang. He picked it up, and when he heard Kathy say hello, his heart began to race. *Thank God.* It was going to be all right, after all. They could work something out. Figure out how to be friends again.

It took him a moment to sort out what she was saying—not that she planned to come out for a ride or that she wanted to see him. But that Delia was critically ill. In intensive care at Children's.

Dread hit his gut, nauseating him. He closed his eyes, but the memories were still there...Delia holding out her hand to give Arriba a carrot, then giggling because it tickled; hugging a new foal, so excited it bubbled out of her in laughter; lying still as death, her smile erased, her voice stilled.

It can't be real. I can't bear it if it's real.

The phone beeped in his ear, demanding to be hung up. He stared at it with no memory of the conversation after Kathy's first words. Had he even responded?

He fumbled with the phone, dropping it to the floor. As he bent to pick it up, the nausea hit in earnest, and he barely made it to the bathroom. Afterwards, he sat on the floor, his whole body shaking as if he were freezing, and with the cold came the memory of the way he'd felt immediately after losing Meg. He'd been nauseated then, too. And in so much pain, he didn't believe he would survive it. Hadn't wanted to survive it.

Kathy's voice saying those appalling things...Delia.

It couldn't be real. But it was. As real as losing Meg.

The memory of that day slipped back, as insidious as a flame blackening the edges of a piece of paper before becoming a conflagration. He had to stop it. Couldn't go through it again. He pushed the images and memories frantically away, Meg somehow entangled with Delia.

Think of something, anything. The colicky mare, riding Sonoro, training a fractious foal. He focused on the coolness of the tile, the smell of his clothes, the rasp of his breath, the sour taste of vomit in his throat. Gradually, he pulled himself back from the brink.

After a while, he forced himself to get up and strip off his clothes. Then he stood under the hot shower until the water ran cold, trying to wash it all away—the pain, the fear, the helplessness.

Not succeeding.

When he got back to Denver after that weekend, Alan lay on his bed, staring at Meg's picture. Remembering the day he lost her. Remembering his last sight of her, so unlike herself, so utterly and emphatically still, the gold of her hair darkened. Remembering how he vowed he would never let himself care enough for somebody to hurt that way again.

But he'd screwed up. Twice over. And now, thinking about Kathy and Delia, he felt...something he didn't want to name.

The memories of the past months, and the sad, restless feelings they evoked, stuck like burrs he couldn't shake off. Kathy grinning at him after he spilled the beer. Laughing as she missed a tennis ball. Standing in his mother's kitchen, her hair shining like the copper pans in the late afternoon slant of sunlight.

He'd chosen loneliness over the possibility of pain, yet pain had come anyway.

Elaine insisted talk would help. But then most women seemed willing to delve into their psyches with the abandon of a flea-market treasure hunt. For him, it was the worst possible trespass. Better to let the problem lie, walk around it, do something physical in order to stop thinking about it. Not dredge it up and examine it in minute detail. Examination only made it that much more difficult to go on.

He stared at Meg's picture, remembering the trial and error that had taught him what worked best to keep the memories locked up.

In the beginning he hadn't been able to manage it. Every waking hour, Meg's absence was a heavy weight that slowed and muted word and act. Simple things, like cooking a meal, answering the phone, shaving took all his energy. If it hadn't been for Charles, he wouldn't have made it. Charles, showing up at random times, opening blinds, turning on lights, heating up soup and watching him while he ate it. Charles insisting he go to a ball game. Charles pushing back when Alan told him to get lost.

When the fall term at DSU had started, Alan began teaching, emerging from his apartment as if from a long convalescence. Gradually the students and the teaching began to distract some of his thoughts. Weekends at the ranch with Sonoro, Siesta, Cormac, his parents helped as well. As did hard physical labor. All of it more effective than talk.

But what about now? With Delia critically ill, Kathy slipping beyond his reach and his position at DSU ending.

Was silence courage? Or cowardice?

Alan called the hospital at least twice a day. An impersonal voice would say only that Delia Garibaldi was still in critical condition. He called Grace and Frank, but all he ever got was an answering machine. He finally left a message, saying he was thinking about them.

He knew where Grace and Frank were, of course. With Delia. And he could see them if he drove to the hospital and waited outside the ICU until they came out. But what good would that do? It wouldn't help Delia. And Grace and Frank didn't need the awkward words he'd be able to string together.

Even as he made excuses, he knew they were weak. Knew with the clarity of self-knowledge that was Meg's best and worst gift to him what the real problem was. He couldn't face either the reality of Delia's sickness, or the possibility he might run into Kathy at the hospital. Even though he missed Kathy and wanted to see her. Wanted back what they'd had—that easy, undemanding companionship, something that was probably no longer possible.

Best then not to see her at all.

Kathy, one kind of pain, Delia another. He tried to pray for the little girl, but the part of him that believed in a loving God had shattered when Meg died. In spite of that, an incoherent, useless, *Please. Please don't do this. Please don't let her die,* played continuously in his mind, accompanying everything he did.

He moved through the days automatically, finishing up his classes for the year, relocating to the ranch for the summer, cleaning stalls, exercising horses, readying equipment for the summer trips to regional fairs. And always it was there, the fear that the next time he called the hospital, the voice would say Delia had died. Or maybe they wouldn't even tell him that.

He carried that burden of worry and guilt alone, knowing, if he told his parents, it would put in motion a persistent and unrelenting concern. Sickness, birth, death meant food. The ranchers' way. His mother would cook and insist he take the food to the Garibaldis.

He shuddered, remembering the casseroles covering the table and kitchen counters and filling every cubic inch of refrigerator and freezer space after Meg's death. He'd no more been able to eat any of it than he could fly.

By the end of the week, he could take it no longer—the Garibaldis' silence and the refusal of the hospital to give him any information. He drove back to Denver Monday morning, determined to sit in the ICU waiting room, until someone told him what was going on.

Alan startled to the feel of a hand on his shoulder. Frank. Looking years older than the last time Alan saw him. The other man slumped into the chair across from Alan.

"How..." It was all Alan managed. His throat was so dry the word came out parched and cracked.

"We turned the corner. Yesterday."

"Thank God."

"Yeah." Frank looked at him with bloodshot eyes. "How about a cup of coffee?"

"Sure. Good."

The two of them went to the cafeteria, and Alan sat, mostly silent, while Frank described what the previous weeks had been like.

"Is there anything you need me to help you with?"

Frank shook his head. "Mostly we're living at the hospital."

"You'll let me know when she's well enough for me to see her?"

"Probably won't be for a while yet. Guess I better get back."

Frank stood and extended his hand to Alan. "Thanks for coming. That's the important thing. To know you're thinking about us. Appreciate it."

සෝ

Alan accompanied his parents and four of the TapDancer horses to the fair in Pueblo. After they arrived and settled the horses, they went to dinner, and Alan, knowing he could no longer put it off, told them he'd been denied tenure.

His mother, looking troubled, touched his arm without speaking.

"Shows they don't know a thing about how to run that place." His father's voice was gruff. "Have you decided what you're going to do?"

"I'll have next year to find another position. Hopefully, I'll find something in Denver or the Springs."

"Oh." His mother's face clouded over in sudden comprehension. "But that would be terrible, if you had to move. We love having you at the ranch."

"More than love having you. You're a big help." His father cleared his throat. "Matter of fact, we could use you full-time, if you've got any interest." He held up a hand to stop Alan's response. "Nope. Don't want an answer now. You got a year to think. Just let me know."

"Thanks." The word was raspy and uneven, and it wasn't enough, but it was all he could manage. It overwhelmed him, their support and love. Offering whatever was in their power in order to spare him more distress.

But what he couldn't tell them was the distress from the tenure decision was a pinprick compared to his worry about Delia, and his sorrow over how things had ended with Kathy.

Chapter Sixteen

Kathy was running on the jogging path that circled Cheesman Park when a man ran up beside her. She glanced over at him feeling uneasy, then relaxed when she saw who it was.

"Thought it might be you," the man said. "Not many people have hair that color. It's good to see you again."

"Do we know each other?" Actually, she'd known immediately who he was. The Greg-look-alike district attorney she seemed doomed to run into whenever she had a relationship end.

He was wearing a T-shirt from an Ironman competition in Penticton, wherever that was. Not only a show-off with that T-shirt, but gay? That was Cheesman's reputation anyway—as a place gays hooked up—although Kathy had never personally observed it. But then she didn't go to the park after dark.

"You did it again. Charles Larimore. We played tennis, last fall. You run here often?"

"Occasionally." Actually, she ran in Cheesman almost every day because it was handy and the jogging track was compressed dirt instead of pavement, and its reputation, if anything, made it seem safer.

"Funny, I haven't seen you before."

"Yeah. Funny." She kept her tone ironic, not wanting to encourage him. But actually, it wasn't funny, it was odd he chose to run here.

"I've got five miles to go. Maybe I'll see you again sometime."

Not if I see you first.

He pulled away, moving at twice her pace.

Over the next two weeks, she did see him, several times. He always caught up to her, never the other way around, and he always slowed down to talk to her a minute or two before pulling away. He usually managed to make her laugh, and underlying the humor she learned he had a sharp intelligence. Gradually, she stopped feeling uncomfortable at the thought of seeing him, and just as gradually, he began spending longer intervals with her before picking up his pace.

She began to look forward to seeing Charles Larimore, and even felt a tiny pulse of disappointment when she didn't. But when he asked her out, she said, no thanks. The second time he asked and she declined, he put out a hand and signaled her, then he stepped off the path. She followed.

"What is it?" she said, thinking he had a cramp.

"You telling me no because you really don't want to go out with me, or are you seeing someone?"

"Seems to me I recall something about a girlfriend."

He looked at her for a moment before starting to grin. "Seems to me someone was prevaricating when she acted like she didn't remember me."

Kathy felt the blush warming her cheeks, but she hoped Charles wouldn't notice. She bent over, hands on her thighs, taking deep breaths as a further distraction.

Charles reached out and lifted her chin. "You really did a job on my self-confidence." He sounded serious, but his eyes were full of mischief. "Nice to have it back."

"About the girlfriend." She moved so his hand no longer touched her.

Charles looked abruptly sober. "I no longer have her."

"And why is that?" Not that she cared. Exchanging a few words with him two or three times a week was one thing, actually going out with him was a whole other thing. One she wasn't yet ready for.

"Irreconcilable differences."

His serious look stopped her from saying that wasn't much of an explanation.

"Just to set the record straight," he said. "I enjoy talking to you. I thought it would be pleasant to share a meal and more talk. No strings." He took a couple of deep breaths examining her while he did it. "I'll keep my hands to myself. Promise."

What he was offering, she could handle it, couldn't she? In fact, going out with him might be just the thing to take her mind off her current troubles. Worth a try at least.

"Okay," she said.

He grinned. "Lucky you agreed. I was about ready to change tactics."

"To what?"

"Better I keep that to myself. I might still need them."

An hour later, he picked her up at the Costellos and took her to a microbrewery. They went through a pizza and a couple of beers as they exchanged the usual get-acquainted litany: careers, schools, birthplaces, family make-up, hobbies.

Charles's personality was so different from Greg's that gradually the physical resemblance ceased to bother her.

When, true to his word, Charles didn't even attempt to kiss her goodnight, Kathy decided it was okay to accept another invitation.

The day Delia woke up, Kathy had come, as usual, for her evening visit. Already, the shimmer of summer pollution was stretching over the eastern plains, and the mountains, hazed with blue, carried only warm weather apostrophes of snow.

"*Tía* Kathy." Delia's voice was a thread, and she appeared as fragile as paper-thin glass, but the smile was all Delia.

"Hello, baby. You sure gave us a scare." Kathy took Delia's hand in hers.

Delia frowned, shaking her head as tears welled out of her eyes. "I can't hear you."

Shocked, Kathy looked at Grace.

With tired eyes, Grace looked across the bed at Kathy. "It's the antibiotic they used. It saved her life, but it damaged her ears."

As Grace's meaning sank in, Kathy's stomach cramped. "Is it permanent? The damage?"

"There are things, maybe later, that can help, but..."

Dizzy, Kathy leaned against the bed, looking down at the little girl with the bright eyes and enchanting smile. Not fair. Delia had already lost the tips of two fingers and four toes to the infection. Wasn't that enough of a price for her life?

It was what Emily had faced. A sick child. The long days and nights of worry.

And years of difficulty afterwards.

ℰↃ

Excerpt from the diaries of Emily Kowalski
1937...

Jess moves Bobby to a cot in the kitchen before he leaves for work every day, but I fancy Bobby would enjoy going outside. I saw a picture of an apparatus called an invalid chair in the Sears catalog, and I pointed it out to Jess. He said it was too expensive, and besides, it was too big for Bobby. He was gruff, and it upset me.

Then last weekend, after a long spell in his workshop he brought me a chair he'd made for Bobby. It is very clever. He used the wheels from the baby buggy, and the chair part is the perfect size. I made cushions so it will be soft, and yesterday we tried it for the first time.

When Jess put Bobby in the chair, I watched him carefully, and I swear, his eyes sparkled. He is aware, I know he is. Just because he can't walk or talk, it doesn't mean he no longer feels.

I have started reading to Bobby. He loved to be read to before he got sick. Today, he moved his arm, just a little, and seemed to point to one of the books. Jess doesn't believe me, at least not yet, but he is home so little.

We are both trying to find ways to deal with what has

happened. For Jess, it means working long, hard hours. For me, it is taking care of Bobby and trying to convince my heart that someday my life can be as it once was, even though I know that's impossible.

Today, I tried to paint again. The brush felt awkward in my hand, the colors clashed and I was unhappy with the result. I wonder if I have to be happy in order to paint. Or perhaps there is nothing wrong with the picture, only with the eyes full of sadness looking at it. I wanted to ask Jess for his opinion, but he's always so exhausted when he gets home. He is studying again, this time for a Ph.D. while teaching at the same time. He often nods off over his books after dinner. Still, he is lucky to be working, and it is one of the blessings I count when I try to pray.

Yesterday was Bobby's seventh birthday. I remembered when he was tiny, and we counted his age in days. It was such a happy, hope-filled time. Every day was an adventure that brought changes. Jess and I were changing as well, affected by the wonder and delight of seeing our dear Bobby grow.

That has all stopped now. When Jess comes home, I have no exciting stories to tell him about what words Bobby has learned, or how far he has crawled, walked, or run.

That awful illness has made a mockery of time, for after all, what is time but the measure of change. Now the only change in my life is that Bobby keeps getting bigger and harder for me to take care of.

And I feel as if I have lost Jess as well. We seem to have nothing to talk about anymore. How could we let this happen? Where has the ease between us gone, the sharing of every small detail of our days? Isn't it enough that we have lost touch with our dear Bobby?

ଈ

The next time Kathy visited the hospital, Delia asked when Alan was coming to see her.

"He hasn't come to see her?" Kathy assumed he had been stopping by during the day, so he wouldn't run into her.

"He sent a card. And he called." Grace seemed to be avoiding her eyes.

Given his reaction to the news Delia was critically ill, Kathy couldn't understand why he hadn't come. He'd been so upset, he hadn't even been coherent.

"He'll come soon," Kathy wrote for Delia. *If I have to drag him here myself.*

Easier said than done. Kathy's connection to Alan had frayed, and now, learning he hadn't tried to see Delia, it snapped. But Delia, the only person in the world she would be willing to do it for, was asking her to pick up those strands and attempt to reconnect them.

It took Kathy most of the next morning to work up the courage to call Alan, and she breathed a sigh of relief when she got his voicemail. A further relief when his voice on the recording had a hollow quality that made it seem unfamiliar. His message said he was away from the university for the summer but would be checking his voicemail on a regular basis. She left a message saying Delia was improving and was asking to see him.

She debated whether to add she always did her visiting in the evening, then decided against it. If he wanted to avoid her, let him work that out for himself.

Two days passed with no word from him. Delia insisted on keeping the stuffed animal he'd sent, a unicorn, in bed with her and wanted to see his card at least once a day.

Kathy gave him points for sending Delia the unicorn, but he lost them with his continuing absence.

Feeling more and more irritated, she finally called TapDancer Ranch. She braced herself for the sound of Alan's voice, but Stella answered the phone. They talked briefly with Stella saying they'd been away and just returned. In response to Stella's questions, Kathy told her about Delia's illness. "Oh, my.

We wondered why we hadn't seen you. Does Alan know?" Stella said.

"Of course. I'm hoping to talk him into visiting Delia."

"I see."

Kathy thought Stella sounded worried, but not surprised to hear Alan hadn't visited Delia. Curious.

"He's out in the pasture with his dad. They'll be in for lunch in half an hour. Why don't you call back then."

Curious as well, Stella not offering to have Alan call her.

Kathy almost didn't call him back. She'd tried twice. Let his mother do the nudging from here on out. But then she pictured Delia asking about Alan, and she knew she couldn't let herself off the hook until she'd actually spoken to him. Besides, who was she kidding. She wasn't just doing this for Delia. She wanted to see Alan again as badly as Delia did, even if she was upset with him. Something wasn't right about his responses either to kissing her or to Delia's being ill, and even though she was furious with him, she was also worried.

She picked up the phone and dialed, her hand shaking, her heart pounding. Once again, Stella answered. "He's washing up. I'll get him for you."

While Kathy waited for Alan to come to the phone, she distracted herself by staring at the way the light caught in one of the leaded glass panels over Calico's front door and transformed into a rainbow of color.

When she heard Alan's voice say hello, the phone nearly slipped from her hand. She gripped it tighter and spoke carefully, trying to keep her voice even. "Alan, Delia asked me to call you. She wants to see you. I need to know what to tell her. About when you're coming to see her."

There was a pause, then he cleared his throat. "I...umm...prob—"

Anger swept through Kathy. The weeks of worry and stress while Delia fought for her life, and now Alan, not saying he'd be right there, not even asking any questions about Delia. Making her do all the work. It was too much.

"Have you ever considered getting yourself a warning label?" she said, cutting across his stumbling words.

"Warning label?"

"Warning. Don't let yourself care for this man, because although he gives a darn good imitation of having a heart, he doesn't. That little girl loves you, Alan. Doesn't that mean anything to you?"

There was a beat of silence before he responded. "You don't understand."

Kathy was too far gone in anger to analyze either his words or his tone. "You've got that right. I can't even begin to understand how you can do this to a child. It's unforgivable. Delia's been hurt enough. Dammit, Alan, you can't just cast her off like this. She needs you now more than ever—"

A click. He'd hung up.

She held the phone in her hand, staring at it, before setting it carefully back in its cradle, knowing if she didn't move slowly, she might fly apart. She propped her head in her hands, closed her eyes and took several deep breaths.

It had felt good, telling Alan off. Lord knew he deserved it. But now in the aftermath, the good feeling was abruptly gone, leaving her hollow and shaken, as if she had just smashed something that would never be whole again.

"Hey, girl, you don't look so good." Jade slid onto the chair next to Kathy's desk. "What's up?"

"I just called Alan to ask when he's coming to see Delia." Her voice shook. She stopped, took a breath, tried again. "He tried to make some excuse and I...I told him off. He hung up on me." And of all the ways she could have imagined the conversation playing out, that wasn't one she'd even considered.

Jade looked surprised. "He hasn't come to see Delia?"

Kathy shook her head, feeling too upset even to cry.

"There must be something powerfully wrong in that man's life," Jade said thoughtfully.

It was what Kathy thought herself whenever she remembered the way he'd looked the last time she saw him. But no matter what it was, how could it justify him turning his back on a child?

In spite of the fact his mother told him who was calling, when he first heard Kathy's voice on the phone, Alan's heartbeat boomed in his ears until he could barely make out what Kathy was saying: that Delia was better, that she was awake and asking for him. By then he was a word or two behind, struggling to catch up. As he stammered out the beginning of a response, Kathy's tone changed abruptly from businesslike to angry.

The crime she accused him of, not one of commission but omission. With a flash of righteousness, he opened his mouth to defend himself. After all, Frank had told him it made no sense for him to drive all the way in from the ranch to see Delia until she regained consciousness. Frank had also said there was nothing else Alan could do at the moment to help. That all any of them could do was wait and pray.

But with a stab of pain, he realized the truth in what Kathy was saying. He *had* been unable to deal with what was happening with Delia. Sure, he'd made some of the motions: calling the hospital, leaving Frank and Grace a message, sending Delia a card and a present. But he hadn't gone to the hospital right away, and he'd worked hard to keep what was happening at arm's length.

Feeling the deep fatigue of regret and sorrow wash over him, he broke the connection with Kathy. He continued to hold the receiver against his ear, in case his mother checked to see what was keeping him, while he focused on finding a way to breathe around the huge boulder that seemed to be lodged in his chest.

When he was finally able to breathe normally, he joined his parents in the kitchen for lunch. After lunch, he drove to Denver to see Delia.

Chapter Seventeen

"I won't be around for the next couple of days," Charles said. He and Kathy were sitting on the steps of the Cheesman Park Pavilion, cooling down after a run. "The Olson trial is heating up."

Kathy enjoyed hearing about Charles's cases. She knew from the way he talked, he loved what he did for a living. He told her he viewed his work like a jigsaw puzzle; his job was to fit together the pieces for the judge and jury.

She also liked talking about his cases because it was a good way to keep their relationship friendly and casual. "What would you do, if you were trying a case and realized the guy wasn't guilty?"

He shrugged. "If I discovered new evidence, I'd have to share it with the defense. But if something comes out in testimony, it's up to the defense and the jury to pick up on it."

"And if the jury didn't see it?"

When he didn't answer, she looked over at him and found him staring off into the distance with a meditative look. Finally he shook himself. "That's why we have an appeals process." Then he turned and looked at her. "Have dinner with me Saturday."

She twisted slightly to look him in the eyes. "Same ground rules?"

He held his hands up in mock surrender. "See, Ma, no hands."

Charles took her to a quiet Italian restaurant for a leisurely dinner. As they finished eating, he glanced at his watch. "Tell you what. Do you like to dance?"

"Won't that make it difficult to keep your promise? You know, the one about your hands."

"I'll keep it strictly on the up and up." He grinned at her. Then he shrugged. "I like to dance, and it's good exercise."

"So what you're proposing is a workout." Kathy tilted her head, trying to decide if it was a good idea or a terrible idea.

"Whatever. The place I'm thinking about plays swing. You ever tried it?"

Okay. She could do swing. Swing was impersonal. "I'll have you know Cincinnati was a hotbed of swing when I was in college."

At Monk's Haven they ordered drinks and chatted until the band returned from a break and began playing "Little Brown Jug".

Kathy quickly learned to trust Charles's lead, and by the time the band segued into "A String of Pearls", they were dancing together as if they'd been doing it for years.

Then the band switched tempo and played "Moonlight Serenade". Before Kathy could suggest a break, Charles pulled her into his arms. The sudden vivid memory of the last time she'd been in a man's arms washed over her. Alan. She misstepped and Charles's hand tightened, steadying her.

When the dance ended, she excused herself and went to the ladies' room. She stared at her image in the mirror, remembering the way Alan had looked saying he was sorry he'd kissed her. And how that made her feel. As if he'd slapped her. The sting of it worse somehow than Greg saying he'd "clicked" with someone named Julie. Because after watching Alan with Delia and the animals, seeing how gentle and caring he was, she didn't believe he'd ever hurt someone deliberately. But he had. He'd hurt her, and he had to know it, because she wasn't any good at hiding her feelings.

She had to stop thinking about Alan. It was simple to do, after all. Just no more looking back. And after a while, it would fade, and everything would be all right.

Except, this time that approach didn't seem to be working.

When the band called it a night, Charles settled the bill, and taking her hand, walked her to his car. In spite of his promises, she expected him to invite her back to his place. She'd already prepared her refusal.

To her surprise, he drove her directly home. After she opened the front door and turned to tell him goodnight, he leaned forward and kissed her gently on the lips.

"That might be the letter, but it's hardly the spirit," she said, meeting his eyes.

A question, one she didn't want to answer, altered the shape of his eyebrows and mouth. She met his look for a long beat before he pulled her into his arms and kissed her again.

It was an expert kiss, and she enjoyed it, but she felt none of the longing she'd felt kissing Alan. She tried to stop thinking about that and concentrate instead on this moment, this man.

A good thing Charles didn't know her well enough to realize her heart wasn't in it.

But it could be. She just needed more time.

She hadn't expected to start dating so soon, didn't even want another relationship. And yet here she was, drifting into one. But maybe it was okay, this drifting. Neither one of them making any special effort.

Only. That was how it started with Alan.

And look how that turned out.

ℬ

Elaine showed up at the ranch and asked Alan to go for a ride with her. "I found a shooting star growing here a couple of years ago," she said, when they arrived at the lake. She swung off Siesta and turned to loosen the cinch. Cormac trotted off, busily following rabbit and chipmunk trails.

"Near the aspens," Alan said.

When they located the flower, Elaine knelt to examine it then looked up at him. "The folks told me the tenure decision went against you. I was sorry to hear it." She looked back at the flower.

Feeling relieved they'd gotten that out of the way so painlessly, Alan walked to the edge of the lake, and after a moment Elaine joined him. He picked up a smooth stone, enjoying the warmth and heft of it in his hand before he threw it. It skipped, touching the lake three times, like a bird taking sips of water. Circles formed on the surface of the lake, slowly expanding and intersecting, then dissipating.

Cormac came up to him carrying a stick. Alan tossed it and the dog bounded after it with a happy bark.

"Mom told me Kathy called you the other day," Elaine said.

Hearing Elaine say Kathy's name was as unexpected as a dash of water in the face, and it was almost more than he could manage to answer her calmly. "Did she."

He worked to keep his expression disinterested as he wrestled the stick from Cormac and threw it again. Of course, it should be no surprise Elaine knew about Kathy. His mother had no doubt provided a full report.

"Mom and Dad liked her," Elaine said, verifying his assumption.

He focused on the middle of the lake, struggling to keep his tone light. "You're fishing."

"They said she came out to ride last fall and this spring. Almost every week."

"They also report she came with another woman? And a child?"

Cormac was back with the stick, and when Alan didn't move to pick it up, the dog nudged his leg. Alan threw the stick as hard as he could, remembering, suddenly, the day he'd watched Delia pet a foal and realized the child he and Meg had been expecting would have been that age if Meg hadn't died. The thought clamped tight around his chest.

"You didn't fool them," Elaine said.

He swallowed, but there was no easing the tightness. "Wasn't trying to."

"They don't come anymore."

"They have other things to do." Like fight for life in an ICU.

Cormac was back. Alan bent over and buried his hands in the thick ruff of Cormac's neck while the dog wiggled with delight.

"Alan, why haven't you gone to visit that little girl?"

In confusion, he stared at Elaine, unable to answer. It had been only a few days since Kathy accused him of the same thing. But Elaine didn't even know Kathy. Besides, after Kathy's phone call, he had visited Delia. She'd been sleeping. He'd spoken to Frank, and they'd left it that Frank would call to let him know when Delia was home and ready for visitors.

Cormac squirmed and, whining softly, reached up and swiped a tongue at Alan's face, catching him on the nose. He sucked in a breath, then stood up.

Elaine stepped closer and laid a hand on his arm. "I love you, Alan, but I can't stand by watching you continue this way."

Cormac stuck his head between them, demanding Alan continue to play with him. Rubbing Cormac's head, Alan moved away from Elaine's touch.

"Alan...Please. There are things that can help you."

"Don't." He bit off the word, took a breath and tried to speak calmly. "You can stop worrying. I'm fine."

"Fine? You think you're fine? How can you think that? You abandoned that child, Alan. Where's the 'fine' in that?"

Not Delia. He hadn't abandoned her. But he had abandoned Kathy. He dragged in a ragged breath.

When did it end? Being half-alive.

"I know you loved Meg," Elaine said, a catch in her voice. "But you can't spend your life mourning her. You do that, you might as well have died, too."

Yeah. Without Meg he was as good as dead anyway. He stared blindly at the lake.

"You're dishonoring Meg's memory."

He turned abruptly and walked away.

"And you're turning into a sour, disgruntled, ugly person no one is going to want to be around." Elaine began to cry. "You have to stop it, Alan. Please stop it."

Why couldn't she understand? He would stop it, if he could figure out how. He took a quick hitch on the girth, swung into the saddle, and kicked Sonoro into a lope. Running away as he had for five years. From Elaine. From the meadow and its tiny lake. And from the memory of a cool, bright morning that had dawned so hopefully and ended so hopelessly.

ഇ

"This weekend's supposed to be beautiful," Charles said, slowing to a walk as he and Kathy finished their run. "We could go to the zoo, if that isn't too dorky a suggestion for you."

"I love the zoo. But I already have a date to go there." She didn't know why, but sometimes an urge to tease Charles just came over her. "You could join us if you like."

"Wouldn't want to horn in." His tone was stilted.

"No. Really. I mean it. It's time you met Delia."

"Delia?"

"The person I promised my Saturday to. She's six going on sixteen."

He wiped a hand across his mouth. "You have a daughter?" Did his voice sound odd or was that her imagination?

"She's the daughter of a friend. But Delia and I are best buddies. Why don't you come with us?"

"Sure. Okay."

Kathy glanced sideways at him, but Charles was taking a drink from his water bottle, so she couldn't see if he looked as uncertain as he sounded.

"There's something you need to know. Delia just got out of the hospital. She was terribly sick, and she's still pretty weak." Then Kathy took a breath and said the hard part. "As a result, she's deaf."

He was momentarily silent. "I, uh, don't know any sign language."

"That's okay. We're all just learning. Can you be at my place at ten-thirty?"

"Sure."

When they parted, Kathy watched Charles walk to his car, thinking how odd it had been—Charles sounding unsure about spending time with a little girl versus a big girl.

Saturday at the Garibaldis', Kathy introduced Charles to Grace.

"*Mira.* Frank's getting Delia dressed. Come on in," Grace said.

They stepped inside as Delia came down the hall with her father. Delia's eyes lit up, and she rushed up to Kathy, giving her a fierce hug.

After introducing Charles to Frank, Kathy turned to Delia and using gestures spoke slowly. "This is my friend, Charles."

Delia gave Charles a solemn look, then extended her hand and said, "Hello."

Charles looked startled, but he recovered quickly and took her tiny hand in his large one. Kathy's heart squeezed with pain at the memory that evoked of the way Delia and Alan always greeted each other. She pushed the thought away. It belonged to the past.

As they wandered around the zoo, Delia and Kathy practiced signs, and Charles joined in. Watching Delia make a sign, Kathy was amazed, as she had been from the first, at how quickly Delia was adapting to the loss of her hearing. Much more quickly than the adults. Delia was already learning to read lips when people spoke slowly, and while Kathy's signs felt awkward and slow, Delia's were already quick and fluid in spite of her shortened fingers.

"Grace Garcia de Garibaldi," Charles said, as Delia watched the polar bear swim. "I'm trying to think where I've heard that name before."

"Grace wrote a children's book. The *Post* had an article on it recently."

"Umm. That could be it."

Kathy glanced at him and saw that he had a preoccupied look. But then, he turned and saw her staring and smiled. "Can you teach me how to ask Delia if she's hungry?"

They took a ride on the miniature train and, after that, it was obvious Delia was tired. Charles gave her a piggy-back ride to the car, and when he set her down, he moved his hands the way Kathy had shown him.

Delia laughed in delight at his clumsy signs, then nodded an emphatic yes.

Charles turned to Kathy. "I don't know how to ask her what she'd like to eat."

"We always go the same place. The cafe at the Tattered Cover Book Store. Then if she's not too tired, we look at books."

"You didn't mind having Delia with us, did you?" Kathy asked Charles after they took Delia home.

"She's a cute kid. I enjoyed it...a lot." He sounded surprised.

Kathy was relieved Charles and Delia had gotten along. Given the odd way he'd reacted to her first mention of the little girl, she had wondered if he didn't like children. But he'd treated Delia with the same care and affection Alan did.

Alan. She was through thinking about him. Wasn't she?

Chapter Eighteen

The phone rang at Calico, and the caller, a woman, asked to speak to Kathy.

"This is Elaine Francini-Galt. I believe...that is I think you know my brother Alan?"

Surprise, quickly followed by dread and a mélange of awful images, almost cut off Kathy's breath. "Is he...all right?"

"Oh. Yes. Of course. Sorry. I-I hope it's okay I called. I need to see you. To talk to you."

Kathy loosened her grip on the phone. "I don't understand."

"Please. Meet with me. I'll explain then."

After she hung up, Kathy sat for a time, her heart still beating too fast, thinking about it. The strangeness of Elaine wanting to see her, and her own panic in that first moment when she thought Elaine was calling to tell her something had happened to Alan.

When she arrived at The Rondel, Kathy knew the woman sitting in the corner had to be Elaine. Her resemblance to Alan was unmistakable. Clamping down on the flight of butterflies taking off in her stomach, Kathy greeted Elaine as she slid into the seat across from her. Seeing Elaine had a glass of wine, Kathy ordered one as well.

Close up, Elaine's resemblance to Alan was startling, and it made Kathy feel like crying. Ridiculous, of course. She was over Alan. Still, if that were true, why had she agreed to this meeting, and why did she still wake up at night, her chest tight with a memory of weeping?

"Sorry I'm late." Kathy said. "A phone call ran long, but I didn't know how to reach you to let you know."

"Here, let me give you my card." Elaine pulled a holder out of her purse as the waitress set a glass of white wine in front of Kathy.

Kathy paid for her drink then accepted the card from Elaine.

Elaine Francini-Galt, Ph.D., Clinical Psychologist.

The busyness of getting out the card had camouflaged Elaine's nervousness, but now it hit Kathy in waves—the lip biting, the flickering glances, the fidgety hands. Not that Kathy was feeling all that calm and cool herself.

"Thank you for coming." Elaine's voice was jerky, and after a quick glance at Kathy, she stared at her wineglass as if it were a teleprompter that had just failed.

Kathy waited. Finally, Elaine took a breath and looked up, her eyes full of distress. "I wanted to see you. To ask why-why you're no longer coming to the ranch."

Kathy drew in a quick, surprised breath, but because of the misery in Elaine's eyes, she spoke gently. "You need to ask Alan that."

"He won't talk to me." Elaine looked down at her wine, blinking rapidly. "Please. I don't usually do this sort of thing, but I really need to know. Was it your choice? To stop seeing him."

Kathy looked away from Elaine, struggling with a mix of feelings. There was no easy answer. She may have chosen, but only after Alan made it impossible for her to choose otherwise.

"It's just. You're the first woman he's spent time with since—" Elaine stopped speaking and swiped at her eyes while Kathy tried to figure out the missing part of that statement. The first woman he'd spent time with since...what?

"Did he ever talk to you about Meg?"

"Meg?" The single syllable took all Kathy's effort.

"His wife."

Kathy stared at Elaine, letting the words sink in, take on weight and substance. Alan married. An answer of sorts. Not that it should matter. But it did somehow.

"So he's married." She shivered and wrapped her arms around herself.

"No. You don't understand—"

"Why?" Kathy's voice caught and the word came out as a whisper. But after that one word, she had no idea what came next, what was left to know.

Feeling dizzy, she closed her eyes, but it only made the vertigo intensify. Why was Elaine asking all these questions? She'd done her job. Told Kathy Alan was off limits. But then Elaine also knew they were no longer seeing each other, so what was the point?

"She died. Meg did."

Kathy's eyes snapped open, and she stared at Elaine, feeling whipsawed, trying desperately to fit it all together.

"Five years ago. We thought when you started coming to the ranch... We all thought, maybe..." Elaine focused on her wine glass as she rolled it back and forth between her hands.

Kathy took a breath to steady her voice. "Why are you telling me?" And why hadn't Alan told her. They'd been friends, after all. He could have just said it, that night in the garden, or the time they went to the lake, or the day in the barn.

Elaine's eyes glittered with tears, and she bit her lip. "We used to be so close. I miss him so much. This spring was...better." She stifled a sob, then sat clutching her arms. "I'm sorry. I didn't mean to..." She stopped, her lips trembling. Then she loosened her arms and leaned her elbows on the table, her hands covering her face as she sobbed.

"It's okay." It wasn't, of course. Nothing was okay about any of this. And watching Elaine weep, Kathy wanted to weep as well. But her tears seemed to be as frozen as her emotions.

"I'm so sorry." She reached out and laid a hand on Elaine's arm, waiting while the other woman took deep steadying breaths.

Elaine raised her head and, again, her resemblance to Alan took Kathy's breath away. Only this time, the resemblance was to Alan as he'd looked that last day, with haunted eyes and sharp lines of pain etched in his face.

It hurt to look at Elaine, and it hurt to breathe. "I'm sorry," Kathy said again.

"No. I am. I had no right." Elaine's mouth quivered, and she took a careful breath. "Grabbing at straws. Stupid. I know better. I just thought, or didn't think. Not your fault." She scrubbed at her eyes.

Kathy wondered how Meg had died, but it wasn't something she could ask. She sat waiting until Elaine stopped crying, then she stood, trying to come up with something more to say, but there was nothing. Nothing that could lift the sorrow that filled both their hearts. She reached out to touch Elaine, then pulled her hand back.

Outside The Rondel, she took a deep breath and looked toward the mountains. The sun slid behind the clouds piled on top of purple peaks. She watched, until it reached a small gap and blazed through, dazzling her.

Getting into her car, she glanced at the clock. Only six-thirty. And yet it seemed as if hours had passed since she sat down across from Elaine. She started the car and waited for a break in traffic to turn onto Colorado Boulevard, trying to push away the conversation with Elaine and focus on her driving, telling herself to stop when lights turned red, to start again on green.

By the time she arrived back at the Costellos', she knew there was no way she could walk into the kitchen and answer cheerful questions about her day while Mrs. C bustled about reheating her dinner.

Instead, she turned in the opposite direction, and walked over to Cheesman Park, to the white pavilion on the eastern edge that looked like a Greek temple. She picked a spot on the steps well away from the scattering of people and sat down, leaning forward, resting her elbows on her knees.

The clouds had thinned, and the sun cast a golden sheen over trees, grass, and people. She watched a man playing Frisbee with his dog as the sounds of cars, an occasional burst of music from a radio, the yelp of the dog and fragments of conversation blurred together, into silence.

So that was why Alan shied away from closeness, why he'd said they could be only friends.

Someone essential. He'd been talking about Meg.

Sorrow that only death could ease. And his reaction when she'd brought that up. She hadn't understood it then, but she did now.

And the look he sometimes had. That day they'd ridden to the lake and she'd recited the poem was the first time. But it had been a mostly happy day as he teased her about semi-misanthropy and a trout's fishy viewpoint. The light shining on his hair—gold, sorrel, and brown—and her hand, arrested from touching. His eyes, usually so serious, but glinting with humor as he looked up at her after drying her feet.

Without that one day...

But maybe she had already loved him.

And now she could no longer deny it.

Chapter Nineteen

Excerpt from the diaries of Emily Kowalski
1940...

Jess has arranged for one of the neighbors to come in three times a day to help me with Bobby. I didn't realize how tired the physical effort of lifting Bobby was making me until Edna started coming. She is a big strapping woman who could probably lift Jess if she had to, so Bobby is no problem for her.

I like Edna. She is a bit gruff and no nonsense, but I think she has a kind heart. I hope we will be friends.

Today Jess had a surprise with him when he came home. A dog. A full-grown German shepherd. My dismay must have been obvious when the two of them came through the door, because Jess's smile faded as he looked at me. I turned to go back to the kitchen, but then Jess must have let go of the dog, because it padded past me right up to Bobby.

I felt a flash of fear. After all, it was a very large dog. Then I noticed its tail waving gently and saw it was licking Bobby's hand, and I was surprised to find tears running down my face.

I never did answer Jess's question about whether we could keep Brad.

Brad has been with us a week, and already I hardly remember what our lives were like without him. He belonged to one of Jess's students who moved and was no longer able to keep him. Jess agreed to bring him for a visit, to see what I thought about the idea of us adopting him.

It's a good thing Jess didn't ask me beforehand, or he would have gotten an earful, but it has turned out well. Brad is an easy addition, and he seems to have appointed himself Bobby's guardian, staying always right by Bobby's side.

I have continued to help Bobby exercise his hands and arms even though the doctor tells me I may as well save my energy for other things. Although it may do little good, it makes me feel better if I am doing something rather than letting Bobby just sit there.

And then today, an amazing thing happened. I left Bobby and Brad alone for a minute, and when I walked back into the room, I discovered Brad had helped himself to a sock from the darning basket. He was pulling on one end while Bobby held the other. Brad was growling fiercely, but I could tell he was playing with Bobby.

I stood there, I'm not sure for how long, watching the two of them and saying one of those wordless thank yous to God for this small miracle. And then, just like that, I was crying again. I seem to cry at the drop of a hat these days. But later I found myself laughing at something Edna said. It felt like the first time I'd done that since before Bobby got sick.

Today I took Bobby outside in his chair, and I set up my easel and painted. Usually, I can't stand to have anyone watch me paint, but having Bobby there calmed me, and I talked to him as I worked.

I tried the sunset again—the one Bill and I shared so many years ago right after he got back from the war. This time the colors flowed, and I liked the contrast of the black fence and the bare limbs of the tree against the deep orange-red of the sky. I felt good when I finished, and I realized that while I was painting I'd forgotten all my troubles.

I think that is why Jess works so hard and long—in order to forget, for a time.

1941...

Jess gave me a record player for my birthday. I left it sitting in the corner next to the couch until last week when I finally played one of the records. I discovered I felt better, getting rid of the silence. Now I play music most of the day.

When the music is on, I notice Bobby's eyes look brighter somehow. And I fancy that if I watch carefully, I can tell which records he likes best. I think, like me, it is the happy music of the Benny Goodman and Glen Miller orchestras. I even found myself twirling into a dance-step to "In the Mood" this morning.

I also play the radio, and when I do, Bobby's eyes get that same happy shine. I've begun to follow a schedule so we can listen to what I think of as our programs—"Coast to Coast on a Bus" for Bobby and "Pepper Young's Family" for me.

Our days are filling up with sounds—music sounds and radio sounds—and it's certainly better than silence chopped into small pieces by the ticking of a clock.

And even if I'm wrong, and Bobby isn't aware, in some ways it doesn't matter. I am beginning to live again, and that has to count for something.

1942...

Yesterday, we received word Bill has died. The day had dawned bright, beautiful and hot, but with that news, the world seemed suddenly darker and colder.

The last time we saw Bill, it was winter. Now, down by the pond, the dogwoods are blooming. They look like pink and white butterflies floating among the bare branches, but it is a sight that brings me no pleasure.

Bill came for Christmas. When he walked into the kitchen with Jess, I took one look at him and knew it would be our last visit together. He was only fifty-four, but he looked seventy, his hair gone white and lines of pain etched into his face. Only his eyes and smile were the same.

I hugged him, pretending I hadn't seen, but Bill knew, and

he whispered, "It's all right, Emmie. Don't worry, we'll talk later."

For the rest of the evening, we all pretended it was an ordinary family visit, with Bill asking Jess questions about the college teaching he is doing, and Jess and I asking about colleagues and friends we left behind in Chicago.

Later, I sat in the rocker knitting while Jess read Bobby a bedtime story. With Jess's voice as background music, I thought about Bill and that conversation so long ago that marked the change in course for both our lives. Afterwards, Bill left Red Oak and met his Kiara, only to lose her almost immediately. And I left Red Oak and met Jess, and we had Bobby who is now thirteen years old but can do no more for himself than a tiny baby.

I wonder if everyone can trace back to one moment in time when a single choice set their whole future in place. And if so, how many of us would choose differently if we knew where that choice would lead?

The next morning, when Bill walked into my kitchen I had a cheerful fire going. Bobby was in his chair, Brad was asleep on the hearthrug soaking up the warmth and we had Christmas music playing. Bill kissed me good morning, saying, "My word, Emmie, this surely does look and feel like Christmas."

I fixed him breakfast and then sat with him, sipping coffee while he ate. When he finished, we talked.

"I need to ask you something, Emmie. Something that isn't easy to put into words. I need to know if you blame me for urging you to leave Red Oak."

"Funny, but I've been trying to figure out how to ask you if you blamed me for telling you not to marry Doris Goodwin."

"Good God, of course not. Why would you think such a thing?"

That made me smile. "Perhaps the same reason you think I blame you for encouraging me to leave Red Oak."

We sat and looked at each other until I started giggling, and then I was laughing so hard I had tears in my eyes. Bill fished out a handkerchief, and when I finished wiping my eyes, he asked if I remembered one evening after he came home from the war, when I'd followed him out to the far pasture and we talked.

"Of course I remember. If we hadn't talked, I might never have left Red Oak," I said.

"Perhaps that would have been better."

"Perhaps it would have been worse. Besides, I would never want to give up Bobby and Jess."

"You know, Emmie, now that I'm at the end, and I can look all the way back to the beginning, I wouldn't trade either. I know I took the right path. Kiara...even though we had only a short time together, it was worth any pain to have that. And in the end, I got to make a difference in so many children's lives."

He stopped talking then, and we sat in the sunny kitchen with cups of coffee warming our hands. And then, I spoke into that comfortable silence words that surprised me. "I'm lonely, Bill. Lonely for Jess. He works too hard. In order to cope, I think."

Bill took my hand in his, and we sat for a time thinking our own thoughts and comforting each other with that touch.

On Christmas Eve, Jess came home early, and we had a wonderful evening. Our memories flickered and sparked like the bright lights on the tree we put up together after dinner.

It was a special Christmas. Not because of the presents or the flurry of snow that came on Christmas Eve and glittered in the light from the windows, but because it was, as I had suspected, and now know for sure, Bill's last Christmas.

Before he left, he told me in stark terms what was going on with his body.

Cancer.

There was little to be done except to put his affairs in order, and he was doing that. He had come to say goodbye, so I wouldn't feel badly about being unable to attend his funeral.

Of course, every time we hug someone who is leaving for work, or church, or to go to the store, deep down we know it could be the last time, but it's knowledge we hide from ourselves. But, saying goodbye to Bill a week after he arrived, I knew for certain I would never see him again, and I had to be quite stern with myself and let him go.

Bill left behind one final gift—a way into a new beginning

for Jess and me. Shortly after Bill left, Jess came home early and told me to dress up. He had arranged for a neighbor to stay with Bobby, so he could take me out.

We went downtown to the brand new French restaurant, the Maisonette. Jess ordered champagne, and when he raised his glass to me, I knew what Bill had done. "Em. To us, to our love, and our family. I want to beg your forgiveness."

I had no idea how to answer, but as I looked at Jess through the shimmering light of the candles, I saw once again the young man who made my heart skip with joy when Bill introduced us the first time. And I remembered him waiting for me to walk down the aisle to take his hand when we married. And it was really quite simple.

"I understand, Jess. It's all right."

After that we sat looking at each other, forgetting the champagne and ignoring the waiter. Eventually we ordered, but we were too busy talking to eat much.

And, oh my, the talk. We shared our feelings about Bobby, our pain that he would always be an invalid, and the added pain of being unable to have other children. In that sharing, we pushed away the darkness that had wrapped around our lives as if we were shedding a heavy cloak.

I have always believed that healing must come from inside. But Bill has shown me it is sometimes called forth through the actions of others.

Chapter Twenty

Alerted by Cormac, Alan walked out of the barn to find Delia squatting down to pet the dog. She didn't look up until he reached her. Then she gave him a solemn look before she stood and threw her arms up to him.

As he lifted her and swung her around, she giggled. With a catch in his throat, he felt how light she was. He gave her a careful hug, then set her down and looked at Grace.

"I'm glad you're here," he said.

Grace hugged him, but without her usual exuberance. She looked tired and almost as frail as her daughter. Delia snuggled her hand into his. In the barn, she reached into her pocket, pulled out a carrot, and held it out to the pony.

His throat tightening, Alan noticed the two shortened fingers. He reached out to take her hand in his, but the little girl was busy patting Arriba.

He touched her shoulder, and she looked at him. "You all set?" Alan asked.

Delia cocked her head frowning, before responding with a nod.

For the first time, the news Frank had given him after Delia woke up was made real, and Alan felt like the earth had tipped out from under him, leaving him sliding into space.

He busied himself, helping Delia into the saddle and adjusting the stirrups. With his back to Delia, he faced Grace and spoke softly. "How do I communicate with her?"

"We're all learning sign language, and she's beginning to read lips. And we write things out for her."

"Come on, Alan. Arriba's ready to go," Delia said.

They were the first words he'd heard her speak, and her voice had a strange new flat quality. He led Arriba out of the barn, and Grace walked alongside.

When they entered the riding ring, Grace stayed by the fence while Alan continued to lead the pony in a circle.

"Alan, why didn't you come see me in the hospital?"

He wanted to say, *But I did*, until he realized that as far as Delia was concerned, he hadn't come. He stopped walking and met Delia's gaze. Sitting on the pony, she was nearly level with him.

He knew what she was really asking. She needed reassurance he loved her, not excuses. And the fact he had come, and she'd been sleeping wouldn't be enough. He should have tried harder to see her.

He spoke slowly and carefully. "I'm sorry."

Delia shook her head and frowned. Grace walked over to them, and Alan turned to her. "I want to tell Delia I'm sorry I didn't visit her in the hospital."

Grace pulled a card and pen out of her pocket and handed them to him. He printed carefully, then handed the card to Delia. She read his apology, mouthing the words silently, then she gave him a serious look. "It's okay. I understand."

∞

Charles slid into the booth across from Alan. It was the first time they'd managed to have lunch together in a couple of months.

"I've got good news and better news," Charles said.

"Oh?" Alan glanced up from the menu.

"Tiffany and I finally called it quits."

"As if I haven't heard that before." Charles and Tiffany, off again, on again ever since they met.

"No this time it's for good. But the better news is I've met somebody."

"And why am I not surprised?" *Heavy lunch and skip*

dinner, or light lunch?

"Her name is Kathy Jamison."

Alan froze, the print on the menu going out of focus. No. It couldn't be. Of all the women in the world. How could Charles... He took a breath and plunged ahead. "The Philly sandwich looks good."

But Charles refused to be diverted. "I met her jogging. And she plays a mean game of tennis." He looked at Alan with a loopy grin on his face.

Alan cleared his throat, hoping he could manage to sound normal. "So what happened with Tiffany?"

"She started dropping hints about her biological clock."

"And you, as we know, are anti-kid. And why is that exactly?" Alan had wondered for years but never felt comfortable asking. Right now, though, he'd do whatever it took to keep Charles off the subject of Kathy.

"I was one, remember. Let's just say kids cause problems. And they tie you down. Limit your options."

"So does any relationship." It was something Alan had never understood about Charles—his inability to commit to Tiffany. Because Charles had been a good and loyal friend, even when Alan pushed him away.

"At least with a woman there are compensations." Charles looked up from his menu, the loopy grin back. "Did I mention she's a redhead?"

Definitely not the Philly sandwich. Soup. And he was going to have a hard time swallowing *that.*

That evening, Alan stood in the dark of his apartment, looking out at the sky, knowing it was going to be another night when sleep would be elusive. He didn't even need to close his eyes to picture Charles talking about Kathy with that happy expression. No question, Charles was attracted. And Alan knew how women responded to Charles being attracted to them. The surprise was how Alan had reacted to knowing the woman who attracted Charles was Kathy.

How could he not have known? So focused on missing Meg

he'd missed how he felt about Kathy.

But, really, he had known.

And now, thinking about Kathy with Charles...

Would talk help that? But what else was there?

He reached for the phone, and not letting himself second-guess it, punched in his sister's number. "Laine, I need the name of someone to see."

During the pause that followed, he knew what she must be thinking, but, thank God, she didn't say it. Instead she asked only if he preferred a man or a woman, and when he said it didn't matter, she gave him three names.

He hung up, shaking. He'd taken only a single small step, and yet he was as exhausted as if he'd just spent hours slogging through deep snow.

But he could still back out, not call the people Elaine recommended, although that would mean his already shaky relationship with her would get shakier.

But there was such a slim chance it was going to do any good.

Besides, he'd left it too late.

&

The conversation with Elaine had ripped open the wound left in Kathy's heart by the loss of Alan. Gone in an instant the careful stitching of weeks of busyness, of progress towards...closure. God, she hated that word. Implying, as it did, that one could walk through a door, close it, and forget everything on the other side.

Hemingway was right. True sorrow never went away. But maybe that was a good thing. Because denying her sadness over Alan, would be a denial of her best self.

Before meeting Elaine, anger had overlaid Kathy's memories of Alan. And that anger had worked, as it had with Greg, as an antidote to pain. But now, learning about Meg had stripped away anger, leaving a sadness that limned even her brightest days with darkness and sudden, unexpected sorrow.

More than anything, she wanted to help Alan. But if his family had been unable to do anything for him, what could she do?

In spite of its hopelessness, the question churned endlessly until she felt like an astronaut in orbit, twisting, floating, turning, always ending in the same place. With no answers.

It was such an effort, to act normal.

Friday, knowing she couldn't face seeing Charles, she called and canceled their date, then early Saturday she got up and drove west until she was deep in the mountains. She took the Silverthorne exit and, turning at random, ended up on a narrow road that at first clung to the steep mountainside then dropped into a valley alongside a dancing stream.

She pulled off in a wide spot. Through the open window she could hear crows calling and the chitter of a squirrel. The smell of warm pine drifted through the window and brought with it the memory of the day she and Alan had ridden to the lake. They'd gone only once, but that day shone with a clarity missing from all her days since.

After a time, she got out of the car and followed a faint trail toward the stream. The dark shadows of trout were clearly visible against the sand and gravel of the streambed, and she smiled remembering the awkwardness of her casts, feeling again the touch of Alan's hand guiding hers along the flank of the fish.

As the memory faded, the familiar sense of helplessness and loss replaced it.

Eventually, she walked back to her car and drove until she encountered a road sign telling her where she was. If only it were as easy to navigate her internal landscape. To see clearly where she'd been and where she was going. And to understand what her choices would mean now that she'd reached a fork in the road.

On Monday, Jade stopped by Kathy's desk and raised her brows in question. "Alan?"

Kathy nodded, unable to speak, knowing from the face that had gazed back at her from the mirror this morning why Jade was asking the question.

"Come on." Jade pulled Kathy to her feet and steered her toward the door. "Kathy and I are taking a break," she told Columba and Polly, as she opened the door and nudged Kathy through. "Let's walk over to the playground. This time of day, it should be quiet."

As they walked, Kathy told Jade about the meeting with Elaine and what Elaine had told her about Alan—that he had been married and his wife had died. "I was so angry with him. But now..." Kathy's voice wobbled.

"Did Elaine say how Meg died?"

Kathy shook her head. The same question had niggled at her ever since her meeting with Elaine.

"Maybe Alan was involved somehow," Jade said. "You know. Like a car crash where he was driving, or maybe she died in childbirth."

"Why do you say that?"

"It sounds like he's having trouble letting go. Sometimes, that's because a person feels guilty."

"I think he just really misses her. I think she was essential."

Jade led the way to the swings where she and Kathy sat side by side.

"There must be something I can do to help him."

"You're in love with him."

"Yes." It was a relief to finally say it.

Jade touched her gently on the arm. "He's the only one who can decide to let go of the past. There may be nothing you can do."

It wasn't what she expected Jade to say.

Chapter Twenty-One

Excerpt from the diaries of Emily Kowalski
1945...

The turn of the new year always makes me melancholy. And yet this year should be different. Everyone is saying this may be the year the war will end.

There was great rejoicing after D-Day, and we all thought the soldiers would be home soon, but it continues. The news is not as dark, still there are boys who made it through D-Day who will not come home.

The country has been caught up in war and it has seemed frenzied at times. There are so many changes, but I feel in spite of that, little is happening to me. I'm like one of those flies caught in amber that I remember seeing a long time ago in the Chicago museum.

Looking back, though, I can see I haven't been as frozen as I sometimes feel. It started when I banished the silence with music and our radio programs. And now I've begun to paint again, and Jess and I have found our way back to each other. And Brad has been a Godsend, and of course the wheeled chair. All of it has helped.

VE Day has been declared but there is still the war in the Pacific. That seems to go on and on. Meanwhile, our lives proceed relatively untouched. I have been able to do little for the war effort because of Bobby.

The war is over. That is the headline, the largest one I have ever seen. It fills most of the front page. We have dropped something called an atom bomb on Japan. The papers are saying it has saved many American lives, but I can't bear to look at the pictures, and it is hard to feel joyful at this ending that has been bought at such a price.

1947...

Yesterday was my forty-seventh birthday. When I saw Jess's gift, I was too angry to even react at first. Four goats, for pity's sake. What on earth was he thinking!

They arrived with big pink bows around their necks that they immediately tried to dislodge. One goat rubbed against a tree then twisted her head to pull the bow loose. Brad bounced among them, barking happily.

I turned to Jess, who grinned at me and said, "Happy Birthday, Em."

It was a good thing I was speechless, because it surely wouldn't do to say something unkind in front of either Bobby or the man who delivered the goats.

I was turning in a circle watching the goats, when I noticed two of them approaching Bobby. My breath caught in fear, and I moved to ward them off, but Jess stopped me, putting his arm around me. Then we both watched as Brad joined in, and the three animals touched noses. Bobby's hand moved toward the black goat, who came close and nuzzled him. Then, doggone it, I was crying, standing in the circle of Jess's arm, feeling all sad and happy at the same time.

Jess thought of everything. A gift, a cake a neighbor baked for him, and candles. We kept Bobby up later than usual, and for the first time in a long time, we laughed together. Then Jess tried to sing "Happy Birthday", and it made me laugh even more, for Jess is no singer.

The goats escaped from the yard and ate all the roses along the cemetery fence. Father Larry was fit to be tied, although he didn't suspect the goats, thank goodness.

Then last week, Jess had to come home from work in the middle of the day to collect them. There's a farm stand across from the cemetery, and that's where they were, helping themselves to the fruits and vegetables, blocking traffic.

Jess said the owner tried to chase them away with a broom, but as he chased one, the other three circled him to get more to eat. When Jess arrived he told them, "That's enough, girls," and they all fell right into line and followed him home like angels.

Jess is the only one they pay attention to. If he can't figure out how to keep them in the yard, we'll have to get rid of them. I would hate to do that, as two of them seem to have a special relationship with Bobby, and that makes it worth putting up with their shenanigans.

Chapter Twenty-Two

After brief meetings with each of the therapists Elaine suggested, Alan chose Dr. Angela Taylor, both because of her age and the serenity of her manner. Although, now that he examined her more closely, he could see she was younger than the nimbus of soft white curls indicated.

"Why don't we begin with you telling me why you're seeking therapy at this time," Angela said, sitting back, her hands resting quietly in her lap.

A reasonable question. Just not one he was prepared to answer fully yet. How to say straight out, *I'm here because I couldn't save my wife, and now I can't let her go.* He shut off the thought and searched for a less direct approach.

"My way isn't working. I decided to give my sister's a try."

"And your way is?"

"Keeping busy. Trying not to think."

"What made you decide it wasn't working?"

He remembered Charles talking about Kathy, and a sick, helpless feeling took over his gut. He'd blown it with Kathy, and suddenly and surprisingly, it was too late to do anything about it.

He shifted, trying to blank out the memory of the happy shine in Charles's eyes and focus on where he was, sitting in a room with a woman he barely knew to whom he'd given permission to ask him the most personal questions.

He thought they'd ease into it, though, take it slow. Chat comfortably for a time before she asked the questions he knew he was going to have to face. He held his arm, massaging a sore spot on his biceps, trying to come up with something that would satisfy Angela, perhaps even mislead her for a time and give him breathing room.

"I was denied tenure."

"On what basis?"

"The new department head wanted all faculty writing fiction."

"And what do you write?"

Suddenly on his internal video screen he pictured a quail mother frantically trying to lead a predator away from her nest. Feigning a broken wing, even. That's what this felt like. Angela, a large cat waiting to pounce, and he the distraught bird with no defense except obfuscation. Although that made no sense since he'd chosen to be here.

He pulled his thoughts back to focus on the question she'd asked about his writing. "Non-fiction. For education journals." There. That was better. A calm exchange of information. If they kept it up, he'd get through this. The only difficulty? The main issue he was working so hard to avoid was right there beside him, as overwhelming in its power and relentlessness as a charging rhinoceros. Not that he'd ever been in a position to have a rhinoceros charge him, but very likely, if one ever did, it would feel like this.

"Did that make you angry?"

Angela's quiet voice snapped him back from the African veldt. Back from the heat and the buzzing of insects and the tall, crisp, yellow grass. But the rhino came back with him.

"No."

"What else?" Angela said.

He frowned. What else what? Oh, he supposed she was still asking why he knew his way wasn't working. He shook his head, giving her what he hoped was a rueful look.

She stared back at him. "How long have you known about the tenure decision?"

"Month, six weeks maybe."

She cocked her head, waiting and, suddenly, he felt ten years old again, called on the carpet for racing one of the horses and then not rubbing it down afterwards. He had no idea what more she expected him to say. Wasn't it obvious? Denial of tenure was a huge blow to the ego. Couldn't they simply explore that for a time instead of her dismissing it with hardly a sniff?

"If you need job counseling, I can suggest someone for you to see."

It was a clear challenge, and one he didn't know how to meet, because he wasn't yet ready to tell her why he was really here. He was like a diver standing on the cliff watching the march of waves so he could time his dive when there would be deep rather than shallow water beneath him. But right now he couldn't make sense of the wave patterns, had no idea whether to walk away or simply fling himself into space and hope for the best.

"Alan, you know why you're here. But we can't get started until you share that with me."

He inventoried the part of the office visible over Angela's shoulder. An aquarium sat below a framed print. He focused on the print, a Vasarely. Meg had always argued Vasarely's paintings were merely form and color masquerading as art, but he found the mathematical precision and color choices satisfying. And right now the print, art or not, was an anchor.

There was one other thing he could tell Angela. She probably heard it all the time anyway.

"I had a relationship end." There, that should do it. No tenure and unlucky in love. At least an hour's worth of talk there.

After a pause, Angela spoke. "Was the relationship important to you?"

His ear began to itch. He scratched it, trying to figure out how to get out of answering. He didn't know why he'd mentioned Kathy anyway. Well not mentioned her exactly, but mentioned that he'd had a relationship. He didn't want to talk about anything more than the tenure decision this first time. Once Angela helped him with that, he could figure out how to handle the other issues himself.

But she wasn't making it easy for him, asking questions followed by long silences. Silences were meant to be shared with someone you knew well. Like Meg.

The urge to bolt overwhelmed him, and it took all his self-control to remain seated. He shifted in the chair, then realizing that made him appear nervous, stopped moving and refocused on the print. The colors smeared together. He blinked, trying to recapture the crispness of Vasarely's design.

"Alan?"

He glanced at Angela, then away, speaking quickly. "You know, it's funny. But if you tell someone standing in front of a boulder not to think about a pebble, what happens? They forget the boulder and all they can think about is the pebble." Not that he expected her to make a bit of sense out of that. It was simply a piece of misdirection. It might even get them to the end of this hour. Then he could leave and not come back.

"So what's your pebble, Alan?"

He shrugged. "Tenure. Ended relationship. Take your pick."

She made a sharp movement with her head, obviously dismissing his response. He'd clenched his hands so tightly they'd begun to ache. He pulled them apart and placed them on his knees.

This talk thing wasn't working any better than he thought it would. They'd exchanged less than a hundred words, most of them his. Wasn't she supposed to do part of the work? Hell, if all she was going to do was sit there, he might as well pick out a tree and talk to it.

"Your pebble," she said again, her voice firm, inflexible.

His pebble. Meg.

Suddenly he could bear it no longer. The guilt, the sleepless nights, the long, dreary days. Trying not to remember. Trying not to feel. It wasn't working. Had never worked. Time. It was supposed to get easier, better with the passage of time. But it hadn't. Instead it had become more and more difficult. But letting it out. Putting it into words. No, he couldn't.

The images and pain he'd tried to hold at bay swept in and over him. Like the water had Meg that day. "I let her...Meg. My wife. She died." He didn't realize he'd spoken aloud until Angela responded.

"How did she die?"

He sat breathing hard, as if he'd run up a steep hill and couldn't quite catch his breath. In between breaths, words pushed their way out, in spite of his efforts to stop them.

"Alaska. We were visiting Alaska. Meg wanted to take a picture. She climbed down to the beach. She was walking back to the car when...sh-she, her legs got trapped. Then...t-tide came in." His voice jerked to a stop and he sat, shivering, focusing on the Vasarely, but no longer able to see it. Seeing instead a wide expanse of water, the same blue as the sky, edged with its smooth curve of silvery-gray glacial silt. Looking nothing like something that could kill you. So beautiful it made you cry.

"You stayed with her?"

The calm tone of Angela's question erased the vision, but not the pain, a roaring black hole of anguish. "They wouldn't let me help."

"Who wouldn't let you help?"

"The rescue team." He tried to wrench his thoughts back from their dark spiral. He had to pretend this was just a story. Not something real. But it was too late for that.

"I have a sense you think it was in some way your fault Meg died," Angela said.

"They told me it wasn't." Mostly they'd left him alone while they waited for the tide to go back out so they could recover Meg's body. But every once in a while one of them would come and squat beside him, offering a cup of coffee, a sandwich, a few words.

"And do you believe that?"

"I should have known how dangerous the tidal flat was."

"How would you have known?" Angela's voice, a soft thread of sound, was his only lifeline in the deadly swirl of memory.

"It was my idea to go to Alaska. I did all the reading, planned what we'd do. I was responsible." *For keeping Meg safe.*

Alaska hadn't even been her first choice. They'd flipped a coin. Alaska this time, for him. Next time, the Caribbean for Meg. He scrubbed his hand across his eyes.

"Do you think Meg blamed you for not knowing?"

"She's dead." The words were harsh and too loud. In their wake, he sat panting, struggling to find his equilibrium in a world that tipped and spun around him.

"So you have to do the blaming for her." Angela's voice was soft, but her words sliced into him. "Did you commit yourself to a life sentence?"

A blazing pain started in the back of his neck and spread to his forehead. He couldn't answer. Could barely manage to keep breathing.

Angela waited a moment and then said, "Did you cry afterwards?"

What kind of question was that? Unable to speak, he shook his head no, then looked back at the Vasarely.

There was a long beat of silence before Angela spoke again.

"Alan, before our next meeting I want you to take a look. See if the dangers of Alaskan tidal flats are widely known."

"What good will that do?"

"Facts and feelings interconnect, and sometimes facts are the easiest place to start the untangling."

Alan hadn't told Angela the complete truth about crying. There had been that one time on the trip he'd taken to Puerto Rico with his dad six months after Meg's death.

It happened the last day, after they'd spent four days driving around the island, checking out horses kept in everything from sheds to fancy stables. They had bought four mares in foal and a yearling that had the makings of the stallion needed to establish a breeding program at TapDancer. To celebrate their success, they spent the last day on the beach at *Bouqueron*, swimming and talking about the horses and his dad's plans for the ranch.

In the early evening, they drove to *La Parguera* for dinner, and afterward they took a small boat out to the phosphorescent bay, something the horse agent had suggested and then arranged for them.

They putted along, a half mile out from the nearly invisible shore as the sky darkened and the stars appeared one by one. The waters were choppy, and a stiff breeze blew spray into their faces.

When they entered the bay, the waves smoothed out, the breeze turned soft, and the wake began to glow. Looking over the side, Alan saw the glittering tracks of large fish darting away from the boat.

In the middle of the bay, their guide cut the engine, and they drifted in the darkness watching the flashes of light in the black water. His dad stayed in the boat, but Alan slipped over the side into the water. He swam with slow, easy strokes, his body outlined with a pale halo of light. He stopped to tread water and lifted his hand. The water flowed down his arm in a sparkling stream, as though he were dipping up thousands of tiny diamonds.

For a moment, he could almost hear Meg's delighted laughter and see the sparkles caught in her hair.

Ocean water had mixed with sudden, unexpected tears.

∽

When Grace told Kathy she and Delia had been to the ranch to see Alan—that in fact Alan came to see Delia in the hospital, but Frank had forgotten to mention it—Kathy had to steady her breathing before she could speak. "Oh. And how is he?"

She and Grace were sitting on the Garibaldis' back steps watching Delia play with a friend in the warmth of the summer day.

"He's always been quiet, *verdad*? But it's a different quiet now. *Mas tranquillo.* But he seems...subdued. Sad." Grace sounded thoughtful.

Kathy, knowing the reason for that sadness, felt like crying. She blinked, trying to focus her eyes on the simple scene of Delia and her friend teeter-tottering.

"What happened between you two?" Grace said, speaking quietly.

Kathy knew it wouldn't do any good to say there'd been nothing between her and Alan. "The usual, I suppose."

"I have no idea what you consider usual, *querida*," Grace chided gently.

"How about inequality? He wanted friendship. I wanted more."

"Oh, Kathy. I'm so sorry. I thought—"

"Yeah me, too. Guess we were both wrong."

"And what about Charles? Do you think you might be serious about him?"

Kathy pulled her lip in and chewed on it. "I don't know. I think he wants to be more than friends. And I'm not ready yet."

The irony of that hit her, almost making her laugh. But if she started laughing, she might not be able to stop it from progressing into sobbing.

Grace patted Kathy's arm. "*Mira*, Kathy, if you like, I'll have a small dinner party. Ease the way for you and Alan to be friends again."

"Thanks, but no. I don't think he'd want that." And it would be unbearable for her as well. Too much between them was broken.

"I think he misses you. He asked how you were doing."

A sudden flare of hope pulsed through Kathy. "Did you tell him I was seeing someone else?"

Grace shook her head. "I didn't know what to say so I just told him you were fine."

Yeah. Fine. That was her, all right.

Chapter Twenty-Three

One night, shortly after her trip into the mountains, Kathy awoke from a dream so vivid, it took her a moment to realize she was in her bed in Denver and not in Emily's house in Cincinnati.

In the dream, Emily had led her out of the kitchen and down the hall to a small study. A wing chair upholstered in faded rose brocade sat in one corner with a floor lamp leaning over it like a curious stork. Across from the chair and lamp sat an old-fashioned maple desk.

As Kathy glanced around the room, two paintings caught and held her gaze. One was of a sunset, glowing through the black tracery of fence and winter-bare trees. The second was an old-fashioned portrait of a young boy in a high-backed chair. A German shepherd sat at the boy's side.

Bobby and Brad. Kathy recognized them as surely as she recognized herself.

Eventually she drifted back to sleep, but when she awakened the next morning, it was with an emphatic statement ringing in her mind. *My name is Bobby.* She stretched and sat up. Then, remembering the dream and the picture of Bobby and Brad, she picked up one of the index cards she kept handy. On it she wrote: "My name is Bobby". Then she added a description of her dream.

A dream about Emily and Bobby was hardly a surprise given she'd been re-reading the diaries. What was odd though, was how vivid and coherent it had been. Not the weird jumble of people, images, and events that were her usual dream-fare.

That evening, as Kathy helped Mrs. Costello do the dishes after dinner, the phrase from the morning kept running through her mind. *My name is Bobby. My name is Bobby,* and accompanying it was an urge to write.

It was the first time she'd felt like writing since Delia's illness and the break with Alan. Amanda, with her 'orses and vintage dresses, had faded so completely Kathy had given no thought to the story in weeks.

When Mrs. C went off to water the garden and watch television, Kathy got a notebook and pen from upstairs and returned to the kitchen. She opened the notebook to a fresh page, and sat quietly for a moment, before beginning to write.

My name is Bobby Kowalski. When I was younger than I am now, I had a bad sickness. It was something called men-in-jeans, and I almost died. I don't remember any of that, of course. I just heard Mom telling the lady who comes to help wash and feed me all about it. She said, "Oh the poor little man."

I'm not a man. I'm a boy. So maybe someone else had the men-in-jeans. Still, it is most odd that I can no longer move my arms and legs or make a sound.

Kathy's pen flew across the page, the words flowing out of the tip as if on their own. She had no idea where they were coming from; they were just there, one following the other in a steady stream, as fast as she could write them down.

Not an answer to her question about Alan, but a respite, because while she wrote, the unproductive spinning of her thoughts stopped.

"Kathy, I didn't realize you were in here working." Mr. Costello stood in the doorway. "Came to catch the light. Thought the missus forgot. We're going up to bed. Don't stay up too late."

"No, I won't, Mr. C. Good night."

Kathy looked back at the page, but the pen remained quiescent in her hand, and her brain no longer teemed with words straining to get out. She sighed, stood up, and carrying the notebook, went to bed herself.

In the days that followed, she continued to work on the

Bobby story, and sometimes, it felt like Emily was sitting with her, reading over her shoulder and smiling.

Writing the story was giving Kathy a chance to catch her emotional breath and to ignore her problems for a time. An additional relief as well, when Charles, caught up in his latest case, was unable to see her. He called daily, but their conversations were brief, hurried affairs, always ending with Charles promising to find time to get together soon. Kathy, glad he was busy, didn't push.

Occasionally, she had a day in which no new ideas for the Bobby story came, but she felt no impatience when that happened and no fear he had deserted her as Amanda sometimes had. When it happened, she simply closed the notebook and went for a run.

Invariably, after a short break, a fresh torrent of ideas was there to guide her the following evening.

A quiet pattern began to emerge from those days—a mix of her work at Calico and long runs followed by evenings spent writing—all of it acting like a gentle massage on her sore spirit, easing the tight painful knots of loss.

She still had no answers to her Alan dilemma, but it felt good to be able to stop searching for a time.

80

Alan sat down at the computer a half dozen times before he finally typed "Alaskan tidal flats" into the search field. He read through the list that came up, and decided on the *Anchorage Daily News* website. On that site he typed in "Turnagain Arm", the name of the inlet outside of Anchorage where Meg had died. That search brought up the headlines and first two lines of a number of stories. He worked his way through the list until he found himself reading Meg's name. He stared at the screen for a long time before he followed the instructions to pay for a download of the story and printed it out. Not yet ready to read it, he put it away and went out to do chores.

The next morning, he got up at dawn, saddled a sleepy Sonoro and calling softly to Cormac, rode out. By the time he reached the lake, the sun was well up, and the dawn's promise of clear skies was fulfilled.

He dismounted and walked through crunchy grass to the water's edge where he picked up a small stone and rolled it in his hand before tossing it into the water. He watched the slow tide of ripples circle the splash until they reached the shore by his feet with a tiny sibilance.

When the water stilled, he pulled the pages he'd printed the day before out of his pocket, then sat on a boulder near Sonoro, who was greedily cropping the dry grass.

The article, dated two days after Meg's death, described her accident and also reviewed a number of similar incidents. A geologist from the University of Alaska was quoted as saying the tidal flats of Turnagain Arm were treacherous because of the unique nature of the silt washed down from the surrounding glaciers. "The angular granules are surrounded by water in a delicate balance. Pressure, as from someone walking, can disrupt that balance, causing the granules to become more mobile, even liquefied, for a moment. Then they reposition themselves and lock together in a new, more compact structure, possibly trapping the person whose footstep set off the chain of events." The article went on to discuss how extraordinarily difficult it was to free such an individual, and with forty-foot tides, victims had to be freed quickly.

Two of the rescues described in the article were of locals, and the Alyeska fire chief was quoted as saying it was past time for the public works department to post additional warning signs along the Turnagain Arm road.

It meant the danger wasn't well-known, wasn't something he'd missed through carelessness or inattention. It was what the rescuers had told him afterward, but he'd been unable to believe it. He thought they were trying to comfort him, when nothing could comfort him.

And now? Could he accept it now?

He re-read the first part of the article, letting the words sink in and begin to overlay his previous thinking. Choosing to accept those words, would change...what exactly?

Guilt. The thought gusted over him like a quick, sharp breeze.

Guilt had been the underpinning of all his thoughts about

Meg's death—the conviction that had he been more observant, done something more, Meg wouldn't have died.

Letting go of that...

He sat breathing slowly, staring at the scene in front of him without seeing it.

After a time, he looked back down at the pages and continued reading the discussion of rescue options that had been considered before being rejected. The first: using SCUBA gear to allow the victim to continue breathing if rescuers couldn't beat the tide. Rejected, because unless the victim could also be kept warm, they would quickly succumb to hypothermia in the frigid water.

But as the tide came in, one of the rescuers had given Meg a length of hose. Alan had tried to believe it was going to keep her alive. It didn't, of course. But maybe it helped. Maybe it gave her a feeling of control. To keep breathing until hypothermia set in, or to drown. He didn't know which he would pick. Perhaps having the choice was the important part.

The second option that had been considered and rejected was amputation of the trapped limb. Rejected because of the remoteness of the rescue site, the difficulties inherent in actually doing it and the potential liability to the rescuer.

Both of Meg's legs had been trapped to mid-calf. He would have let them do it. Even that. Anything to save her.

Cormac ambled over and put his head on Alan's knee. Absently, Alan stroked the dog's smooth head and silky ears as he continued to read.

The next part described his actions. The account was provided by one Jim Little, the man who'd stopped to help them. When Alan started to climb down to where Meg was trapped, Jim had grabbed him, told him not to be a damn fool. That he wouldn't be able to do any good, and he'd bollix things up if he got stuck, too. Jim had been big enough, in spite of his name, to make the order stick.

And Jim had been forced to intervene a second time. When the water began to cover Meg, Alan had flung himself toward her, not thinking, simply reacting to his need to hold her, be with her. Jim had tackled him and pulled him back.

He remembered the taste of dirt in his mouth, the pain in

his ankle, the cut on his cheek. When he got back to the hotel twelve hours after they'd left, he noticed for the first time the front of his jacket was stained with mud, grass and blood.

How had he managed to forget all that?

As Angela stood to greet him, Alan thought what a close thing it had been—his decision to return. And he'd made a further decision: to see it through.

"I looked at the information on tidal flats as you suggested," he said after they were seated.

"Did it change your thinking in any way?"

He frowned, staring at the Vasarely print. "It says the danger isn't well-known." Something he'd been repeating over and over to himself since reading it.

His feelings had not yet altered, but he thought it was possible they eventually would.

Angela waited for a moment, but when he didn't add anything more, she said, "Tell me about Meg."

He didn't want to talk about Meg, but the only way to avoid it was to walk out, and he'd promised himself he wouldn't do that. "She was the best and bravest person I've ever known."

"What was something brave she did?"

They were eleven when he'd first known how brave Meg was. "There was this bully. In grade school. He picked on the little kids. Meg stood up to him."

"What happened when she did that?"

"He pushed her over, kicked her." It had seemed to happen in slow motion. As Ted's leg moved in an arc toward Meg's face, Alan had flung himself past Meg, trying to take the blow himself, fear and anger turning his vision red.

He'd only partially deflected the kick, but he did manage to pull Ted to the ground. After that everything was a blur of dust, sharp pains, deep aching blows, and low guttural sounds. When Mr. Dodds ended it with a sharp blast of his whistle, Alan was hanging onto one of Ted's arms, and Meg was right there, hanging onto the other.

"Did you get involved?" Angela asked, speaking gently.

"Not soon enough."

"Was Meg injured?"

"She ended up with a broken tooth and a black eye." He'd teased her that she looked like a pirate.

"What about you? Were you injured?"

He shook his head, rubbing the finger Ted had broken. "Some bruises, a black eye. No big deal."

"Meg wasn't the only brave one."

He shook his head, looking from the Vasarely to the fish circling their tank. Meg had been the one to take a stand. He'd gotten involved only to save her.

"Did you ever talk to Meg about that day?" Angela asked.

"She said it wasn't bravery. When she saw Ted push Rosita, and Rosita started to cry and no one lifted a finger to stop it, she was so angry, she didn't even consider the consequences before she jumped in. She said bravery is when you know exactly what you're facing, know you're likely to get hurt, but you still choose to do it."

"Do you agree with that?"

"I think she knew what could happen." Meg simply ignored those kinds of calculations when she saw someone in trouble. But he didn't. Except when Meg was involved, and then he, too, simply acted.

"Tell me what you did, Alan. After Meg was trapped."

He'd known therapy would be difficult, just hadn't realized it would be this difficult. He took one breath, then another. "Meg was about ten feet from the bank. I got as close to her as I could, and we talked while the team worked to free her." He stopped speaking, trying to shut off the memories.

Angela spoke softly. "What did you talk about?"

I can't do this. The words were a scream of anguish inside his head. Frantically, he tried to focus on the Vasarely. Failed. Meg, raising her face to his. The water coming. The rescuers scrambling to get out of the way. Meg, turning to look and his voice. "No. No. Don't look. Look at me. Look at me. I love you. I love you."

He found he was rubbing his head, hard. He had no idea how long Angela had been waiting for an answer, watching him with those clear blue eyes that seemed able to read his most private thoughts. It could have been ten seconds or ten minutes.

"Do you ever think about your relationship with Meg before that day?"

"I try not to."

"Does that work?"

"Nights are bad sometimes." Especially when all he could remember was how Meg had looked after they'd freed her. It was why he'd hung her picture in his bedroom. To counteract that awful image.

"So you've pushed all your memories down deep inside, only they refuse to stay there," Angela said, jerking his thoughts back again, as if he were a foal she was halter training.

Angela let the silence stretch before speaking more briskly. "Our time is up for today, Alan. What I want you to do this week is write about Meg. Start with when, where and how you met. Then write down whatever you remember about your time together."

No. He couldn't do it. Wouldn't do it.

Chapter Twenty-Four

Excerpt from the diaries of Emily Kowalski
1948...

Jess has finally finished his work for his Ph.D., and he is now a full-time faculty member at Xavier.

The summer has gone by so swiftly. Already, as I look out the window, I see leaves drifting down. By the pond they have formed big piles the goats run through in joyful abandon, just like I think Bobby would do. Oh, there's really no sense writing, if I'm going to get all teary.

Bobby's birthday. Today, he's eighteen. Thirteen years since the meningitis.

This is the hardest day of the year for me. It is one of the few times I can't help thinking about what might have been and grieve.

Bill told me the last time we were together that he felt good about his life, because teaching made it possible for him to change for the better the lives of so many children. It strikes me that Jess and I have done the same. A procession of youngsters, Jess's students, have moved through our lives. Some needed extra tutoring, some needed feeding up, and some just needed loving to alleviate their homesickness.

A few of them have been in the war. Sometimes I can tell because of the external wounds, a missing arm or a limp, but mostly I can tell from their eyes. They have the same pain and confusion I saw in Bill's eyes when he returned from war nearly thirty years ago. I think they need to get used to feeling safe again.

The ones who have been in the war are especially gentle with Bobby.

I enjoy the students, but Bobby is at the center of my heart. His quiet spirit infuses this house, and he is the one who has helped me find the courage to look for joy in my life.

1953...

As I start a new year, it has become my habit to put down where I am with my life and as always, everything revolves around Bobby. I lived thirty-five years up to the day Bobby got sick and now Bobby is twenty-three and it has been eighteen years since that day.

In the beginning, I was so weighed down with sorrow, I didn't write anything at all, so the woman who survived those first months after Bobby came home from the hospital is a mystery to me.

I do remember that at first I was angry about Bobby's illness and what it did to him, to our family. Then the anger faded, and I went numb. I was numb for a very long time.

I don't know what eventually convinced me to live once more. I didn't just get up one day and decide, today I start living again, but I have come to realize that over a period of time, I made many small choices that had that effect.

The music and the painting started the process, and of course my love for Bobby and Jess helped, and it was hard to mope surrounded by the menagerie Jess put together. Before he stopped we had Brad and the goats, ducks and geese for the pond, and cats, chickens and guinea hens.

But whatever the reason, I have found a way back to happiness—a very different happiness than I ever envisioned, but happiness nonetheless. I now believe that when something happens that brings unimaginable pain, it is essential to stop feeling for a time in order to survive.

I take Bobby outside as much as possible and let him interact with the animals while I paint. Two of the goats and one of the cats seem to be his special friends, and they come over to greet him whenever we come outside.

Brad spends most of his day at Bobby's side, sleeping, with his gray muzzle resting up against Bobby's chair. Brad is getting old. I wonder what we will do when he dies. He and Bobby are so attached to each other that the thought makes me very afraid.

I am still trying to paint the sunset Bill and I shared so many years ago, but somehow I am never satisfied. I have also tried to paint Bobby over the years, but I can't seem to capture his gentle spirit with paint or pen. I've been more successful painting the animals, and those are the pictures I think Bobby likes best.

1954...

Today has been a typical Cincinnati winter day. Cold, dark, somber. I took Bobby out when I went to feed the animals, but as soon as we finished, we came back inside to warm up. I made us hot cocoa and settled Bobby by the fire, and as a special treat, I read him once again the story that seems to be his favorite, *The Little Prince*.

I often wonder what my dear Bobby thinks of this life of his, and I wish so much that we could talk about it. All we have, though, are looks and touches. It isn't enough.

Still, in spite of everything, he brings me so much happiness. I know if I were to say that to anyone other than Jess, that person would think I was demented, but I love Bobby so very, very much.

1956...

Once again I have been unable to write, as I struggle to find my way. When I descend too far into sorrow, language deserts me. It's as though I've been set down in the middle of a vast plain of sand that sifts around my feet, holding me fixed from my attempts to run for help and silencing my cries with its vastness.

The last time I picked up a pen to place my thoughts in this book, it was winter, and Bobby sat beside the fire waiting for me to read to him. Now it is summer, and the flowers on Bobby's grave bloom and dance in the breeze that cannot dry my tears.

Brad is gone, too.

My life, which was filled with activity, is now empty and quiet, and I have no heart to play music or paint. Once again, I can hear the clock snipping the hours into little pieces.

I didn't want to hold onto Bobby any longer. He had been trapped in his poor, frail body so long. It was cruel to hold onto him. But I never expected to miss him so. How can it be that I miss him so?

Even the goats have been subdued. They skipped their annual predation on the cemetery's roses, as if they know it is where Bobby has gone.

I look out the window and see in my memory as clear as the day it happened, the black goat dropping petals in Bobby's lap. Only later when Father Larry came by to complain his roses had been stripped did I understand what I had seen.

I smile as I write this, and I wonder if that is proof the darkness will eventually fade. As it did before.

Chapter Twenty-Five

"I've read *Bobby and Brad*," Grace said. "It's a beautiful story, Kathy. I loved it, and so did Delia. She thinks the goats are *graciocos*, funny. But it made me cry."

Kathy propped her chin in one hand, with the phone in the other listening to Grace.

"I think you should show it to Columba and Polly."

"I'm not even sure it's a children's story."

"Whatever it is, it's special. I think more people need to see it. Children who are worried and scared about being sick or different. And their sisters, brothers, parents. Anybody who's hurting. You need to share it."

Kathy slowed to a walk, her breath coming out in pants. Cheesman was deserted this morning except for a man walking a dog in the distance. When she pulled in a deep breath, it made her chest ache. Still August, but the early morning air was chilly.

So how much longer was she going to continue this way—dating one man but unable to stop thinking about another. Stuck in neutral. Kept from moving forward by regret and the feeling there had to be something she could do to help Alan.

She knew Jade was right in saying he had to choose healing for himself. But there must be something she could do to encourage him to make that choice. It had to be right there on the tip of her mind, if she could just grab hold of it.

Your own heart needs to heal as well.

The thought was as clear as the urge to write the Bobby story had been. Shaken, Kathy stepped off the path. She caught her breath, then turned toward the center of the park and started running, picking up her pace until she was sprinting as fast as she could, up and down the grass covered slopes, to the very center.

There she stopped, bent down and sucked deep gulps of air into her burning lungs. Then she straightened and began turning in a slow circle. Surrounded by a huge, modern city, yet she was completely alone in this wide, silent expanse.

Still turning, she looked up at the sky, at contrails crisscrossing the blue, seeing it clear at last.

She'd focused on Alan and his wounds, avoiding the bruises on her own heart. Not one essential loss, but years of small losses, wearing away at her, until it had become so much easier to let go than to hang on. The pattern formed by too many goodbyes when she was still too young to notice. A pattern that had eventually distorted all her relationships.

She'd called Greg dishonorable, and he had been. But she'd been dishonorable, as well. Doling out her love for him. Waiting to make sure it would come back to her before doling out more.

No wonder he'd fallen in love with someone else.

Loving Alan had changed that, changed her. She loved Alan without counting the cost, and just like Jade said she would, she had no doubts.

She was exhausted from trying not to feel the pain of that certainty. A pain that intensified every time she thought of what she'd said to Alan the last time they talked. Words she now knew were not true.

So which would be worse? Letting him go without a fight, or reaching out and having him turn away? Either would be painful, but her only choice was to decide if she had the courage to take a chance.

Then it would be Alan's choice—to accept her love or to live in the past with the memory of the woman he'd already lost.

ॐ

In order to meet with Angela, Alan was spending more time in Denver that summer than he usually did. After his second therapy session, he returned to his apartment, still resisting the assignment she'd given him, to write about Meg.

After a restless night, he decided he had to at least try. That way he could tell Angela with a clear conscience he couldn't do it. Then she'd have to come up with another suggestion. That was her job, after all.

He pulled out one of the old notebooks he'd used in the past to write his story ideas. Without looking at what he'd written when Meg was still alive, he turned to a fresh page and picked up a pen. After a moment of hesitation, he began.

"I met Meg Adams the first day of school when we were both six years old."

The pen stopped moving, and he sat staring at the page, adrift in memory.

In the beginning Meg had been like a second sister. His mom called Elaine, Meg and him the tootling trio, Meg's mom called them the gruesome threesome. They'd shared everything. Bikes and braces. Horses and homework. 4H projects.

Without realizing it, he'd begun writing again, the words pouring out in spurts and runs, long convoluted sentences and short fragments as the memories flashed. He grabbed at them before they could fade.

Meg, always drawing. Everywhere they went, even out to round up calves, she'd have a small sketchbook tucked in her pocket. How many hours had he spent, watching the quick, sure movement of her pencil. A rabbit frozen into immobility next to a tumbleweed, one of the horses, head up, checking the wind for rain, a calf bawling for its mother. And then she'd close the book and smile at him, and he counted that full payment for his patience.

When hunger and fatigue forced him to stop writing, Alan closed the notebook. Without looking at what he'd written, he went to the kitchen, opened a can of soup, and turned on the television for company. He ate and watched the movements on the screen without any memory afterwards of what he'd eaten or seen. When it was late enough, he went to bed.

He stayed in Denver the next day and spent it writing,

stopping only to open a can of something when his stomach growled, going to bed when he could no longer keep his eyes open.

At the end of those two days, looking at the filled pages, it hit him. He was writing and had been for two days, scarcely lifting his hand from the page.

His hand ached, something he hadn't noticed until now. He gently bent it back, stretching the muscles, then he curled and uncurled his fingers to ease their stiffness—a good stiffness, a good ache.

"I've written about Meg," Alan said.

Sometimes Angela made no attempt to help him out by responding immediately. This was one of those times.

"I think it's helped."

Still no response.

He sighed. "Writing about her, I've been able to remember some of the good times again."

"Do you know anything about the grief process, Alan?"

He shook his head, relieved to let her do her share.

"When we lose someone we love, most of us react at first by denying it's happened. We say things like, 'I don't believe it', and 'it can't be real'. Then when it becomes real, we get angry. At God. The universe. Ourselves."

Alan sat still, letting Angela's words fill the space between them.

"Some people get stuck in the denial phase or the anger phase. Blocked, if you will, from moving on. Sometimes that block is guilt. It's only after the disbelief and anger fade that we're able to begin to accept. And only once we accept, that we can live again."

He knew she was looking at him, but he kept his eyes on the aquarium behind her.

"Alan, is Meg buried here in Denver?"

"Yes."

"Do you ever visit her grave?"

He shook his head, still staring at the aquarium.

"Perhaps a good place to think about your grief would be Meg's gravesite."

"You're telling me that's what I should do?"

"No. I'm asking you to think about difficult issues. And suggesting a place that might help you with that thinking."

"I can't."

"This work you're doing, Alan. To overcome grief and guilt. It's difficult. As difficult as getting stones to float."

"You're saying it's impossible."

She shook her head and refused to say more. It was one of the maddening things about Angela. She never argued and rarely explained. All she did was plant these squibs that would later explode just when he thought he'd managed to forget them.

He bought another notebook and spent more time in Denver writing about himself and Meg. As he wrote, Angela's suggestion that he visit Meg's grave hovered at the edge of his conscious thought. By the time he filled the second book, he was tense, irritable and sleeping poorly.

He awakened Friday morning at five, still exhausted, but knowing he'd be unable to sleep anymore. Resigned, he got up, made coffee, then sat down to write more about Meg.

No words came. He sat staring at the blank page, his vision blurring with sudden rage. It was too damn hard. All of it. And there wasn't a scintilla of evidence that any of it was doing any good.

Changing what one thought about something was easy. But changing what one felt...that was like trying to change the course of a river. Or getting stones to float.

He threw the pen down and stumbled over to the balcony door. The trees across the street were barely visible. But as he watched, the contrast between foliage and sky grew more definite. Another day beginning. Another day without Meg.

He moved automatically, showering, dressing, eating. But instead of driving back to the ranch, he turned north and drove until he reached the entrance to I-70 west. It wouldn't do any good. Going to the cemetery. But he'd paid Angela for her advice, and this was it. Visit Meg's grave.

At the cemetery, he parked and got out. The air was still cool, but it was going to be another hot day.

It took him thirty minutes to find Meg's grave. All he remembered from the day they buried her was looking up from the gravesite and seeing the small hill with its tall tree, the mountains behind, solid, eternal, aloof from earthly sorrow.

He stood looking down at the gray granite marker.

Margaret Adams Francini

Meg

1966 - 1993

They'd asked him what to put on the stone. He told them to put any damn thing they pleased.

Be not afraid.

His breath caught in surprise.

He and Meg had been in eighth grade, Elaine in ninth.

"Bet you guys don't have a clue what words appear most often in the bible," Meg had said.

"Of course we don't. We're Catholics," Elaine said.

"The, and, but," Alan said. "Oh, and begat."

Meg had taken a playful swipe at him, which made his horse pretend to shy and Elaine's horse to flick its ears and snort.

"Think you're so smart, huh?" Meg said, grinning at him. Then her look turned serious. "Be not afraid. Three-hundred and sixty-five times. Just to make sure we get it. How cool is that?"

"What's to get?" he asked.

Meg shook her head, giving him her boys-are-hopeless look. "That we don't have to worry. Just do our best, and everything will turn out okay."

Except it hadn't.

Without Meg he'd lost it all—tears, words, joy. He stood, bent over Meg's grave, and the memories slipped out, floating away like clouds laden with rain heading for the plains.

He looked again at Meg's marker. It was unpretentious. Just like Meg. The only decoration was an anemone, the first spring flower, carved along one side. He glanced around at the artificial flowers on several of the graves and real flowers in plastic vases, browning and dropping their petals, on others. Should he bring flowers to Meg? She had loved flowers, the wildflowers best of all. The anemones, columbine, buttercups, and fireweed. But pick a wildflower, and it dies within a day.

No, this was better. This simple marker with its plain patch of grass.

After a time, he walked back to his car and drove to the ranch, feeling lighter.

"I visited the cemetery," Alan said.

"Did you." Angela's voice, as always, was calm.

"I think...I no longer feel the same way about what happened to Meg."

"What's different in how you feel?"

"I feel sad. But not..." He looked past Angela. Gradually, he became aware of the fish, lazily circling their tank. "I can see it wasn't my fault." Still easier to say than to feel.

"Saying the words. It's a start," Angela said, as if she had read his mind.

They sat quietly for a time. He watched the fish, letting the words play again in his head. *Not my fault. It wasn't my fault.*

Maybe if he said it a few thousand more times...

∞

"I've found the one," Charles said, when Alan answered the phone.

"The one what?" But Alan had a sinking feeling he knew exactly what, or rather whom, Charles was talking about.

"When the time is right, I'm asking Kathy to marry me."

The awful feeling in Alan's gut intensified. He tried to speak. Stopped, cleared his throat. "That's fast."

"I've known from the beginning. But it doesn't pay to rush."

That last statement was pure Charles, but the other part, about his being certain of this relationship from the first, that couldn't be more different.

Alan struggled for something to say. "Doesn't this one have a biological clock?"

"She can have as many kids as she wants. If need be, we'll get a nanny." Charles sounded as giddy as a small child with his first bicycle. Only he wasn't a child. And Kathy, most decidedly, was not a bicycle.

If Alan could just pretend Charles was talking about some other woman, he could manage. He had to manage. After all, he'd thrown away his right to step between Charles and Kathy. "How are you going to manage that on a DA's salary?"

"I'm going to join Peters and Lipold. They've been after me for a couple of years. It'll triple my salary for starters."

But Charles loved being a district attorney. Had refused to even consider giving it up for Tiffany, whose tastes matched her name. Alan's free hand came up in a distracted movement to rub his temples. He had to get off the phone. He couldn't listen to Charles rhapsodizing another minute. But if he hung up, Charles would know something was wrong. He took a breath and focused on the cadence of Charles's comments without actually listening to the words, adding in umm's and uh uh's where it seemed appropriate, until finally Charles said, "Got to go. Promised Kathy I'd call."

Alan stood unmoving after he hung up.

It was hard enough knowing he'd lost Kathy through his own cowardice. How was he going to manage if his best friend married her?

Chapter Twenty-Six

Angela rose to shake Alan's hand as she always did at the start of their sessions. After they seated themselves, she spoke briskly.

"Are you ready to discuss your relationship now?"

"Relationship?"

"Yes. The one you mentioned during our first meeting."

He'd forgotten he'd told Angela that. He shifted, trying to ease the immediate tightening in his neck and shoulders. "It was no big deal."

"Wasn't it." Angela's tone was gentle. "Perhaps it ended because you were afraid. Of losing her, like you lost Meg."

Pain moved from his neck into his head. *You think everything is about Meg.* He'd said that to Charles.

"How long ago was it, Alan? That this happened."

He cleared his throat and took a careful breath. "May."

Angela regarded him steadily, while he tried not to squirm. Finally he couldn't stand the silence any longer, even though he knew it was a tactic on Angela's part. "Kathy. Her name's Kathy. And I couldn't deal with...my feelings. For her." He could get up and leave any time. It was his decision. So why didn't he? Why did he sit here talking about Kathy in a voice that even to his ears sounded strained? Not that there was much to tell, except...

"There's one other thing you need to know." He took a deep breath. "My best friend plans to marry her." He glanced at Angela. For an instant he thought he saw a look of pity on her face. But no. Angela never gave any hint of what she was thinking.

"You don't want that to happen."

"No."

"Are you going to do something about it?"

"I don't think... No." Five, six. Was one of the fish missing?

"Love brings pain. You can't avoid it, Alan. Nobody can. But denying love brings pain as well."

He sat counting fish, trying not to think about any of it.

"Kathy is unfinished business," Angela said.

℞

"*Voilá,*" Charles said, opening the door to his apartment.

Kathy stepped past him and looked around with interest. Abstract art prints on the walls, a clear vase holding a large arrangement of silk flowers in shades of turquoise and teal sitting on a glass coffee table. And...chintz covered furniture? If she'd had to guess whose apartment this was, she would have said a woman desperately trying to look hip and failing miserably, not a man whose interests included vintage Porsches and Ironman competitions.

"It's ah...very..." The only word that came to mind was "feminine". She bit it off.

"I think the word you're looking for is clean. I know. I need to redecorate." He gave her a rueful grin.

She tipped her head. "Irreconcilable differences?"

"Yeah. This was one of them. Have a seat. Try to make yourself comfortable. I need to check on dinner."

Instead of sitting down, she followed him to the kitchen.

He opened the oven door and squinted at whatever was inside. It smelled as good as something from Mrs. Costello's kitchen.

"Congratulations on the verdict," she said. "We saw you on the news. Mrs. C thought you looked very distinguished."

"And what about Ms. J. What did she think?"

"Fishing for compliments, and before I've even had a bite to eat." It was pleasant trading gentle barbs with Charles. A relief, actually. He was so...uncomplicated. She'd missed him this past month when he'd been too busy to see her.

"Missed you," he said, catching her thought. "Although it was superior planning on our parts to both be busy at the same time."

True. While he'd concentrated on the trial, she'd focused on the Bobby story.

"So, how goes the writing?" he asked.

"Good. I finished the story."

"Hey that's terrific." He came around the counter and pulled her into his arms for a hug. He rubbed his cheek against hers. "Let's not do that again. Get too busy to see each other." Then he tipped her face up and kissed her.

She kissed him back, then moved casually out of his arms. "So, what's for dinner?"

He gave her a sharp look before turning back to the stove. "Roast chicken with all the trimmings."

She knew he was used to reading the body language of jurors and witnesses, and right now, although he wasn't looking at her, he had to be wondering why she'd shortened the kiss and moved away. Not that her instinctive withdrawal hadn't been a surprise to her as well.

When the food was ready, they carried it into the dining room where the table was set with fresh flowers and candles. A thoroughly domesticated man, Kathy thought, looking across at Charles. Except there was nothing domesticated in the look he was giving her.

And then she knew. Actually, she'd known for some time, but had refused to face it, even after putting it into words for Grace. He was no longer going to be satisfied with kissing.

But she wasn't yet ready to take that next step.

And maybe she never would be.

Looking at Charles, she was struck anew by his sheer physical beauty, surprised as well by her own reaction to that beauty. Indifference? Or maybe the better word was unmoved.

And she knew why.

He wasn't Alan.

It was as simple and as complex as that.

When they finished eating, Kathy insisted on helping Charles put the food away.

"Screw leftovers." He steered her firmly into the living room. Soft jazz floated from the stereo, and he took her in his arms and began to dance.

When the music ended, he kissed her, gently at first, and then with steadily increasing passion. Heart sinking, she broke off the kiss.

"What is it?" His hands moved from her waist to lightly grip her upper arms.

"I'm sorry, Charles." She took a breath. "I think I know what you're hoping. And it's only fair to tell you, it isn't going to happen."

He gave her a searching look. "And what exactly is it you think I'm hoping?"

She swallowed, feeling suddenly unsure. What if she'd misread the situation? Wasn't it presumptuous to assume just because he put flowers and candles on the table he was planning a seduction?

But another look at his face, and she knew she had it right. She met his gaze. "You're hoping to seduce me."

"So why isn't it going to happen?" He still held her lightly.

Clamping down on her nerves, she pulled away and led him over to the couch. "We need to talk."

"Uh oh. Usually when a woman says that, it means I'm not going to like what she has to say." His tone was flippant, but his face was solemn.

She tried to smile, but it felt like a grimace.

He sat next to her and put his arm along the back of the sofa, and she wished she'd sat in one of the chairs.

"I really enjoy our time together." Her throat tightened, and she had to stop speaking in order to shut off the tears. Charles was a thoroughly nice man, and he'd done nothing to deserve this.

"But you're planning to save yourself until we're married."

Married? But Charles couldn't be that serious. They were just...friends, weren't they? "I...well, I think sex. Sometimes it obscures things." And it needed to mean more than *thanks for dinner.* Or *let me check to see if I still love you.* She shuddered at the sudden, vivid memory of that last time with Greg.

"You okay?" Charles leaned toward her, his brow furrowing.

No. She wasn't okay, but she nodded anyway, then stared down at her hands. "I want a relationship built on more than physical attraction. And I want to fall in love first." She glanced at him. "I'll understand if you feel differently and decide you don't want to see me anymore."

It hurt more than she expected it to. Saying that last bit. She'd come to depend on Charles and enjoyed his company in all sorts of ways. As someone to look for when she went jogging, someone to go out with Saturday night, someone to share parts of her life with. She didn't want it to end. But it wasn't fair to hang on to him if all she was looking for was companionship, and he wanted more.

Charles eased his arm from behind her, then sat sideways looking at her. Under that scrutiny, she felt like a defense witness who had just given him the perfect opening.

"You ever been in love?" he asked.

She thought she had, several times. Except, looking back, she now knew she hadn't been. Not really. They'd all been quick, bright flares, easily blown out with the cross wind of a single unkind word or thoughtless act. She'd gotten singed, but none of it had touched any deeper than that. Until Alan. That feeling of certainty Jade had described, overlaid now with loss. It reached all the way to her core.

"Once."

"What happened?"

She shrugged, looked away. "He...he didn't feel the same way about me." And if she let herself think about what those words meant, she'd start crying.

"You get over it?"

"No. I thought I had. But no." In spite of her efforts, tears filled her eyes. "Sorry." She wiped the tears away with the back of a hand. Charles handed her a handkerchief.

He waited while she wiped her eyes. Then he sighed.

"Guess I could use that help in the kitchen, after all." He took her hand and pulled her to her feet.

She discovered he was serious about the kitchen help. After they cleared the table, he loaded the dishwasher, while she rinsed off plates and bowls then handed them to him.

"It was a delicious dinner." She tried to smile, but it wasn't much of a success.

"Yeah. I'll make someone a lovely wife."

"That you most definitely will." She was relieved he was starting to joke again.

"Actually..." he said.

"Actually, what?" She glanced at him as she handed him another plate.

He shook his head sharply. "Got a question for you, actually. You ever done any teaching?"

"Sure," she said, puzzled. "While I was working on my masters at Iowa. And I taught a seminar at DSU last spring. Why do you ask?" She rinsed another bowl and handed it to him.

"Did you enjoy teaching?"

She nodded, handing him a plate. "If you get an enthusiastic group of students it can be a real high. Good thing, because the pay is peanuts."

"So what did you get out of DSU for your efforts? Reserved parking, an office?"

"Enough money for dinner and a movie if I stuck to McDonalds and Blockbuster." She was finally able to give him a real smile.

"You didn't happen to meet an Alan Francini at DSU, did you?"

It was the last thing she expected him to ask. She almost dropped the pan she'd started to rinse. She had to swallow before she could speak. "You know Alan?"

Charles nodded, taking the pan from her.

She turned away and concentrated on gathering together a handful of silverware. "Isn't that a coincidence." She had to clear her throat, but she thought she'd managed to sound casual, although she felt anything but. "How well do you know him?"

When Charles didn't answer, she glanced at him. He was frowning at the wall over the sink, but she didn't think he was seeing it. Then he blinked and looked at her. "Yeah. I know Alan."

He hadn't answered the question she'd asked, but she wasn't inclined to challenge him. And he looked too strange for her to ask the other questions swirling in her head. *Have you seen him recently? Do you know how he is? Did you know Meg? Do you know how Meg died?*

Later, when he took her home, he kissed her lightly. "I want to keep seeing you. But I think it's better if I don't." His look was strained. Meeting his eyes, she felt a surge of sorrow. Before it could overwhelm her, she pulled away and hurried into the house.

In the days that followed, she gradually stopped expecting to see Charles running in Cheesman or to hear his voice when she answered the phone.

She was surprised at how much she missed him.

Chapter Twenty-Seven

"I plan to get drunk," Charles said when Alan answered the phone. "And I could use company. How about it? You in, or are you going to consign me to crying on some stranger's shoulder?"

The tone was much too flat to be a joke.

"Why don't you come over here?"

"You got anything besides beer?"

"Nope."

Charles sighed. "I'll be there in an hour."

When Charles arrived, Alan got a bottle of beer out of the refrigerator. "We drinking to anything special?"

Charles opened the whiskey he'd brought and poured a large amount over a small amount of ice. "Yeah. Sure. Why not." Charles tapped his glass against Alan's bottle. "Let's drink to experience." He took a gulp.

Alan frowned. "We talking any experience in particular?"

"Believe I need to finish this before I'll be ready to get into particulars." Charles saluted Alan, tipped up his glass, drained it, then reached for the bottle and poured a refill. He was obviously serious about getting drunk, even though normally he wasn't any more of a drinker than Alan was.

Halfway through the third drink, Alan could tell the whiskey was taking effect. Charles set the glass down carefully and blinked as if he were having trouble focusing.

"Particulars," Charles said. "You asked what particular experience prompted this evening's visit. Believe I'm almost ready to," he stretched his neck, "tell you the whole frigging story."

Alan sipped his beer, ready to distract Charles if he tried to drink anymore. But Charles seemed to have forgotten the whiskey.

"All started by chance, you know. I saw her running in the park and asked her out. Turned me down. After I promised I wouldn't touch, finally went out with me. Should have known something wasn't right."

Alan froze, barely breathing.

"Hard not touching. God, that hair. So damn...silky." Charles's fingers moved, caressing the air. "Took it slow, though. Seemed like that's how she wanted it." He wiped at his mouth, then looked around as if trying to figure out where he was. "Elusive. That's the word. Didn't want to go slow any more. Made a move, she stopped me cold."

The relief hit Alan like a fist. All these last weeks he'd avoided Charles, because seeing him, all he could think about was Charles and Kathy together, talking, laughing...making love.

Charles's head wobbled, and he shifted as if to rebalance it. "Says she loves someone else, but he doesn't love her. Think I know who she meant, though." Charles's head nodded up and down in a slow rhythm.

Alan's relief turned to regret. *She loves someone else.* It was still too late. Alan looked across at his friend, whose eyes were now closed. Charles swayed gently as if he were responding to a phantom breeze. Then he opened his eyes and looked at Alan, although Alan wasn't at all sure what he was seeing. "'Magine that. Funny, huh? Waste, though. Don't you think? What the hell good is pain if there's no chance for any happiness?"

Charles stopped talking abruptly, and sat silently for a time, then his eyes drifted shut.

Alan lifted Charles's legs onto the couch, propped a pillow under his head and draped a blanket over him. Then he poured the rest of the whiskey down the drain, turned out the light and sat nearby.

As Charles slept, Alan, feeling a deep sadness, kept watch.

In the morning, Charles sat up groaning and holding his head. Alan handed him a glass of water and two ibuprofen.

"Just shoot me," Charles said.

"Think you can handle a cup of coffee?"

"God, no. Tea, maybe."

After a cup of tea, Charles picked at a piece of toast. "Really made an ass of myself, huh?"

"Incoherent," Alan agreed. "Although one thing was clear."

Charles touched his head and winced. "Yeah. I'll bet. Kathy."

"I take it she broke up with you."

Charles shook his head, then stopped moving abruptly and rubbed his temples. "I broke up with her."

"Why?"

"That incoherent, huh? Damn. Figured it would be a lot easier to tell you while I was drunk. Blew it. Hell of a thing, a hangover."

Alan waited impatiently while Charles poured more hot water into his cup and re-dunked his teabag. Then Charles closed his eyes. "Sorry. Bit nauseated." He took a careful sip of tea, then raised bloodshot eyes to Alan's face. "I was damn slow, but I finally put it all together. Did you think I wouldn't?"

Alan froze, trying to meet Charles's look.

"One. She's an editor. Two. She taught a seminar at DSU last spring. Three. She says she met you, but you acted like you didn't know her. Four. Grace Garcia de Garibaldi, although damned if I can figure out how she fits in. But, what the hell. You see where I'm going with this." He stopped speaking and his hands went up to clench his arms, rubbing them as if he were freezing. "You and Kathy. You lied about knowing her." He narrowed his eyes, frowning at Alan. "A witness lies, means he has something to hide."

Alan's heart squeezed into a tight aching lump. He tried to remember why he hadn't told Charles he knew Kathy. Partly it had been the shock. But that wasn't the whole truth. He'd like to believe he'd done it to allow Charles and Kathy to discover what they might mean to each other, but he knew the main reason he hadn't said anything was because he simply couldn't bear to talk to anyone about what happened with Kathy.

"So I asked myself. Why didn't Alan just say, hell, Charles, old buddy, Kathy Jamison, huh? You're talking about that editor Hilstrom foisted on me last spring."

Alan found he was clenching a case knife in one hand and a mangled piece of toast in the other with no memory of how either got there.

"Only one answer to that," Charles continued. "Something happened between you two." He nodded, his lip sucked in. "Know you'll find it hard to believe. Went the noble route. Told her I'd better not see her again. But then I got to thinking. Didn't solve a thing."

Charles lifted his head and stared at Alan with those awful eyes. "Bottom line. I'm only going to be noble so long. You do something soon, or I'm back in the game, and this time I'll do everything I can to get her to forget you and love me."

"Why are you telling me this?"

Charles shook his head in irritation, then winced. "Giving you a sporting chance. We've been friends too long." He stopped and lowered his head into his hands.

Then he looked at Alan again, his face haggard from more than too much whiskey. "For God's sake, man, how could you let her go?"

He hadn't let her go. He'd pushed her away.

But now. The anguish he'd felt when Charles said he planned to marry Kathy had been replaced with an agonized hope.

Hope as fragile and tentative as a foal trying to stand the first time.

ℬ.

In the wake of Charles's visit and his revelations, Alan felt restless and uncertain. To distract himself, he once again pulled the box containing his writing out of the closet and sorted through it, pulling his stories together in one pile, his novel in a second. He returned the research materials and computer disks to the box.

Charles had been wrong. Not a thousand pages. Only five hundred. He split the pile into three parts, tapping the stacks to straighten them, then he picked up his first page, realizing he could no longer even recall the beginning.

He read the first two pages before coming to a penciled comment from Meg, his most effective editor and critic. The sight of that familiar writing startled him, but the pain of memory seemed less intense than in the past. Seeing the note, he recalled that right before the trip to Alaska he'd printed out the novel and given it to her to read.

He looked at the piles of pages, suddenly curious to know how far she'd gotten. He flipped through the first two piles to find notes scattered throughout. Then he picked up the third stack and discovered she had written her usual note on the last page. It meant she had finished before they left on the trip. Likely she planned to go over it with him when they got back.

He put the pages down without reading any of her notes. He wasn't ready yet, but soon he might be able to take up all these pages and all these words and begin to work with them again.

Alan walked in to find Angela had cleared off the small table that held drinks, her notes, and the ever-present box of tissues. In the middle sat a clear bowl of water. In the water were stones, and they were floating. *Getting over grief and guilt is as difficult as getting stones to float*, Angela had said. He'd thought she was telling him it was impossible.

He looked from the bowl to Angela, then leaned forward, reaching out to touch the stones. Real. Hollowed out, maybe.

"Pumice," Angela said.

He cleared his throat, trying to think what to say, feeling his heart fill. Not with pain or sadness, but with relief.

Angela was letting him know he was going to be okay.

80

"I finished reading your story," Jade said.

Kathy looked up from the galleys she had been checking.

"I didn't want to talk to you about it until I came up with the right word to describe my reaction."

Kathy winced. "Ouch."

"No. That definitely isn't it." Jade said thoughtfully. "More like wonderful, delightful. Touching." She smiled at Kathy. "You should show it to Columba and Polly."

"They might hate it."

"They might love it and want to publish it. And if I didn't expect that to be their reaction, I wouldn't suggest you show it to them." Jade turned serious. "It's a wonderful story, Kathy, and you know it." Jade pursed her lips, then took a breath. "And I know the perfect illustrator."

Kathy felt slightly dizzy. "Maybe we better see what Columba and Polly think before we get carried away."

"Kathy, you busy?"

Kathy looked up to see Columba and Polly standing by her desk. It couldn't be about her story. She and Jade had talked only yesterday afternoon.

"Let's go over to my desk, shall we?" Columba said.

There was no privacy at Calico Cat with all their desks scattered around the single large room. Walking to Columba's desk, Kathy looked over at Jade who gave her a thumbs-up sign.

After sitting down, Columba spoke in her usual slow, definite manner. "We've both read *Bobby and Brad.*"

"And we absolutely adore it," Polly chimed in with a grin.

Columba frowned at Polly, "Never can keep any decorum around here, can you, Poll." Then she gave Kathy a slow smile. "We want to get it into production as quickly as possible."

"Aren't you jumping the gun, girlfriend? She hasn't said we can have it," Polly said.

"Well of course we can." Columba looked suddenly unsure. "Can't we?"

"I can't imagine taking it anywhere else," Kathy said, happy laughter bubbling up and out.

Jade walked over to join them. "This a private party, or is the illustrator welcome?"

"What, Jade? You mean it?" Kathy said.

"If you gave this to someone else, I'd never forgive you. No more free advice for starters."

Grinning from ear to ear, Kathy hugged her friend.

"Group hug." Polly said, joining in and pulling Columba with her.

"But do you have time?" Kathy asked, when she caught her breath.

"I've already worked up two sketches. If you like them, I think this project will practically draw itself."

Jade pulled two sheets of paper out of her portfolio and walked over to one of the tables where she laid them out.

"This is what I'm thinking for the cover." She pointed to a sketch of a wide field bounded by a fence. Running toward the fence were a boy and a German shepherd. She had added a wash of color to indicate a sunset.

"And this is a portrait of Ethel, Bethel, Bobby, and Brad." The picture showed a small boy sitting in a high-backed invalid chair placed on a stone path in a garden. In front of him were two goats and a German shepherd. Startled, Kathy realized she was looking at the boy from her dream.

She turned to Jade and found the other woman giving her an intent look.

"I'm having trouble finding the right word to describe what I think," Kathy said.

"Ouch?"

"No, that's definitely not it." Kathy shook her head and smiled. "Wonderful, delightful. Absolutely perfect."

Jade started smiling, too.

"That's exactly how I pictured them," Kathy finished.

"Okay," Columba said. "I sense a plan here. Let's see if we can't set a record. I'd love to have this ready for the Christmas season."

"You're talking next year of course," Jade said.

"After all, you did say the pictures were drawing themselves," Columba said.

Jade rolled her eyes.

Kathy left the dirt path and jogged over to the Cheesman pavilion and halfway up the steps before stopping to sit down. The steps were cool and the pavilion and park were mostly deserted in the early morning.

She wrapped her arms around her knees, staring at the park, unseeing, trying to empty her mind as she waited for the sun to come up, but her thoughts kept pulling away, returning as they always did these days to the puzzle that was Alan.

Okay, she could admit it to herself, couldn't she—why she hadn't tried to contact him after the meeting with Elaine?

Because she was afraid. Afraid, he'd reject her again. And if he did, that final break would be the worst thing that ever happened to her. But as long as she didn't act, she could pretend that everything would work out. Somehow.

Deep down, of course, she knew it wouldn't. She could hardly expect him to want to see her after the angry words she'd flung at him the last time they talked. She closed her eyes, fatigue weighing her down. She was so damn tired. Tired of the regret. Tired of not knowing what to do. Tired of waking up at night knowing that although Alan lived nearby, he might as well be on Jupiter.

So much broken between them—shattered by his actions and her words, words she'd used to try to make him hurt as much as she hurt.

Sticks and stones may break my bones but words will never hurt me...

Not true. Words had the power to wound much more deeply than sticks and stones. And the wounds never healed.

With her arms still wrapped around her knees, she rocked, trying to ease the pain in her heart, although she knew there was only one way to ease it. The words she'd used to hurt Alan were choking her.

She needed to apologize.

But where and how to do it, that was the issue. If she phoned, she knew she would have trouble speaking, and even if she managed it, he might simply hang up when he recognized her voice. Not that she would blame him.

Maybe it would be better if she went to his office. She pictured herself opening the door and waiting for him to look up, and a shiver rolled through her. She clenched her jaw to keep her teeth from chattering.

Okay. A written note, then. She could manage that. Take her time. Figure out just the right words.

And just maybe the right words were already written. *Bobby and Brad.*

"Mira, Kathy, I think more people need to see it... Anybody who's hurting."

Chapter Twenty-Eight

The first evening seminar of the autumn semester had been followed by a longer than usual discussion between the visiting author and the graduate students. Alan yawned, feeling the long day settle over him.

He picked up his mail and glanced through it quickly on his way upstairs. As usual, it was mostly catalogs from companies he'd never bought anything from and never would. Some bills. And a large white envelope that slipped out of his hand and fell to the floor.

He bent to pick it up and read the return address. Calico Cat Books.

Kathy? His heart stumbled into a faster rhythm as he fished out his key and opened the door. He dumped everything on the couch except the white envelope, which he opened. He eased out the contents—a small spiral bound book and a handwritten note.

The signature on the note was Kathy's. Heart pounding, he began to read.

Alan,

The last time we spoke, I said something I would give anything to be able to retract. But once said aloud, words can never be reclaimed. All I can do is tell you that I no longer believe those words, and I regret having said them. I hope you can forgive me.

I'm sending you a story. A peace offering of sorts. I'm sorry

we lost touch.
   Kathy

I'm sorry we lost touch. He was sorry, too. He re-read the note, feeling a weight lift from his heart. Such a relief to know she was no longer angry with him, and maybe that relief would free him to finally think about his last meeting with Charles, something he'd been avoiding.

He carried the note and Kathy's book into the bedroom, leaving them on his nightstand while he got ready for bed. Then he re-read Kathy's note, and on the burst of optimism it ignited, picked up *Bobby and Brad* and began to read.

ଚ୍ଚ

My name is Bobby Kowalski. When I was smaller than I am now, I had a bad sickness. It was something called men-in-jeans, and I almost died. I don't remember it, of course. I just heard Mom telling the lady who comes to help wash and feed me all about it. She said, "Oh the poor little man."

I'm not a man. I'm a boy. So maybe someone else had the men-in-jeans. Still, it is very strange that I can no longer move my arms and legs or make a sound.

My mom's name is Emily, and she's beautiful. She has soft, brown hair, and her eyes are the same color as the sky on a sunny day. Dad's name is Jess. He's tall, like a tree, and his voice sounds all low and rumbly. If a bear could talk, and it was friendly, I believe it would sound exactly like my dad.

Mom takes care of me, while Dad goes to work. My favorite part of the day is when she reads to me. In the books are pictures of dinosaurs and trucks, horses and trains, ships and treasures. And the people in the stories have adventures.

I would so very much like to have an adventure.

Today, Dad brought home a dog from work. The dog came right over and licked my hand. He's black on top and tan underneath with pointy ears and a bushy tail.

He cocked his head at me, and I heard the words, "Come play with me," inside my head. It felt strange and tingly.

"Ah, perhaps you cannot," he said. Then he laid his head on my lap, and his fur tickled my hand, making me want to laugh.

"I wonder what your name is."

It was only a thought, because I can't talk, but he heard somehow and answered, "Brad."

"How did you know I asked you that?"

"Ah. That is an enigma."

I didn't know what that was, a nigma. I decided it must mean he didn't understand either.

Just then, Dad cleared his throat, and I looked at him. He was smiling at Brad and me, but Mom had tears in her eyes.

I was very afraid it meant Brad couldn't stay.

Brad has been here since the snow left. He stays by my side all day and sleeps beside my bed at night. When I tell him to, he goes and nudges Mom's hand. She comes and tries to figure out what I need.

Sometimes, it's only to know she will come.

Yesterday was Mom's birthday. A large red truck arrived with her gift—two goats. Mom clapped her hands, and Dad laughed. The goats jumped and bucked and Brad barked. It was very exciting.

One goat came over to me and said, "What's wrong with you, little boy?"

I heard the words in my head, the way I hear Brad. "You talk. Like Brad," I said.

"Of course I talk," said the goat. "Who is Brad?"

"Brad is my dog."

"Aha. And who are you?"

"My name is Bobby. What's your name?"

"I'm Ethel, and this is Bethel," she said as the other goat joined her.

"How do you do, Ethel and Bethel."

"We do very well," answered Bethel. "Especially if this is going to be our home," she added, looking around.

"It is. You're my mom's birthday present."

"We've never been birthday presents before, have we, Bethel?"

"I don't believe so, Ethel."

Brad joined us, and I told him the goats' names. When I looked over at Mom and Dad, they were watching Ethel, Bethel, Brad and me, and Mom had tears in her eyes. I would have worried except the last time she cried, Brad came to live with us.

After dinner, we had a cake with candles. Dad lit them, then he turned out the lights, and it was like we brought the stars inside. Then Mom blew out the candles, and she and Dad laughed together like they used to before I got sick.

Something has changed since Ethel, Bethel, and Brad came to live with us.

I think perhaps they have helped us remember how to be happy.

&

Alan looked up from the page. The blank wall at the end of the bed met his distracted gaze. It was still a habit, to stare at that spot, even though he'd removed the picture of Meg.

He'd done that after he took the notebooks full of what he had written about her out to the ranch, ridden to the lake on a rainy day and built a small fire on the shore. Angela hadn't suggested a ritual burning, but it seemed the right thing to do. Once or twice, the fire had flared, and he'd felt the sharp pain in the tips of his fingers as he let loose another page.

When he returned to Denver afterwards, he walked into his bedroom and stared at Meg's picture for a long time. Saying goodbye, letting go, letting her go, his memories of the two of them floating like the bits of charred paper had floated above the flames of his small fire.

Finally, he'd reached up and taken the picture down. Carefully, he dismantled the frame and removed the photograph which he placed in the box where he kept all the pictures Meg had painted.

Abruptly, he pushed away the memories of Meg and looked back at Kathy's book.

℘

Today, Ethel and Bethel brought me a present—a red petal from a flower they said is called a rose.

"Taste it, Bobby, you'll love it," said Ethel.

"But why would I want to eat something so pretty?"

"Because it tastes even better than it looks," said Bethel. "See, Ethel, I told you we should eat all the roses ourselves. Bobby has no emaciation."

"You mean appreciation," said Ethel.

"I know what I mean," Bethel said.

When the goats argue about their big words, it's sometimes hard to know who is right, but I think probably Ethel is.

Ethel placed the petal on my tongue. It was soft, and when I bit down, it did taste very good.

"Thank you, Ethel. Bethel. But where did you find a rose?"

Ethel and Bethel looked away without answering.

This evening when we finished dinner, a man named Mr. Pitzer came to visit. "A vandalism so abominable I can hardly speak of it."

He used big words like the goats do. I didn't know what

they meant—abominable and vandalism. They must be bad though, because he sounded very upset.

"All the roses along the cemetery fence have been eaten. Hundreds of them. Not a single petal left behind."

I didn't know what that was either—a cemetery. But Ethel and Bethel knew, because they'd been there. Brad figured it out, just like I did. He started to giggle, then he laughed so hard his leg thumped. I laughed, too, inside, remembering how good the one petal Ethel and Bethel shared with me had tasted.

Dad frowned at us. "What is the matter with the dog? Could he have fleas? We'd better put him outside until we can check him over. We certainly don't want him giving Bobby fleas."

Brad stopped laughing. He got up, came to me and put his head in my lap. We both looked at Dad.

"If I didn't know better, I'd think he understood me." Dad stared at Brad.

"Well of course he did," I answered. Then I remembered. Dad couldn't hear me.

"Do you think so, Jess?" Mom asked. "I believe he and Bobby communicate somehow."

"What makes you say that?" Dad asked.

She frowned. "It's mostly a feeling I have."

"Perhaps Brad having fleas is a small price to pay then."

Brad and I sighed with relief.

As he was leaving, Mr. Pitzer asked Dad one last question. "Do you think deer ate my roses, Jess?"

Brad and I sat very still.

"Could be," Dad said, slowly.

After Mr. Pitzer left, Mom and Dad looked at each other. Then they started to laugh.

"Oh, Em. It had to be the goats. I'll have to check. See how they got out." Dad wiped laughter tears from his eyes. "We can't have them stripping Pitzer's roses. They're his pride and joy."

I fell asleep that night remembering the taste of the rose petal and the sound of Mom and Dad laughing about Ethel and Bethel's adventure.

The roses weren't the goats' only adventure. One day the phone rang while Mom and I were eating lunch. Mom said a lot of "Oh, nos," and "Are you sures". Then she called Dad. "Jess, Mr. Tuppen just called. He has the vegetable stand. You know, the one by the cemetery. He said we better come get our goats, or he'd shoot them. He sounded awful angry. What are we going to do? I can't leave Bobby."

I guess Dad said he would take care of it. Mom was still upset, though.

After a while, Dad walked into the house laughing. "Em, your goats are notorious. I got an earful from everyone at the vegetable stand. Seems they've been all over the neighborhood, practicing their own version of neighborly visitation. Folks didn't want to trouble us with it, but now we know we have to do something about it."

Brad went outside with Dad. In a few minutes, he came back, chuckling. "You ought to see those silly goats now. Your dad hobbled them."

"What's hobbled?" I asked.

"It's tying two of their feet together so they can walk, but they can't run. Ethel and Bethel are hopping mad. Or they would be if they could hop."

"Can you get Mom to take me out? I want to talk to them."

Brad went over and put a paw on Mom's lap, and she put down her mending. "You want us to go outside, is that it? Just a minute, I need to get Bobby a sweater."

"Can you find Ethel and Bethel?" I asked Brad when we got outside.

"Sure," he said, trotting off. He disappeared for several minutes, then he returned with a short rope in his mouth.

"What's that, Brad?"

Both Mom and I asked the question, but I was the only one able to hear Brad's answer.

"It's a hobble. Ethel and Bethel must have chewed them off, and now they've disappeared again."

It turned out, he was exactly right. When Dad got home,

the goats were just getting back. Dad laughed as he told Mom how they'd jumped over the gate back into our yard. Brad and I laughed too, until we heard Dad say, "Em, I'm afraid we're going to have to get rid of the goats."

"Isn't there something we can do, Jess? Bobby loves them."

"If we can't keep them in the yard, we'll have no choice," Dad said.

"Oh, Brad, can't you do something?" I said. "I'd miss Ethel and Bethel terribly if they went away."

"What can I do? You know Ethel and Bethel. Nothing ever stops them from doing exactly what they want."

"Why don't you tell them Dad said they'll be sent away? Maybe that will make them behave."

"That's a good plan," Brad said.

I could hardly wait to get outside the next day. "Did Brad talk to you?" I asked the goats.

"In the assertative," said Bethel, nodding.

"You mean affirmative," snorted Ethel.

"I don't understand why you're always correcting me, Ethel," said Bethel. "My language is ever more poetic than yours. I think you're just jealous."

"Poetic my hoof, pathetic is more like it."

"Brad talked to you, right? What do you think?" I said. When the goats start speaking in that snippy tone, Bethel always ends up sulking.

"Your mother doesn't even have any roses," grumbled Bethel.

"But I love you, Ethel, and you too, Bethel. You must stay in our yard, or Dad will send you away. And we'll never see each other ever again. And I'll be awful sad."

"We're being selfish, Bethel. Bobby can't run at all, and here we are complaining we have to stay in this yard," said Ethel. "After all, you must admit, it is a very pleasant yard."

"You are precipitously correct, Ethel. The place we were before this wasn't nearly as comfabable."

"Precipitously indeed," Ethel muttered. "I suppose you mean precisely. And as for comfabable. The word is

231

comfortable."

"And, you're nice, too, of course." Bethel said, ignoring Ethel and turning to me. "I suppose we can try. If it's too bad, we can always run away later."

"Oh, please don't do that," I begged.

"Since you asked so nicely, we'll try," said Bethel.

Once they promised to stay in the yard, the goats had to find new ways to have fun. On hot days, they ran through the sprinkler or squeezed onto the chair swing Dad hung from a tree. When it was cooler, they chased the chickens and guinea hens.

Then one day, Mom went back inside for a minute, leaving her paints and a fresh canvas set up. Before I could stop them, Ethel and Bethel got into the paints and smeared them all over their tongues and noses. Then they wiped their noses on the canvas, all the time making faces and saying "Ugh, yuck."

Maybe they expected the paints to taste like roses.

When Mom came back, Ethel and Bethel ran away. Mom stood with her hands on her hips watching them, and then she looked at the canvas. It was a mess but quite a pretty mess. Like a rainbow that twisted itself into a tangle.

ℰℭ

Alan stopped reading abruptly, the memory sharp and clear of a painting Meg had given him when they were in grade school. When he asked her what it was, she had giggled and said it was a rainbow that decided to tie itself into a bow.

He still had it. That picture. It had fallen out of one of his books, when he and Meg were unpacking in their first apartment. He'd put it carefully away, teasing her that one day it would be worth a fortune. An early Meg Adams.

He opened eyes he hadn't realized were closed and looked once again at Kathy's story, trying to read more quickly, just to get through it, trying not to let it surprise him again.

∞

Mom is teaching me to talk with my fingers. She holds my hand and asks me questions, and I answer with taps. One tap for yes, and two for no. The first question she asked me was, did I want a cup of cocoa. I tapped once.

The cocoa was warm and creamy, the best I have ever tasted.

I am getting bigger, and I barely remember the time before I got sick. Brad says I am growing up. He told me most boys my age go somewhere called school in order to learn to read and write, paint and play music.

Then Brad said those other boys have forgotten how to talk to animals.

It's all right that I can't read stories, because Mom reads them for me. But I would like to paint and play music. Still, I can't decide if I would give up talking to Ethel, Bethel and Brad for school.

Mom has been reading me stories from a brand new book. They are called fairy stories and are about princesses, wicked witches, fairy godmothers and spells.

"Do you think I could be under a spell?" I asked Brad. "And that's why I can't run or speak?"

"Do you mean you used to run and speak?" Brad said.

"Yes. And I even threw stones into the pond."

"I suppose you could be under an evil spell."

"Then that means I need a fairy godmother to come." I was very excited. "You must help me watch for her."

"I would be happy to do that," Brad said.

The goats don't like fairy stories. They think they're too scary. Their favorite story is *The Three Billy Goats Gruff.* Dad built a bridge over the stream that runs into our pond, and Ethel and Bethel use it to act out the story. They pretend they are the Gruff family, and they make Brad play the troll.

Whenever Mom reads to me outside, Ethel and Bethel come over and ask me to pick their story. They watch me tap out yeses and nos as Mom holds up the books. *The Three Billy Goats Gruff* isn't my favorite, but I pick it for Ethel and Bethel because they are my friends.

The other stories I especially like are the ones about Doctor Dolittle. I'm glad there's a grown-up who still remembers how to talk to animals. Maybe that means when my spell is broken, and I go to school, I'll still be able to talk to Ethel, Bethel and Brad.

Mom has also begun reading me something called poems. I like them very much and so do Ethel and Bethel. In fact, we like them so much we decided to make up our own. Here is mine.

Someday I know I will run and jump
And sing like the birds in the trees
The day my fairy godmother comes
And breaks my spell for me

"That was very good for a first try, Bobby," said Bethel. "*Trees* and *me* rhyme quite satisfactorily, but I do believe you need to work on your other lines. They don't rhyme at all."

"I think it's perfect," said Ethel.

"Do you have a poem to say for us, Ethel?" I said.

Ethel lifted her head and recited:

Tippytoes, swerves, leaps, and curves
We run in the grass and roll in the leaves
Until we're covered with garlands and wreaths

Ethel said her poem very nicely, but Bethel broke in and said, "Really, Ethel, *curves* does not rhyme with *leaves* and

234

wreaths. It won't do."

Ethel lowered her head, and I thought she was going to butt Bethel, hard. Instead, she shook her head and said in her sweetest voice, "And what, my dear, have you composed?"

Bethel stuck her nose in the air and said, "And wouldn't you like to know that." Then she turned and pranced away.

I think Bethel acted that way because she was having trouble with her poem. Poems can be very hard.

Bethel was gone for a while, but then she came dancing back, singing out:

Clickety Clack Tickety Tack
Feedle Fiedle Foodle Frack
Weedle Wadle Woodle Wack
Tickety Tack Clickety Clack

Ethel snorted.

"You'll notice how all of my lines rhyme perfectly," Bethel said, ignoring Ethel.

I liked Bethel's poem, and so did Bethel. She pranced around for several minutes chanting it over and over, until Ethel stamped her hoof and said, "Enough!"

Bethel may be bigger, but Ethel is the boss.

Now that I know what they're called, I think poems are used to cast spells. I wonder if a poem can also break a spell.

It is something to think about.

It's almost Christmas again, and when Dad comes in from outside, puffs of cold air come in, too. Yesterday, he brought a tree indoors and stood it in the corner. It makes the house smell the same way our woods do on a hot summer day.

Dad and Mom circled the tree with strings of red, blue, green and yellow lights. Then Mom added strings of silver that flutter whenever anyone walks by. It is very pretty.

A strange man has come to be with us this Christmas. When he arrived, Mom rushed over to hug him, laughing and crying. I don't understand it, but sometimes Mom can be all happy and sad mixed together.

Mom dried her eyes and led the man over to me. He is my uncle Bill. Mom is his sister. Uncle Bill took one of my hands in his and talked to me exactly like I was all grown-up. "I am most particularly happy to meet you, Bobby."

I was happy to meet him, too.

He nodded his head as if he understood that. Then he held out his hand for Brad to sniff and patted Brad on the head.

"Your uncle is a good man," Brad said to me later.

"How do you know?" I asked, although I agreed with him.

"He has kind eyes, and he was gentle when he patted me," Brad said.

Uncle Bill is a teacher in a school where boys learn to read and write and forget how to speak to animals. I wish I could ask him questions about that, because I'll be going to school someday.

Well of course my fairy godmother has to come break my spell first. And she does seem to be taking a very long time.

Spring is early this year. Mom and Dad said so. There are no leaves on the trees yet, but when we go outside, I don't need a heavy jacket, and I can smell that warm spring smell.

Today when we went outside, Mom brought along a bowl full of soapy water and blew bubbles. The bubbles floated, spinning slowly and changing colors. Some were pink and purple and some blue and green. One floated over and touched my nose and popped. It tickled.

Ethel, Bethel and Brad chased the bubbles, but whenever

they caught one, it always popped. It was funny to watch them, although I was sad when a bubble popped, because they're so pretty. But Mom blew more, so it was all right.

Mom blew bubbles a long time. I liked it a lot.

Today, Mom got a phone call. It made her cry but not in a happy way. She left the room for a while, and when she came back, her eyes were red, and her nose was all stuffy.

Brad went over to Mom and rubbed his head against her leg, and she started crying again. Then Dad came home and hugged Mom, and she cried some more.

"Hush, Em. You're upsetting the boy," Dad said. "Bill's okay. He's with God."

"What does that mean, Brad? Are they talking about Uncle Bill?"

"I think they must be, Bobby. I was afraid of this. I believe your uncle was ill at Christmas, and now he has died."

"When you die, you have to live with God? But what if you don't want to?" I didn't want to live with anyone but Mom and Dad.

"It's what many people believe," Brad said. "It's a good thing."

I didn't understand how going to live with someone you didn't know could be a good thing.

ᏚᏅ

Amen to that. Alan winced at the memory. How many people had come up to him at the funeral to say, "Meg's gone home to God. She's at peace now." As if that had the power to comfort him when all he could feel was Meg's absence.

What an odd story Kathy had written. It was making him uncomfortable, pulling at memories he'd rather leave untouched. He started to set the book aside, but the words *Little Prince* caught his eye. Intrigued by the oddity of that, he pulled the book closer.

ℰℭ

Mom is reading me a new story. It's called *The Little Prince*, and it's about a boy who talks to a rose, a fox, and a snake. A flower has never spoken to me, and I've never met a fox or a snake, but I have Ethel, Bethel and Brad. So maybe this little prince and I are alike.

At the end of the story the snake helps the little prince go home to his rose. "Where do you find a magic snake like that?" I asked Brad.

"It wasn't a magic snake, Bobby. It helped the little prince die," said Brad.

"Did a snake help Uncle Bill die?"

"No. When people get old or sick, it just happens."

"Are Mom and Dad old enough to do it?"

"No. They're still young. You're not supposed to do it until you get old. When someone young does it, the older people get very upset."

ℰℭ

Kathy had that right. Meg's death had upset the order of things. And it wasn't only the older people—Meg's parents and his—who had been devastated. He rubbed his temples, which had begun to ache. He'd done the right thing, hadn't he? Not telling them Meg was pregnant. Better they not know they'd lost a grandchild as well, although they might have suspected. More than enough grief to go around without knowing for sure, though.

His forced his eyes back to the book.

ℰℭ

Ethel and Bethel enjoyed *The Little Prince*, too. I asked them what they thought of it.

"I do not believe it can be vilified," was Bethel's opinion.

"You mean verified," Ethel said. "I think it must be true. The person writing this story sounds very reliable."

Only one thing worried me. The man who wrote the story was sad after the little prince left his body with the help of the snake.

"It does seem those left behind are often sad," Brad said. "But they don't need to be. You see, I don't believe dying can be forever. After all, the trees and flowers do it every fall, and in the spring, they come back to life."

I looked at the flowers and remembered how the yard looked in the winter, all brown and empty and the trees like bare sticks. But in spring, the flowers come back, the earth turns green and the trees get leaves again. It is always a surprise to me when it happens. I am glad to know it's supposed to be that way.

"They do that to show us there's no need to be afraid of anything that happens to us," Brad said, settling down for his nap.

§

Be not afraid. Yeah. Right.

Enough.

Alan set the book down, and got out of bed. He walked into his living room and gazed at the floor to ceiling shelves, stuffed with books. The bright colors of the Dr. Seuss books caught his eye, even though they were shelved near the bottom in a corner. They were all gifts from Meg, given over a stretch of birthdays and Christmases during grade school. Next to them were the other books she'd given him as they grew up. It was their tradition—Meg always giving him a book.

He bent down and pulled out one of the Seuss books, *One Fish Two Fish.* It was loved almost to pieces, the spine broken and the cover smudged. He opened it to the inscription printed with laborious neatness on the inside cover: To my friend, Alan Francini. Happy Birthday. Your friend, Meg Adams.

He slipped the book back into place. Then his finger traced

the bindings of the other books—books about horses and wildflowers, the poetry anthology with the Gerard Manley Hopkins poem about "couple-coloured clouds" and "stippled trout".

His hand came to rest on *The Little Prince*. Antoine de Saint-Exupéry. He pulled it out and turned to the inscription. In this book it was written in an adult hand.

To my dearest Alan, you are unique in all the world. You have tamed me, my love, and like the fox and the rose, I no longer wish to live without you. All my love, Meg

He hadn't wanted to live without her either. But he'd had no choice. Looking up, he was startled by his reflection in the balcony door. Was that how he looked? A man no longer young. A man stooped with sorrow.

Looking at his reflection, he no longer had the energy to stand. He sank to the floor and leaned back, feeling the welcome discomfort of the books poking into his back. *The Little Prince* lay open on his lap.

He turned the pages of the story, looking at the pictures, reading a few lines here and there. But he knew what he was really doing—putting off reading the rest of Kathy's story. He hurt, and the story wasn't helping, chipping away at the last of the insulation that made it possible, with Meg no longer in his life, to get up every day, go to work, deal with students. Without that insulation, he was skin and bones enclosing a dark, empty hollow.

After a time, he stood, slipped *The Little Prince* into its slot, and went back to the bedroom. He turned out the light and settled himself in bed, then he lay in the dark, eyes aching and heart pumping, knowing after a few seconds it wasn't going to work.

He snapped the light back on and sat up, rubbing his head. Kathy's story lay on the nightstand, glowing in reproach.

He picked it up and read the remaining pages quickly, trying not to think, holding himself in tight so the words couldn't touch him.

80

Today, Brad asked me if I wanted to learn to float with music. When I said yes, he told me to relax, breathe slowly and deeply and pretend the notes were pulling me into the air.

"How did it feel?" he asked.

"I felt like a...a soap bubble. All light and bouncy. I liked it very much."

"You can do the same thing with pictures," Brad said. "Just look at the picture, breathe in slowly and deeply and imagine yourself inside it."

"Sometimes, I pretend I'm running across the field in one of Mom's paintings. Is that what you mean?"

"Exactly. You're making good progress, Bobby. You won't need me much longer."

"No! You can't leave me!"

"Shush, Bobby, I didn't mean to upset you. I'll stay with you as long as I can," Brad said, rubbing his head against my hand.

"You must promise me, Brad. You mustn't go anywhere without me."

"I'll do my best, Bobby."

Mom is painting a new picture, of a man standing by a tree looking at a sunset. It is a beautiful sunset, all deep oranges and reds, and there are clouds that look like lace. I focused on the tree, and Brad and I breathed slowly together.

Suddenly, I was standing in the field, inside the picture, my hand resting on Brad's head. "Come on, Brad. I'll race you to the tree," I sang.

I was very excited. I've waited such a long time to have an adventure. And it was finally happening.

We ran across the field toward the man. My legs felt strong, and my feet thumped against the ground. I jumped and twirled. I felt like my fairy godmother had come at last and made me completely well.

The man by the fence turned to watch us, and I stopped running to look at him. He had the same sky color eyes as Mom, only he was taller, and he wasn't a girl, of course.

He held out his hand to me, and I reached for it, but before I could touch him, he disappeared. I opened my eyes, and Mom was there, leaning over me, rubbing my hand.

"Bobby, are you okay? Oh, please. You've got to be okay."

She looked so worried, but I was excited. I wanted to tell her all about my adventure. How wonderful it was to run and sing and fling my arms into the air. I didn't want her to worry.

I tapped against her hand, once.

"Are you really okay?" she asked.

I tapped again, once.

"Thank God. I was so frightened. I thought you went away."

I wished I could tell her I'd gone only into the picture. Not that far at all.

"Why is Mom so upset?" I asked Brad.

He sighed and laid his head in my lap. I felt the softness of his ears pressed against my fingers, and it made me feel better. "The man in the picture looked a lot like Mom," I said.

"Do you remember your uncle Bill, who visited at Christmas?"

"Do you mean that was Uncle Bill? But he died. And went to live with God. So how can he be in Mom's picture?"

"I don't know how that happened. But I'm certain that was your uncle Bill." Brad moved to lie in his usual place beside me, and when I asked him how he knew that was my uncle Bill, he didn't answer. Lately, it seems like Brad sleeps a lot, and he doesn't always answer my most important questions.

Mom told Dad I'd had a spell. I was very excited when I heard it. I could hardly eat my dinner or go to sleep. I'm sure, now that they know about it, they'll be able to figure out how to break it.

But all they did was take me to the doctor who did the usual poking and prodding. I don't know what the doctor discovered, but I don't think it was good. He had a very serious look. If I could speak, I would have asked him why I sometimes feel like something heavy is sitting on my chest.

After that, Mom put the painting with Uncle Bill in it away, and *The Little Prince* disappeared from the stack of books. Brad slept more than ever and moved more and more slowly, and sometimes Mom seemed to be holding her breath, like she was waiting for something to happen. And every once in a while, my breath would go out, and I couldn't pull it back in right away.

Summer was ending, and the leaves were once again dropping from the trees into colorful piles. Ethel and Bethel chased each other around the pond, snorting and stomping and making the leaves crackle and fly about, but it didn't make me laugh inside the way it used to.

Then one day, Brad perked up. All afternoon, he lay beside me, talking instead of sleeping. "See, Bobby. The trees are dying again. But they'll be back in the spring." For a while we watched the leaves drifting down, then he spoke again. "Do you remember I told you I would stay with you?"

"You promised," I said.

"I don't believe it's my promise to keep. You remember, I also told you when we get old enough or sick enough, like your uncle Bill did, dying just happens."

"But I've been sick a long time, and I haven't died."

"Perhaps love postpones it." He sighed. "You need to know. If one day my body doesn't move, and I look like I'm asleep, I'll still be nearby."

"Brad, please. You can't go. I need you. The doctor found something. I'm afraid."

Brad got up and stood beside me with his head in my lap, and that's when I knew.

"When it happens, Bobby, run right up to your uncle Bill and take his hand. Then everything will be all right."

"Will Mom and Dad come, too, Brad?"

"I think you and I will go first. But your mom and dad will join us. You don't need to worry."

Last night, the first snow of the winter came. When I awoke this morning, big fluffy flakes swirled in the air, and the trees looked like one of Mom's pencil drawings. In the afternoon, the snow stopped, the sun came out and the whole world sparkled.

Brad went outside, and I heard him bark. Mom heard him too. She looked out, then she pushed me over to the window so I could see what was happening. Brad and the goats were jumping about, knocking sprays of snow off the bushes. Watching them made my heart lift and laughter bubble inside me.

Later, Mom took out her paints and placed the picture of Uncle Bill on her easel. Then she put on music and lit the fire. Brad, back in from his romp, dozed beside me. I watched Mom painting and listened to the music, feeling warm and sleepy.

Mom added a woman to the painting. Then I must have fallen asleep for a while, because the next time I looked, the man and woman had been joined by a dog.

I told Brad to look, but he didn't answer. Then I felt the heaviness in my chest. It was happening more and more lately. I stared at the painting, absorbing the colors, trying to ease the pain.

Suddenly, the crushing weight pushing on my chest lightened, and I was floating. I slipped free and landed inside the picture. The grass tickled my toes.

Remembering what Brad told me to do, I walked then ran toward Uncle Bill. As I got close, I saw the dog was Brad. Uncle Bill held out his hands to me, and when I caught them, he swung me in a circle, laughing with me. "Look, Kiara, it's Bobby. Bobby, this is your aunt Kiara."

The woman smiled at me. She was short with dark, curly hair and laughing eyes.

I turned to Brad. "Will I have to go back to being sick?" I asked.

"We may be dreaming, but I don't believe so," Brad said.

Uncle Bill and Aunt Kiara stood quietly while Brad and I talked, then Uncle Bill said, "You're finished with sickness forever, Bobby."

"But what about Mom and Dad? I don't want to leave them."

"Time has no meaning where we are now," Aunt Kiara said. "It will seem no time at all before they join us."

"But they'll miss me."

"Of course they will," Uncle Bill said.

"I don't want them to be sad."

"They will be sad for a time," Aunt Kiara said. "But there are gifts to help their hearts heal."

Then she took my hands in hers and spoke words that sounded like music.

Sky color shimmering like visible laughter
Snowflakes and sunsets and leaves falling down
Rainbows and bells
Waterfalls and light
Books, pictures, memories, tears, stars, and time
An enchantment of comfort for those left behind

She placed her hand gently on my shoulder. "It's okay for you to be happy, Bobby."

I closed my eyes and repeated to myself, "It's okay to be happy. It's okay to be happy."

I took a deep breath, opened my eyes, and smiled at Aunt Kiara, Uncle Bill and Brad, and the light caught a tear on Aunt Kiara's cheek and turned it into a rainbow.

⁛

There. Done. Alan set the book aside, only then noticing the tears running down his face. He stared at the place where Meg's picture had hung, the tears drenching his cheeks, dripping off his chin. Something tight and hard was loosening inside him, as if Meg's death had corroded him, rusting him shut, and now he was being pried open.

It's okay to be happy.

Could it possibly be that simple?

Alan awakened the morning after reading *Bobby and Brad* feeling empty and peaceful, as if the tears had been a heavy burden he'd carried far too long and had at last laid down. Soon he would have to act, and that action would decide the course of his future, but for the moment he felt suspended. Content simply to be.

But after a couple of days, he began to feel a niggle of restlessness. He quieted it by once again pulling the box containing his writing out of the closet. He gathered the pages of his novel together and stacked them on the table.

It took him three nights to get through it all. When he finished, he read the note Meg had written at the end.

Alan,

The story is wonderful, and I'm not just saying that because I'm crazy about you. Although, don't doubt it for a moment, my love, I am. You've made the 1890's come alive again in all their raucous, maudlin, violent, tender glory. And to think, this is only the beginning. Oh, the places you will go!

Meg

If he had read the note shortly after she wrote it, the wording of that last sentence would never have struck him as unusual—a quote from the Dr. Seuss book, of course.

He'd just never expected to go anywhere without Meg.

And with that thought, the peaceful interlude shattered.

Delia, Angela, Charles, Kathy and now Meg. All whittling away at him. Cutting, slicing, occasionally producing a sharp stab of awareness.

Delia: *It's okay, Alan.*

Angela: *Kathy is unfinished business.*

Charles: *For God's sake, how could you let her go?*

Meg: *Oh, the places you will go.*

But what pushed at him most was Kathy. *I'm sorry we lost touch.*

Kathy. All these months, not seeing her but knowing Charles was. A bone-deep ache. A pain so unrelenting, he'd finally done what he had been most afraid to do. Confronted his guilt over Meg's death. Let Meg go.

Sending him the story had taken courage on Kathy's part. If he wanted to complete his healing he needed to respond with equal courage. He needed to see her.

He concentrated, trying to remember what she'd said about living near the Botanical Gardens. In one of the big houses, with an elderly couple named...something to do with comedy, wasn't it? Abbott? No. Costello, that was it.

He found a listing in the phone book for a Louis Costello on the eight hundred block of Race Street.

It had to be the right one.

Chapter Twenty-Nine

Excerpt from the diaries of Emily Kowalski
1990...

This year I turn ninety, although I certainly don't feel that old.

My life has not been the life I thought I would have. When Jess and I married, I thought I was choosing a life filled with children, grandchildren, and even, as I have lived this long, great-grandchildren.

But perhaps if I'd had that life, it would not have had room in it for Bobby. And I could never choose not to have Bobby in my life.

I have seen friends dealing with the hurt of angry adolescents or trying to help children through the pain of bad choices, and I sometimes think I had the easier road.

Bobby never did anything to disappoint or hurt me. He was always mine to love, and he returned my love in full measure. And I have Jess as I have always had him in spite of our losing our way for a time.

When Rose Cameron called to ask if I would meet with one of her students this semester, I almost said no. These last six months I've been awful tired, and lately I've had to work harder to breathe. Of course, that's to be expected at my age.

But after thinking about it, I told her yes. I do so enjoy being around young people, even when they make no secret of the fact they suspect I'm old enough to be personally acquainted with King Tut.

The student came yesterday. Her name is Kathleen Jamison. She stood on my doorstep, her hair like a bright copper penny, with the maple tree all gold and red behind her, and I thought, oh my, how lovely she is.

She reminds me of someone, but I can't think who. I don't believe I've ever known anyone with hair that color.

I'm supposed to share with Kathleen my view of an important historical event that occurred in my lifetime so she can write about it for Rose's class.

If Jess were asked to pick the most amazing thing that happened in his lifetime, he would probably say it was men landing on the moon. But for me, it was the discovery of antibiotics, although it came too late to help our Bobby.

Kathleen was surprised at my choice.

Talking to Kathleen about the past, I realize who she reminds me of. Bill's Kiara. Anyone seeing pictures of them both would not think so, yet I feel it strongly. Perhaps it is some deeper quality of the spirit they share.

Kathleen and I have been talking about life and love. She is so young. All she knows of love is the excitement that comes in the beginning when she meets someone new who may be special.

But I hope she will someday discover the love that grows from the wholehearted acceptance of another and the sharing of sorrow and pain along with joy.

I want to tell her that when you love that way, you never feel old. I look in my mirror and am amazed at the face looking back. When did that happen? But then I look at Jess, and I see only my Jess, the man I've loved since the moment we met.

I think that is why we say love is blind. It isn't really. It simply sees the eternal part of us that does indeed never grow old.

I'm afraid the time for sharing with Kathleen is ending, and there is still so much I want to tell her. I especially want her to know her capacity for sorrow will always be exceeded by her capacity for happiness.

ℰↃ

Sitting on the Costellos' porch waiting for Kathy, Alan shivered, and not just because the evening was cool. He saw the curtains twitch and knew Mrs. Costello was keeping an eye on him.

She hadn't been happy with his decision to wait on the porch, but even if it had been twenty below, this was one time he'd choose a cold porch over having to make small talk with someone he didn't know.

Kathy finally arrived, walking quickly, her head down, watching her step on the uneven slates of the sidewalk. He took a deep breath, bracing himself. She didn't realize he was there until she was halfway up the porch steps. When she saw him, she came to a stop, her eyes going wide with shock, those clear mountain-stream eyes.

"Alan? Oh my goodness. It's...good to see you." Her voice was hoarse, surprised.

Before he could respond, Mrs. Costello opened the front door and stuck her head out. "Oh, Kathy, I'm so glad you're home. This young man refused to come inside to wait for you. He must be half frozen. Make him come in. I've got fresh coffee and some old dead cherry pie."

With that, Mrs. Costello transferred the responsibility for the next step from him to Kathy. Feeling both relief and trepidation, he held Kathy's gaze, waiting for her response.

She nodded slightly. "You'd better come in. I never argue with Mrs. C about food. Her old dead pies are more delicious than everybody else's fresh out of the oven." Kathy had a serious look, but a trace of humor softened her tone, and a hint of a smile hovered on her lips.

Mrs. C took charge of him, hanging up his coat, then briskly herding him back to the kitchen, while Kathy went upstairs to put away her things.

When Kathy walked into the kitchen five minutes later, he waited to see her reaction to the fact Mrs. C had changed her mind about the pie and was insisting he stay for dinner instead. Kathy's lips twitched, as if she were suppressing a smile. A good sign.

He doubted he'd be able to eat, but the warm smells of the food and the comfortable chatter between the Costellos, as a heaped platter of fried chicken and bowls of mashed potatoes, gravy, and peas were passed around, soothed him. He filled his plate and ate with more appetite than he'd had in a long time, warmed inside and out by the food and by Kathy's presence.

"How was your day, dear?" Mrs. C asked Kathy.

"Really good. Jade finished another illustration for *Bobby and Brad*."

"Calico is publishing it?" Alan asked.

Kathy nodded.

"I'm not surprised." He met her gaze. "Thank you for sharing it with me. It should be published." *It helped me heal.* He couldn't tell her that, not yet, but maybe someday soon.

Delight transformed her face, her skin lucent with it, her eyes sparkling brooks.

After a moment, she looked away, but the memory of that look stayed with him, warming him even more than the food.

When they finished eating, Kathy shooed Mrs. C out of the kitchen, then turned to him. "I hope you don't mind doing dishes."

"Seems only fair." They needed to talk and doing it while they washed dishes—he could handle that.

"I better dry since I know where everything goes. Mrs. C hates it when things are put away in the wrong place."

He filled the sink with hot water and added soap as Kathy cleaned off the dishes and set them on the counter next to him. As they worked, he thought about what he needed to say. Keeping his gaze focused on the sink and its contents, he began. "Your note. You didn't need to apologize, but I do. I'm sorry for the way I treated you. I was hoping that...maybe we can be friends again." That wasn't what he really wanted, but it seemed to be all he was capable of asking for at the moment.

Cradling plates with one arm, Kathy reached out and touched him. "I'd like that."

He looked down at her hand, resting lightly on his arm, feeling a mixture of fear and hope, knowing with perfect clarity he was not turning back this time. He couldn't bear to lose her again. He rubbed a hand over his forehead, forgetting it was soapy. Kathy reached out with her towel to wipe the soapsuds away.

"This is harder than it looks."

"Washing dishes? Or talking?"

"Both." He shook his head and gave her a rueful smile. "Talking."

He turned back to the sink, determined to say it all. Bowls and silverware followed the plates into the drainer as he struggled to find the words. "I didn't mean to hurt you." He stretched his shoulders, trying to ease the tension, upset he was making such a hash of it. "But I did. And I'm sorry." He handed Kathy the last batch of silverware and let the water out of the sink.

"I treated you badly as well."

"No. No you didn't." His voice firmed, and he managed to meet her gaze. He raised a hand to stop her from saying more. "Please, I need to know you forgive me."

"Of course I do."

He nodded, relieved. "I'm not doing very well, am I?"

"You're doing just fine. Although there is the small matter of the pots and pans."

He gazed over at the stove then at Kathy, who smiled at him.

He refilled the sink while Kathy carried over the saucepans

and skillet. After he finished washing them, he said, "Can I take you to dinner tomorrow?"

"I'd like that."

"I'll pick you up. Seven? I thought the Indian restaurant. Or do you prefer something else?" He wished they could simply laugh together, but he couldn't think of a way to bring that about.

"Indian's fine." Her tone was solemn, but her mouth curved in a smile.

"Can we..." He stopped and took a deep breath. So many emotions jumbled together. Elation. Exhaustion. Fear. But stronger than fear were love and a growing desire. He wanted to do it right this time. Tell her about Meg. Begin to build something new with her.

"What?" She spoke gently.

"Can we take it slow?"

"As long as you promise not to disappear again."

"I won't."

"I'll see you tomorrow, then." Kathy spoke with the firmness of a promise.

"What a nice young man," Mrs. C said, when Kathy came back into the living room after showing Alan out. "And such lovely flowers he sent you."

"Flowers?"

"You didn't notice, dear? I put them in your room."

Kathy rushed upstairs, her heart beating with gladness, relief flooding through her. Maybe Alan had trouble saying the words, but here was proof he wanted more than friendship.

The flowers, a mix of roses and orchids in a small vase was sitting by the bed. She fumbled open the card.

It was never my intention to seduce you. I intended to make love to you. C

She drew in a deep, shaky breath, letting it sink in—that

the flowers weren't from Alan and what Charles was saying in his note. She didn't want to hurt him, but it wasn't Charles she wanted making love to her.

Alan. She'd almost given up hope. Over a week since she sent the note and the story. With the passing of each day, it felt less and less likely he would respond. So when she'd looked up tonight and seen him, such immense relief had washed through her. He'd come. Thank God.

Then everything turned bizarre. Mrs. Costello inviting him for dinner. Sitting across from Alan with all the words they needed to say to each other silenced by the presence of the Costellos. Until something odd happened. Peace gradually easing the tightness in her shoulders, forehead, and arms.

Grace said Alan was different. *Mas tranquillo.* And Kathy understood now what Grace meant by that. His eyes were free of shadows, and there was an ease to the way he moved, sat, spoke, that was different than before. Like a lake smoothed to mirror stillness after being ruffled by a breeze.

It was one of the hardest things she'd ever done, walking him to the door and staying behind as he drove away. She'd wanted to run after him and insist he take her with him. But he hadn't yet been able to tell her about Meg, and she needed to give him the chance to pick the time and place for that.

Still, his abrupt departure tempered her relief with uneasiness. He had not made his intentions clear. What if he were offering only what he had offered before?

She already knew that wouldn't be enough.

But the only way to find out was to risk being hurt even more than she already had been. A gamble she knew without any debate she would willingly risk.

When Alan arrived at the Costellos the next evening, Mrs. Costello let him in. He watched as Kathy came down the stairs, wearing an old-fashioned burgundy-colored dress, and looking so beautiful his heart felt like an inflating balloon.

Seated across from her in the restaurant, he had to clear his throat before he could speak. "You look wonderful. Your dress. I like it. It's old, isn't it?"

"The term is vintage." She smiled at him. "Amanda insisted I buy it."

"Amanda, huh. How's she doing these days?"

"Locked in a trunk."

He gave her a questioning look.

"The story...it stopped working after Delia got sick."

Yeah. Lots of things had. "At least you ended up with a nice dress. Possibly worn by one of the silver baron's wives."

"More likely, one of their mistresses."

He examined the dress. "The design. It's not exactly right."

"For a mistress, or a wife?" Her eyes danced with mischief.

"For the eighteen nineties."

"What makes you say that?"

"I'm working on a novel set in that time. I've looked at a lot of pictures."

Slowly Kathy began to smile, a wide, wonderful smile. "So, we're writing something other than memos are we, Professor Francini?"

"I never was very good at memos, to tell you the truth." He thought of all the pages of manuscript scattered across both his table and desk at home with that note at the end from Meg.

"What is it?" Kathy spoke softly, her hand on his arm.

He met her gaze, pulling his thoughts back to the present, trying to think how to begin. So many things he needed to tell her, all of them difficult, but he needed to start. "I was denied tenure."

Kathy frowned. "I don't understand."

He shrugged. "Hilstrom said no tenure unless I was writing fiction."

"But you just said you are."

"Too late."

She took his hand between hers. "I'm sorry. What are you going to do?"

"I have until next year to find something else." He liked her taking the initiative to touch him. Liked the feeling of connection it gave him.

"I happen to have inside information that you're a wonderful teacher."

He raised his brows in question.

"Almost had a riot on my hands when the students discovered you weren't teaching the seminar last spring."

"Doesn't count."

"And it's too bad it doesn't. Whoever hires you is going to be really glad DSU didn't keep you."

"Thanks. That means a lot." He was sorry when she let go of his hand in order to pick up her menu, but her words continued to soothe the rough wound Hilstrom had inflicted with her decision.

While they waited for the food to arrive, Kathy filled him in on the sign language classes she was taking with the Garibaldis. "You should see Delia sign. She's learning so quickly, it's amazing."

He agreed Delia was amazing. In fact, the little girl had shown herself to be tougher and more resilient than he was.

"I need to sign up for a class, too. So to speak," he said.

Kathy nodded, then she moved her hands and lips, slowly and emphatically, but without sound.

"What's that?" he said.

Kathy's eyes gleamed with laughter. "That was either, 'Delia will be so pleased', or 'Delia likes to eat porridge'."

It surprised a laugh from him.

"Not that I'm finding it difficult, you understand," she hastened to add.

Later, when he walked her onto the Costello's porch, she pulled out her key and inserted it in the lock, but she didn't open the door. Instead, she turned to him and raised her eyes to his. "I'm glad you came back. I missed you."

He pulled her into his arms and she leaned against him, solid and warm. Real. He rubbed his cheek against her hair. "I want to kiss you, but I don't dare."

"Because of what happened last time?" Her voice sounded

choked.

"Partly that, I suppose. It wasn't what I meant, though." He thought of the barriers still between them. Meg. And the knowledge Charles loved Kathy. So hard to reach for happiness when it meant hurting a friend.

"There's something...before." No he couldn't manage it. Not yet. He had to do it soon, though. "I-I have to go out to the ranch tomorrow. The folks are going to be away. I wonder if you...if you'd come out Saturday."

"I'd like that."

"Come early." He stepped back from her, his hands on her shoulders. "I'll show you how to muck a stall."

"And I'm interested in that because?"

The sudden lightness between them was a huge relief. He drew in a breath and smiled at her. "You have a skill like that, you'll never starve."

"Maybe starving's preferable. But you're on. I'll be there."

"I'll feed you breakfast." He closed his eyes briefly and dropped his hands to his sides. "I'll see you then."

Chapter Thirty

Kathy watched Charles walk toward her. The courts had recessed for lunch, and the restaurant was filling up quickly.

He sat down across from her. His eyes were blue-gray behind a pair of wire-rimmed glasses she'd never seen him wear before. She'd always thought his eyes were too blue to be real, but these eyes were very real indeed, as was the man.

"Thank you for coming," she said. "And thank you for the flowers. They're beautiful."

"Just wanted to set the record straight."

She shifted uncomfortably, trying to meet his gaze. "The man I told you about. He came to see me."

"Alan Francini." His voice was flat. "I know. He called. "

"You're friends?"

"The best."

It was a shock but not really a surprise given the way Charles had acted that night in his apartment. "He hasn't been able to tell me about Meg."

Charles looked surprised. "How do you know then?"

"Elaine told me. Did you know her? Meg."

He looked away, his throat working. "She was his whole world. When he lost her..." His voice sounded raspy.

"Do you know how she died?" Kathy said the words quickly, knowing if she thought about it she wouldn't be able to say them at all. But this could be her best, maybe her only chance to understand Alan.

Charles pinched the bridge of his nose, displacing the glasses. "You know you're taking a hell of a chance."

"I don't understand."

"Being second-best."

Kathy felt like the breath had been knocked out of her. If Charles were angry or speaking vindictively, she could have shrugged it off. But he wasn't. He sounded more sad than anything. Besides, it was what she herself feared most. That for Alan she would be an unequal substitute for the woman he'd lost.

"That's one thing I can give you he can't. A free heart."

"But I can't give you one in return. I'm so sorry. I wish I could."

"If wishes were horses..." He gave her a crooked smile then reached out and took her hand in his. "I don't believe I could eat to save my life. But thank you. For meeting with me, for not leaving me hanging."

"You're a good man, Charles. Any girl in her right mind would find it so easy to love you."

"Just my luck you aren't in your right mind, then." He rubbed his thumb gently across the palm of her hand.

"You and Alan." She stopped, unable to say more.

Charles closed his eyes briefly then opened them and gave her a rueful smile. "Might take a while, but we'll be fine." He lifted her hand to his lips and kissed her palm. "Just be happy." Then he pushed his chair back and stood up.

Her eyes filled with tears. She wasn't in love with Charles, but she cared for him and wished with all her heart she could alleviate his distress—but what would bring him comfort was the one thing she didn't have to give.

He wended his way around tables to reach the entrance, and then he was gone.

It wasn't until he'd left that she realized. He hadn't answered her question about how Meg died.

Saturday morning, Kathy was up at six. Mrs. C already had coffee made, and she insisted Kathy drink a cup and eat a

259

cinnamon roll. "To tide you over, dear."

Kathy drank half a cup and ate a roll, then she pulled on her jacket.

"Here you are." Mrs. C handed her a wrapped package. "Some rolls for that nice young man."

Kathy took the rolls and kissed Mrs. C's cheek before hurrying out to her car.

Driving to the ranch, she felt the way she had driving to Denver when she first moved there—that at the end of the trip, for better or worse, her life would change forever. She let her thoughts drift, not wanting to lean on this new future too hard. It all seemed so unbearably fragile and tentative.

When she arrived at the ranch, she parked in her usual spot, climbed out, and eased the car door closed. She stood for a moment, looking at the barn, the pastures, and the house on the hill, breathing in peace along with fresh air.

Then, ready at last to face whatever came next, she walked to the barn and slipped inside. The warm smells of hay and horse with its slight tang of ammonia wrapped around her. Cormac came up to her, tail wagging, and there was Alan pitching hay. She watched him, feeling a tremulous mix of hope, joy and fear.

She spoke softly. "Good morning."

He turned abruptly, his gaze shifting from her to Cormac. "Some watchdog, you are." He sounded stern, but Cormac simply gave him a doggy grin and wagged his tail. Then Alan smiled at her, "I'm almost done mucking out."

"I hoped you would be."

"Chicken."

She smiled as she went down the line, patting heads, rubbing ears and noses, getting reacquainted with Siesta, Sonoro, Arriba and the rest. When Alan finished, they walked up to the house.

They decided on scrambled eggs for breakfast. Kathy sliced onions and mushrooms and sautéed them while Alan stirred the eggs and put the cinnamon rolls in the oven to warm up. They worked comfortably, as if they'd been cooking together in this kitchen for years.

When their plates were ready, he led the way to the bright dining alcove. There was contentment in the warm food and their being together, but underneath, tension trembled between them.

"I thought we might go for a ride," he said, when they finished eating.

Kathy had already figured out the place Alan would be most comfortable talking about Meg would be on the back of a horse.

She'd dressed for it.

Sonoro's hooves clicked against cold stones as Alan struggled to find the first words—the beginning of all he needed to say to Kathy. His gaze drifted to a stand of golden-leafed aspen and from there back to the trail. He tried to speak, but his throat tightened, and with a flare of panic, he feared he wasn't going to be able to do it after all.

But maybe if he started with a few simple words—*You see, I was married.* Then he could say the other words. *She died.*

He cleared his throat in preparation, but the words clotted and refused to come out. The tension in him squeezed at Sonoro, who moved abruptly into a *paso corto* leaving Kathy and Siesta to follow.

When he reached the lake, Alan dismounted and turned to watch Kathy riding toward him—a woman with red hair on a red horse, the sun catching fire in her hair. The light at the end of his five-year tunnel of darkness.

Kathy swung off Siesta, and Alan held out his hand to her. She placed her hand in his, and he led her to the edge of the water that lay silken and still, mirroring sky, trees and mountains like an alternate reality.

Living with two realities. It was what he'd been doing since Meg's death. Letting the past overshadow the present.

"When we were here before, you asked if the lake had a name."

Kathy stood quietly, her hand still in his, and her calm gave him the strength to go on.

"*Lago de Lágrimas.* Lake of Tears. My...my wife named it." He gulped in some air. "She died."

The only way he knew Kathy had heard was from the slight tensing of her hand in his.

"It was...I lost my way. Stopped living. Then I met you." He stumbled to a stop.

"Someone essential," Kathy said. "You meant Meg, didn't you?"

He glanced at her, shock coursing through him. "You know about Meg?"

She nodded. "Elaine told me."

He looked away, feeling a nerve jumping in his cheek, wondering why he even felt surprised. "All of it?"

"Only that much. That you were married, and she died."

He swallowed, his mouth dry, knowing he still needed to tell her the rest. Get it over with. Then they could go on.

"Meg died in Alaska. A place called Turnagain Arm. She was walking on the beach and got trapped."

Kathy's hand tightened in his.

He braced himself to say the next words. "The tide...she drowned. I blamed myself." There. Done.

Only it wasn't. Because what he'd managed to hold back all these years, finally rose up to meet him. Those last moments with Meg, when they'd both known she wasn't going to be freed in time, and their only choice was how to face it.

Meg's face had been drenched with tears, her mouth quivering, but she had lifted her chin and looked right at him. "Alan, please. Promise me you won't look away. I can't do this without you."

He'd met her gaze even though he felt as if every cell in his body was being sliced and torn. "I'll never get over losing you."

"You must, Alan. Please, I want you to be happy."

I want you to be happy. He'd forgotten Meg said that.

Slowly, the image of Meg receded, and he became aware once again of Kathy's hand in his.

"It's okay." Kathy's voice was soft as a sigh. "I understand why we can only be friends."

Had he actually believed that? That all he wanted from this woman was friendship? Of course, he did want that. And so much more.

Still holding her hand, he turned and met her gaze and found her eyes brimming with tears. He looked into Kathy's eyes, still under the spell of memory. Drifting between past and present, Kathy his only anchor.

He pulled on her hand, and surprise flowed through him at the solidity of her body against his. He folded her in, smoothing his hand along her back. "Kathy, Kathleen. Shhh. It's okay. Shhh." Comforting her, but comforting himself as well.

She put her arms around him and tucked her head into the curve of his neck.

Softly, like a magic incantation, he breathed her name. "Kathy, Kathleen Hope, dearest Kath."

She snuggled against him like someone burrowing into a warm quilt. Silken hair touched his cheek. Her tears wet his neck, mingling with the tears sliding down his own cheeks.

The past loosening its hold on the present. No longer powerful. A last sigh, and then gone, like a reflection in still water banished by the tossing of a single stone.

A woman with red hair and silver tears, lips pressing against his, her arms enfolding him. This moment, this delicate, blessed present.

He took a deep breath of crystalline air and said the words he last spoke to a woman facing death on Turnagain Arm, words he never expected to say again. "I love you."

"Alan. Oh, my dear. I love you, too. So much." Her body shivered against his. "I've been so afraid..."

So had he. But stronger than that fear was hope. He hugged her tighter, then stepped back slightly, and with gentle fingers wiped the tears from the corners of her eyes. "Last chance, Kathleen. If you're wise, you'll run now and not look back."

His hands rested gently on her shoulders, holding her loosely, giving her the chance to change her mind. Tears still welled in her eyes, but she didn't pull away.

"It won't be easy."

"I'm not asking for easy. As long as you love me a little."

"Oh, much more than a little." He gazed in her eyes and seeing the love shining there, gratitude flowed through him for this gift he'd done nothing to deserve. Cupping her face between his hands, he kissed her, and his whole world narrowed down to this.

Kathy warm and real in his arms, her lips moving against his.

Epilogue

Excerpt from the diaries of Emily Kowalski
1990...

I am beginning to see at long last the symmetry and balance in my life.

First came the dreaming time, then the time when I met Jess and we had Bobby, and it seemed that all my dreams had come true. Then the dark time came, when our beautiful dreams turned to stones—dull, ugly stones.

But now I have been given time enough to discover that when I turn and look at those stones, they have a sheen, and in their depths is a dark beauty.

And I know I have lived the life I was supposed to live, and I am content.

About the Author

From an early age, Ann Warner's dreams were to marry a rich rancher and own a racehorse, not necessarily in that order. Instead, she married a man who doesn't even like horses after one stepped on him with deliberate intent when he was ten. And instead of ranching, Ann ended up directing Clinical Chemistry and Toxicology laboratories at two universities. She still doesn't own a racehorse.

But when the protagonist in *Dreams for Stones* turned out to be both a university professor and part-time rancher, it proved to Ann that dreams never completely go away, but continue to influence our lives in unexpected ways.

To learn more about Ann Warner or to send her an email, please visit her at www.annwarner.net.

Life, love and unlikely legacies.

Reversing Over Liberace
© *2007 Jane Lovering*

Willow runs into Luke, the university lust-of-her-life, ten years on and this time around he's interested—she's lost twenty pounds and found fashion. But their meeting turns out to be no accident. What is Luke *really* after, Willow or her new inheritance?

Her best mate Cal is gorgeous and...well...*gay*. Then reveals himself to be more than a mild, unassuming computer geek and she is no longer sure exactly *who* is telling the truth or who to trust.

Is anyone in her life what they seem to be?

Add to the romantic confusion, twelve pairs of rubber boots, two elderly spaniels, a pregnant sister and the unexpected contents of a matchbox and you get a funny, touching story of a woman in search of revenge and getting what she needs, rather than what she thinks she wants.

Available now in ebook and print from Samhain Publishing.

"Luke?" Katie was waiting when I put the phone down, her scandalometer clearly reading into the red. "What's happened?"

"Nothing, nothing," I trilled. "Well, not exactly, we just had a bit of a misunderstanding, that's all."

"Oh, right, about him moving out of the hotel and stopping at the showroom instead?"

"Ah, no. This was another misunderstanding. A different one." Buoyed up and riding on the tide of goodwill that Luke's admission had brought, I told Katie the full background to last night's little, ahem, indiscretion on the lip frontage. When I'd finished, she frowned.

"Do you and Luke ever actually, y'know, *talk*, Wills? Or do you spend all your off-duty time shagging and communicating in mime?"

"What?"

"You do seem to have an extraordinary number of *misunderstandings,* don't you? For a couple who are supposed to be so deeply in love that they're planning to get *married,* there's a lot he doesn't seem to tell you about. And, please God, if you're going around kissing strange men, the reverse is also true."

"Cal...it wasn't...it wasn't *that* sort of kiss." I said indignantly. "And of course Luke and I talk, don't be stupid. It's just, you know how prone I am to grabbing the wrong end of the stick and using it to beat myself."

"Yes, but the stick does have to be held out for you to grasp in the first place." Katie put her hands on my shoulders and looked me deep in the eyes. "I'm worried about you, Will. Okay, so Luke might have good reasons for all the misconstructions that have gone on, but it's more that they've happened than what they've been about that worries me."

"Well, my dear, worry no more." I twirled around on my chair. "I'm going to suggest to Luke that we move into the flat next week and start living together properly. It can't be comfortable for him camped out in the showroom, and we might as well start getting it all together. How do you feel about wearing peach for the wedding?"

"Will, if it makes you happy I shall wear a whole fruit salad," she said solemnly.

"Willow." The door opened and Neil came in. "Bloke for you in the front."

"Good Lord, it speaks. Evolution in action."

"Shut it, frosty knickers."

"What, Clive not with you? Was the separation a success?"

"And you can shut up an' all." Neil grinned. "Dunno 'oo he is. Some weirdo. Bit of luck, he's a mad axe murderer."

He wasn't. It was Cal, loitering about in the front office, looking at the photographs on the walls. (Man Rescues Tortoise—Pictures Inside.) "Hi."

"Hello." Katie was hanging around by my left shoulder like a conscience-devil. "How are you?"

"Fine. I came to..." Cal clocked Katie and began to stammer. "I...I...you, yesterday...quite...upset."

"Everything's sorted now, just another misunderstanding," I said smoothly. Well, I could have belched every word and next to Cal's delivery it would have sounded smooth. "Cal, Katie."

"Oh, so *this* is the guy with the lip action. Pleased to meet you, Cal." And Katie turned round to face me and half-whispered, "Fuck me, Willow, you didn't tell me he was such a *ride*. I mean, look at him."

"Forgive my friend, Cal, she has a form of Tourette's. We normally keep her locked up for her own good."

Cal smiled broadly and Katie went "phwooooarrrr" in my ear. "Chuffin' hell, will you look at the eyes on your man?"

"And she's Irish. Happily married. Quite respectable."

Katie leaned over the desk towards Cal. "But prepared to be unrespectable, if the offer's right." She pursed her lips and Cal's smile grew slightly broader.

"Are you any good with goats?"

"Um."

"So, that's a 'no' then." I hustled Katie to one side with my elbows. "It's fine, Cal. I've spoken to Luke, he's explained. It was something personal."

"Anyway. The brother in Boston? I've got the phone number, if you wanted to ring and introduce yourself."

"What a great idea." Katie derailed the nearest elbow and slotted herself in beside me again.

"Have you got something in your eye?" I asked her suspiciously.

"No, I'm fluttering my eyelashes, can't you tell?"

"I don't think Cal's impressed by fluttering eyelashes, Katie."

"No, but I'm mightily impressed by anyone who can move my goat."

Katie's appraising stare narrowed. "Is that some sort of code, Willow? Is he chatting you up in code? Because if he is, that's really unfair. No one chats me up in code, not even Dan—not that he chats me up anymore. Doesn't even chat much, if you want to know the truth. He sort of grunts and points. I think he learned it off the twins."

Cal and I shared a baffled shrug. "So, do you want to call him now? You can borrow my mobile."

"Well, not right this second. I mean, I'm at work and everything and it'll be the middle of the night in Boston, won't it? Tonight. I'll do it tonight."

"Why are you putting it off?" He tipped his head on one side. "Are you worried about what he might say?"

"No! I told you, Luke and I have sorted everything out. If I ring James and he tells Luke that I called, then it looks as if I've gone behind his back and don't trust him."

"But you *don't*, do you?" The words dropped into a clanging silence. I stared at Katie who didn't even look ashamed of herself. "Come on, Willow. If you trusted him, he wouldn't need to explain himself to you because the situations would never arise in the first place. I mean"—her voice became gentler—"you know I love you, Wills, but you can be a complete and utter zombo where men are concerned."

"Is that a real word?" Cal asked.

"It is on Planet Katie," I answered, a little bitterly. "Kate, you're warping things again. Luke and I are fine. We...oh, sod the pair of you. Give me the number, Cal. I'll call after lunch when it's a civilised time in Boston. Katie can earwig all she likes to make sure I ask the right questions. There. Are you both happy now?"

The two of them agreed that, yes, in this instance they were fairly satisfied with my reply, and Cal left the office, Katie watching his every move. When she noticed his limp, her eyebrows almost twanged.

"Christ Jesus, he even manages to make *that* look sexy. Aw, do an old married woman a favour. Before you marry Luke, shag Cal just the once"—a libidinous look—"and tell me *all* about it."

"*Katie!* I will do no such thing. Anyway, Luke's sexy too, isn't he?"

She stopped boiling over and switched down to simmer. "Yeah, he's sexy, too. But it's different with Luke. He's macho sexy, all swagger and cock-first into a room. Your man there, you can tell he's the kind who'll make you wait, then lick you till you're screaming."

A pause while we thought about this.

"You really do need to get out more, don't you?"

"Tell me about it," she sighed.

Printed in the United States
128431LV00002B/316-339/P